SELF MADE

BELINDA WILLIAMS

SELF MADE: Freshwater #2

ISBN: 978-0-6488099-7-5 (Trade paperback)
https://belindawilliamsbooks.com

Edited by Laura Greaves
Proofread by Rebekah Groves
Cover art by Belinda Williams

Also by Belinda Williams

Read Between The Lines: Freshwater 1

Daddy's Girl: Freshwater 3

Don't Let Me Forget

Heartthrob: Hollywood Hearts 1

Heartbreaker: Hollywood Hearts 2

Heartbeat: Hollywood Hearts 3

Wild Heart: Hollywood Hearts 4

Heartstrings: A Hollywood Hearts novella

The Boyfriend Sessions: City Love 1

The Pitch: City Love 2

Modern Heart: City Love 3

Wish List: City Love 4

Anthologies

(available for FREE digital download):

Bad Things Come In Threes: Winter Heat – Six Sizzling, Fun-Size Chick Lit Stories

The Spring Clean: Spring Fling – Six Mini Chick Lit Tales

Dear Reader

This book is set in Australia, so I've used UK English instead of US English.

This means if you're one of my US readers, you might notice some differences in spelling: colour instead of color; towards instead of toward; realise instead of realize.

You may also notice other differences like my characters' tendency to call their friends "mate" or "mates". Hopefully the Australian colloquialisms are self-explanatory, but if you come across any that you don't understand, feel free to get in touch via the contact form on my website: https:// belindawilliamsbooks.com/contact/

I've tried to refrain from using Aussie slang because this can seem like a language within itself! But if some usage has slipped in, I'll cop it . . . whoops, see? That means I'll take responsibility for it.

I hope you enjoy *Self Made*.

Happy reading,

Belinda

Chapter One

'WELCOME BACK TO *SYDNEY TONIGHT*. I'm Kat Chalmers.'

'And I'm Ant Monticello—the funny one. Just in case you forgot.'

Jessica Jinks smiled brightly and kept her hands out of sight beneath the broadcast desk. To the other members of the television panel, they were simply resting on her lap. In reality, she was holding them together in a death grip to stop them from shaking uncontrollably.

Without turning her head—because she'd been told not to do that unless someone actually directed a question her way—Jess glanced over at the news show's hosts.

Kat Chalmers, her neighbour and good friend, was the reason she'd been dragged into this television appearance. Well, not quite dragged, but extensively encouraged. Kat appeared completely in command of the evening's show in that take-charge manner she exuded on a constant basis. Her long, chestnut hair sat perfectly straight without a strand out of place, and her discerning dark eyes never seemed to miss a thing.

Her co-host, Ant Monticello, also seemed effortlessly comfortable in front of the camera. Unlike Jess, who was anything but relaxed.

Of course they're relaxed, Jess silently admonished herself.

Kat was a broadcast news journalist known the country over for her adept interview techniques. Ant was a comedian. It was an odd pairing at first glance, but one that seemed to be working ever since Kat's much-loved co-host Davey Walters had switched networks earlier in the year.

'As always on a Monday, we have a special guest for you,' Kat told their viewers.

Their *live* viewers.

Jess clenched her hands together tighter. *Why did I agree to this?* Sure, she was used to being in the public eye for her fitness brand, but that was on social media. And social media wasn't live. That was planned. This? This was terrifying.

'A lot of us already know Jessica Jinks thanks to Hi-Jinks, an exercise routine currently taking the country by storm. Tonight we're going to learn more about what it takes to be an Instagram fitness goddess. Say hi, Jess.'

Jess released one of her hands, which was slick with sweat, and waved in the general direction of the camera, her smile so wide it hurt. She wasn't sure how, but she managed to speak.

'Hi. Thanks for having me. I wouldn't say I'm a goddess. Hi-Jinks is all about getting fit no matter what stage you're at.' The pre-rehearsed words were burned into Jess's brain. 'And we're not about looks, either. If you feel good, you'll look good is my theory, so I don't like to focus on scales or mirrors.'

Her elevator pitch, Kat had called it, and Jess kept right on smiling, grateful she'd managed to say it all without stumbling.

Ant tapped his fingers on the broadcast desk. 'I couldn't

help but notice you're kind of gorgeous though, Jess. So that's very easy for you to say.'

They'd also rehearsed this. Despite her clenched stomach and tight chest, Jess was almost starting to enjoy this, especially seeing as she knew what was coming next.

'Now, Ant,' Kat interjected. 'You know better than to judge a book by its cover. For those of you who already follow Jess, you'll know she's not afraid to show us what exercise really looks like.'

The large screen positioned behind the broadcast desk lit up with an image and Jess suppressed a giggle. It was a picture of her, red-faced and sweaty, after teaching one of her very first Hi-Jinks classes a few years ago. She remembered being on a massive high and not caring about the beads of sweat on her forehead or the fact she was bright enough to resemble a traffic light. Not known to anyone back then aside from her friends and family, she'd posted the photo on Instagram without a second thought—and that's when things had gotten really interesting.

Another image came up on the screen. This was one of her curled up in pain on the sand at her local beach. She was cradling her ankle and there was blood dripping down her leg due to a gash on her knee. She'd sprained her ankle while beach jogging after missing an empty bottle half buried in the sand. When she'd fallen, she'd also discovered whoever had been partying had been kind enough to leave broken glass behind, too.

By that stage, she'd gained a following not for posting Photoshopped images of her toned arms or abs, but of what exercise looked like in the real world. She'd posted that ugly shot without a second thought and it had created even more attention.

Ant winced. 'Ouch. If that's what exercise really looks like, I knew there was a reason I don't do it.'

'I was just unlucky that day,' Jess told them. 'Injuries are a very real possibility when you exercise—but they don't need to be if you exercise right.' Jess's nerves began to dissipate as she warmed to a subject she was passionate about. 'I'm sick of hearing about women and men as young as their teens and twenties experiencing life-altering injuries because they thought the workouts they were doing would make them look great and keep them fit. Usually from exercise regimens that give no thought to the long-term wear and tear on your body.'

'Yeah, I mean look at the wear and tear on my body so far, and I don't even exercise,' Ant quipped.

That comment wasn't planned, and Jess found herself smiling thanks to the comedian's well-timed joke. He was being unkind to himself for the purpose of a laugh. Sure, he wasn't fit and toned, but with his olive skin and strong, dark Mediterranean features, his face was striking—made more so by the permanent five o'clock shadow. If it wasn't for his warm brown eyes, which always danced with humour, Jess could almost imagine him as one of those brooding heroes from a romance novel.

'That's abuse you've inflicted yourself,' Kat told him. 'From too much food and alcohol.'

Ant pouted. 'It wasn't abuse, it was genuine enjoyment.'

Everyone laughed this time, and Ant's pout turned upward into a grin.

'You don't have to starve yourself to be healthy,' Jess pointed out. 'Quite the opposite, in fact. You just have to eat the right food.'

'Yeah, see, that's where you've lost me,' Ant said. 'The right food usually isn't the tasty stuff.'

'Oh, I don't know,' Kat interjected. 'Jess is pretty good at knocking up some tasty recipes when the mood strikes her.'

The screen behind them flashed to another picture of Jess, this time of her in her kitchen. The bench was laid out with ingredients and she was resting a hand on top of her trusty blender, which had made many delicious morning smoothies over the years. Her fans followed her for her recipes as well as her fitness inspiration.

Ant pointed at the screen. 'No way. See that? Right there?' He pointed again. 'That's kale. Ain't nobody going to sneak that green muck into my smoothie. And why have a smoothie anyway when you can enjoy real food for breakfast?'

'I think you'll find my smoothies aren't all that bad,' Jess told him.

Ant shook his head and folded his arms together, resting them on the desk a bit like a petulant child. 'I doubt I can be convinced. Get back to me when you invent an egg and bacon smoothie with barbecue sauce.'

Jess screwed up her nose while Kat shot Ant an unimpressed look.

Kat turned back to the camera. 'One of the main reasons Jess's approach to health and fitness has been brought to the attention of the mainstream media is that anyone can do it. Even you, Ant.'

They'd rehearsed this also, and Jess found herself looking forward to what was coming.

'Uh-uh,' he replied. 'I'm aware of my many failings. The key to being at peace with yourself is not to fight them. I accepted that exercise and I don't go together long ago.'

'Or you could try something different and see where that takes you,' Jess said confidently. 'How about a three-month Hi-Jinks challenge, and you can share with us your opinion on exercise after that?'

Ant tipped his head to one side, considering her words. 'Nope. I'm all good. See? I've perfected acceptance—that's got to count for something.'

Kat shook her head. 'You're approaching this from the wrong angle, Jess,' she told them. 'You just need to give Ant the right inspiration.'

The image behind them changed again. Jess tried not to blink at the impossible beauty the picture portrayed. It was a full-length shot of catwalk model, Alicia Travers, who was well-recognised for her role as ambassador of one of the country's biggest department store brands.

Ant's dark eyebrows rose. 'Well, hello, Alicia, my love. This is an unexpected pleasure.'

'Alicia,' Kat said, quite seriously, 'is your inspiration.'

Ant dragged his eyes away from the screen. 'Inspiration? Don't you mean my future wife?' he quipped.

'Not yet, she isn't,' Kat told him. 'But that could all change. If, in three months' time, Jess tells us you've met the requirements of her Hi-Jinks challenge, Alicia will attend Australia's biggest television network awards ceremony—the Logies—with you.'

Ant fell silent. So did Jess.

What the hell? Jess knew about the three-month challenge— that was her entire reason for being on the show. Kat had pitched the idea to Jess one weekend. It was simple: transform Ant over a twelve-week period from a non-exerciser and junk food addict into someone who genuinely wants to exercise and eat healthy. Jess had been unconvinced at first. She'd always hated those *Biggest Loser*-style programs. While the weight might fall off on the shows, it was keeping it off with a healthy approach to life that was harder to achieve. And Jess's approach had never been about losing weight. She'd always focused on fitness—and fitness looked different for everyone.

Despite this, Kat had worn Jess down. Kat pointed out that Ant wasn't particularly overweight, just unfit. She also claimed the PR opportunity for Jess's brand would be huge. Eventually, Jess had been unable to argue.

But this added incentive was entirely unexpected. Kat and the producers must have concocted it.

Jess saw Ant's Adam's apple bob up and down as he swallowed. Clearly he'd been taken by surprise, too.

He looked between Kat and Jess. 'You're serious?'

Jess held up her hands. 'Don't look at me. I've only agreed to work with you, not go on a date with you. That's up to Alicia.'

For some strange reason, the idea of Ant going out with Alicia felt wrong. Not because he wasn't good enough for her —Jess wasn't that superficial. Just because they seemed so different.

Ant cleared his throat. 'So let me get this straight. For the next three months, I get to hang around this beautiful woman sitting right here—even if she is going to torture me with regular exercise sessions and force-feed me kale. At the end of that, I get to have another beautiful woman on my arm for a night.' Ant put a finger to his lips and removed it a second later. 'Hmm. Nope. I don't need to think about it. I'm in.'

Kat smiled. 'You heard it here first. Ant Monticello is going to get fit with the help of Jess Jinks. Each week we'll bring you a weekly report on his progress so we can see for ourselves how his exercise sessions are going.' Kat shifted to face Jess. 'Thanks for taking one for the team, Jess. You've got your work cut out for you.'

'Hey!' Ant protested.

'My pleasure, Kat,' Jess replied, ignoring Ant like he wasn't there because it was kind of fun. 'I think Ant will find exercising isn't so bad after all.'

'But kale. Kale isn't fun,' Ant muttered. 'It's disgusting and you can't make—'

Kat faced the camera again. 'Now, Ant. Jess won't be *making* you do anything. It's all up to you at the end of the day.'

'Do I have to eat kale to go on the date with Alicia?' he asked.

Jess couldn't help herself and laughed. 'You definitely have to try some kale.'

Ant put his head in his hands.

Kat smiled serenely for the cameras. 'We'll bring you an update on Ant's first exercise session next week. Thanks for joining us, Jess.'

'Thanks for having me and I look forward to helping Ant get fit.' And to her surprise, Jess meant it.

Chapter Two

ANT FOUND Kat and Jess after the show chatting in the room where the guests usually got ready.

'I'm glad it wasn't as bad as you thought,' he heard Kat say to Jess as he came to a stop by the door.

'Oh, it was so much better than I expected. With you and Ant up there to guide things, it was almost easy. You guys are pros. Oh, hey, Ant.'

He watched as Jess's friendly manner shifted to uncertainty. It annoyed him, but he didn't show it. She was probably unsure of how the next few months were going to pan out with a lazy comedian for a client. Let's face it, she had the most to lose if this PR stunt tanked. It would reflect poorly on her fitness brand, whereas Ant was used to looking bad in the media, so it would be water off a duck's back for him.

Ant stepped into the room. He had no plans for the PR exercise to fail, and he hoped that Jess would see that before too long.

'You were great on camera,' he told Jess, meaning it.

Despite her obvious discomfort about being on live television, Jess had shone—as Ant had known she would. How could she not? The woman practically glowed in real life with her tanned skin and bright blue eyes that always seemed to sparkle. She exuded positive energy on a permanent basis, and Ant had found himself drawn to her the first time Kat had introduced them.

In reality, it was a cruel irony. He, the goof-off comedian who had failed at any sport and fitness related activity in high school, finding this cute, fitness freak woman impossibly attractive. Ant wasn't going to fight it though. He'd been failing at relationships since he was old enough to crush on girls, so he completely expected his feelings not to be reciprocated.

'Thanks,' Jess replied.

A pink blush flushed her cheeks, making Ant crush on her a little harder. It wasn't every day that you met a gorgeous woman who didn't seem to know that she was gorgeous.

'I mean, I wouldn't say I was comfortable in front of the camera,' Jess continued, 'but it was a lot less frightening and painful than I thought it was going to be.'

'Pain. Now, let's talk about that some more, shall we?' Ant took another step closer to the pair, ignoring Kat's raised brow. She'd worked with him long enough to know that if he wasn't joking, he was usually working up to a joke. 'Just how much pain are you planning on putting me through in your quest for fitness?'

Jess blinked and bit her lip. Ant's stomach clenched in response. Yep, she was completely unaware of her appeal.

Jess released her lip. 'Well, that depends on you, I guess, and how hard you're willing to let me push you.'

Ant swallowed at the delicious thought, which Jess mistook for uncertainty. She closed the distance between them and put what was supposed to be a comforting hand on his arm. The contact twisted his already tight stomach into a ball of pent-up need.

'Don't worry,' she reassured him. 'We'll start slow. I meant what I said on camera. I don't believe pain is the way to get to fit. We'll work up to things. Sure, you might have a few sore muscles when you use them for the first time, but any pain will be good pain. And it will be worth it, I promise.'

Good pain, Ant wondered as he looked into her clear blue eyes. *Is that what this was?* Because spending the next three months in close proximity to her was definitely going to be painful for him, but not in the way she thought.

Kat rolled her eyes at Ant—something she would never do on camera, but did regularly when they weren't filming—and patted him on the back. 'There, there, Ant. You'll survive,' she said without any hint of sympathy.

It was all good and well for her. She'd been training with Jess once a week for at least a year, so she was already fit. Ant was pretty sure he'd never been fit his entire life. Unless you counted his eager eight-year-old self riding his bike five blocks every day to see if the pretty girl in number eight wanted to play with him. She'd been about three years older, so had considered herself far too mature for him. Ant had been hoping she'd be swayed by his innocence and find him unthreatening to be around. But she'd just rolled her eyes, much like Kat did now. Story of his dating life.

Jess dropped her hand and shrugged. 'You can't hate exercise that much, surely?'

Ant resisted a groan. 'Define hate.'

'Loathe, abhor, and avoid at all possible costs,' Kat interjected helpfully.

'See?' said Jess. 'You might not like exercise, but I'm pretty sure you don't feel that strongly about it, do you?'

Ant's repressed groan surfaced in a wince and Jess's hopeful expression turned to one of alarm.

'Seriously?' she said.

Kat turned and patted Jess on the shoulder—this time it was genuinely sympathetic. 'I'm sorry, but you really do have your work cut out for you when it comes to Ant Monticello and exercise. Just be reassured that I have every bit of faith in you, Jess.' Kat tipped her head in Ant's direction. 'Him not so much. On that note, I'll leave you to it. Matt's waiting for me.'

Kat raised her hand in farewell and disappeared from the room to go and meet her fiancé. Jess retreated a step and Ant resisted the urge to close the distance between them again. It was like this whenever he was around Jess—he felt an inexplicable need to be close to her.

'So, I'll see you on Thursday, then?' she asked, less relaxed than she had appeared in Kat's presence.

'That's the plan,' Ant confirmed, trying to sound enthused. He could take or leave the exercise—preferably leave it—but the thought of spending time with Jess again was definitely appealing.

'Are you going to be able to manage six in the morning?' she pressed.

Did he have a choice? He wasn't a morning person, even less so since he'd started working on an evening show.

'With your happy face to greet me, I'm sure I'll manage,' he said, then instantly regretted it.

Jess blinked a few times, then diverted her eyes as she turned to get her bag, the awkwardness shifting to painful. 'Yes, well, it does definitely help to have an exercise group or partner for those times you find it hard to motivate yourself.'

It sounded like a well-practiced line, and Ant wanted to kick himself. Honest compliments with a girl like Jess Jinks were never going to work in his favour. He should have just stuck to his usual jokes, because that's what she expected. What they all expected.

Ant suppressed a sigh. When would he meet a girl that he could just be himself with? Unfortunately, Ant's self wasn't what women were usually interested in. They found him funny and easy to have around, and for whatever reason, those qualities seemed to cancel out his potential as a love interest. Ant had grown used to playing the role of the perpetual friend.

So, that's what he'd do with Jess. Tell jokes. Make her laugh. Then she'd feel comfortable in his presence.

And then what?

Ant honestly had no idea. But he could live in hope that Jess's exercise regimen would work miracles. And then, by the end of their time together, she'd find him impossibly attractive and suddenly want to be with him.

Hey, if that didn't work out, he always had that date with Alicia.

Ant swallowed a laugh. As far as back-up plans went, it wasn't bad. Although, if regular girls friend-zoned him, he wondered what Alicia would think of him. He honestly had no idea.

Jess turned back to him, her bag on her shoulder, catching his eye as she did so.

'Hey.' She stepped in close again, her expression concerned. 'Are you alright? You're not really worried about this, are you? I thought you were just joking around before.'

Ant forced a smile. 'Something you'll learn about me is that I'm always joking. And I'm not worried. I know we'll make this work somehow. I'm doubtful you'll ever get me looking like an Adonis though, it's not in my gene pool.'

Jess frowned. 'Adonis is overrated. I'll be over the moon if you still want to exercise at the end of this.'

Ant didn't want to exercise now, so he very much doubted

it, but didn't say that. 'How about we just start with this week?' he suggested. 'I think I should be able to manage that much.'

He paused. She was standing opposite him with her bag hitched across one shoulder and he was in the way of the door. He couldn't help feeling like she wanted to make a quick escape.

He pushed aside a stab of disappointment. He decided that, in order to win her trust, he should actively try to show her that he was taking this whole thing seriously. Never mind he hadn't taken anything seriously his entire life.

'OK. See you Thursday then.' Jess went to step around him.

'Wait! Is there anything I need to do before then?'

Jess gave him an uncertain look.

'In preparation,' he clarified.

Her eyebrows shot up. 'Oh, right. Sure. Good question. Physically, you don't need to do anything. That can wait until Thursday. But how about this? Can you try not to eat junk food or takeaway this week for me? I'm working on a meal plan for you, which I'll run through with you after our session.' At his horrified look, she smiled. 'Don't worry. It won't involve much kale.'

'Much?' he sputtered.

She grinned and prodded him in the side. 'Got you.'

He put a hand to his chest in mock relief and it wasn't entirely a joke. It wasn't the kale, but the surprising way she caught him unawares with her teasing. He knew in that instant that his pointless crush wasn't going to get any easier over the coming weeks.

Her grin turned into a genuine smile. 'See you Thursday, Ant,' she said as she slipped past him on her way to the door.

He turned to watch her go. 'Hey, from now on it's Adonis to you.'

He was rewarded with melodious laughter as she disappeared into the corridor.

Chapter Three

JESS INHALED the early morning sea air from her balcony overlooking the Pacific Ocean. Gosh, she loved living here. Growing up in one of Sydney's leafier northern suburbs, Jess had always appreciated being surrounded by nature. Then she'd taken a part-time job at a beachside gym in her early twenties to support her university studies and she'd become addicted to the coastal lifestyle ever since.

Something about the ever-changing ocean and the refreshing sea breezes made Jess feel like anything was possible. That, and she enjoyed beach jogging, which was what she planned to be doing shortly when her two neighbours arrived.

Jess enjoyed most types of exercise, so she always tried to mix it up. Sometimes a solo jog was what she needed, and other times it was great to exercise with friends—like she was doing this morning.

Her Saturday morning beach sessions had become a regular routine with her two neighbours, Kat and Em. They'd both taken some convincing at first, as neither was particularly fitness-minded. They'd soon realised that their sessions were a great way to kick off the weekend and shake off stress from the working week.

Jess also occasionally used them as guinea pigs to try out new Hi-Jinks routines she was considering. The fitness brand Jess had built up was a blend of Pilates-style strengthening exercises and aerobic fitness. Her friends gladly included these extra exercises in their Saturday morning sessions because neither was keen to join a gym. In fact, that's how her business had continued to grow. Attracting people who didn't think of themselves as fitness freaks and preferred to avoid gyms, yet who still had a desire to exercise and stay fit was what set Jess apart.

It was her hope that this approach would work well with Ant Monticello, too. Except he had no desire whatsoever to exercise and stay fit.

Jess huffed in relief at the sound of a knock on her front door. She picked up her water bottle and headed down the hall, determined to shake off the feelings of doubt and worry that had plagued her ever since her television appearance.

Doubt and worry weren't natural emotions for her. The truth was, this week she needed the morning exercise session just as much as her friends.

Jess opened the front door, keen to greet her friends and put her troubling thoughts out of her mind. 'Hi! Ready to go?'

'What's wrong?' Kat demanded.

Jess closed her mouth and felt her brow furrow in confusion. She thought she'd been her usual positive self when she'd opened the door.

'Nice one,' Em said, her light blue eyes rising skyward in response to Kat's direct attempt at a greeting. Em was usually honest as well, but this morning she appeared to have more tact than their friend. 'I think what Kat is trying to say is good morning.'

'OK,' Jess said, still feeling uncertain but not ready to answer Kat's question. She felt the need for the sea breeze on her face and the sand between her toes more than ever. 'Let's hit the beach, ladies,' she told them, taking on her familiar role of fitness coach because that made her feel better.

They headed towards the lift together.

'Uh-uh,' Kat said as she pressed the down button. 'You're not getting away with it that easily. You need to talk to us.'

'About?'

'Whatever is worrying you,' Kat replied.

Em nudged Kat. 'Maybe she doesn't want to talk about it.'

The lift doors opened, and they all stepped inside.

Kat shook her head. 'Jess is always Miss Positive,' she said, like Jess wasn't standing right there. 'I want to know what's gotten under her skin so much that she's not her usual self.'

'I am my usual self!' Jess cried.

The other two women stared at her.

All right, maybe she wasn't quite her normal self for her to react like that.

She sighed as the lift doors opened on the ground floor.

'Can we just head down to the beach? I'll feel better once I get some fresh air,' Jess suggested.

Kat went to open her mouth, and Em backhanded her across the stomach.

'Hey!' Kat complained.

'I barely touched you,' Em shot back.

Jess stepped out of the lift, hiding a smile. Jess guessed it wasn't Kat's stomach that hurt, but her pride. She wasn't used to being told to be quiet, but Em wasn't afraid to stand up to her despite being the youngest of their group.

Em might look sweet and innocent with her pale, rosy complexion and her waves of cascading auburn hair, but her feminine appearance hid a determined, confident nature.

Unlike Kat who had already carved out a career for herself as a successful broadcast journalist, Em was still studying at university. *Still* being the operative word. She was working on her PhD. Jess could never quite recall what it was about exactly because it was all a bit over her head—something about the built environment and creating sustainable cities. Something immensely important and inspiring at any rate. It was also something that required a high degree of intelligence, so while Em might only be twenty-five years of age, she was well and truly a match for Kat.

'Let's walk,' Em said, and Jess silently thanked her friend.

She'd meant what she said about needing the fresh air. They headed down the street that followed the headland towards the beach affectionately known to the locals as "Freshie", or Freshwater as it was formally known.

They walked at a brisk rate in companionable silence, basking in the warmth of the early morning sun. Winter was only a few weeks away, so aside from the die-hard surfers and fitness enthusiasts like themselves, the beach would be relatively empty.

Jess actually preferred this time of year, if she was being honest. It was easy to spot the locals, and a trip to the beach was often punctuated by "hello" and "how are you?" Or perhaps, like her friends told her, she was more well-known than she gave herself credit for these days.

Jess's thoughts returned to Ant again. Their first session was going to be filmed down here on the beach, weather permitting. As always when thoughts of the comedian came to mind, Jess found her brow furrowing. She wasn't sure what it was about the man that unsettled her.

For one, he was genuinely nice. Two, he was actually very self-deprecating, which Jess thought was an over-exaggeration because the man had plenty of positive qualities. Sure, he was a bit on the short side and not at all ripped, but it wasn't like he was overweight or bad looking. He was just out of shape, and what he lacked in that department he made up for with his dark and handsome looks. And surely the fact that she was noticing his dark and handsome looks wasn't very professional of her.

'OK, I can't bear it,' Kat muttered from beside Jess. 'Whatever it is that's not bothering you, Jess, you're thinking about it again.'

Em covered a laugh with her hand and Jess actually cracked a smile.

'Fine,' Jess relented. 'It's Ant.'

Kat nodded knowingly. 'Jess is worried about the PR exercise *Sydney Tonight* is hosting involving her and Ant,' Kat told Em.

Em also nodded in understanding, already having been told about it during previous exercise sessions.

'I'm not worried,' Jess interjected. 'More like mildly concerned.'

'We've already been through this,' Kat told them. 'Ant's not going to try to damage your reputation in any way. He's agreed to do his best the next three months.'

'I know,' Jess said, because they most certainly had been through it at length on previous occasions otherwise Jess wouldn't have agreed to it. 'He's just so . . . not serious.'

Kat shrugged and Em smiled.

'That's Ant,' Kat said.

'Yes,' Em added. 'He's a comedian.'

'Does he ever take anything seriously?' Jess asked hopefully.

'Not really,' Kat replied honestly. Jess's face fell, making Kat reach out and pat Jess on the shoulder. 'Don't worry. He's paid not to be serious. He'll make you look good, trust me. It's his job.'

Jess worried her lip with her front teeth. 'I know he won't set out to make me look bad. He's too nice for that. It's just . . . he always seems to be joking. I mean, I'm not super serious myself, but surely he can have a conversation without making a joke now and then, can't he?'

'Not that I've noticed,' Kat answered. 'It's who he is.'

Jess didn't say anything else straight away and concentrated on walking. They were on the flat now, having walked down the steep street that took them from the headland to the expanse of grass overlooking the beach.

'He can be funny and still ambitious,' Em pointed out as they made their way across the grass. 'He's one of the country's best-known comedians. You don't land a job on *Sydney Tonight* with the likes of Kat without being ambitious.'

'She's right,' Kat agreed. 'I'd actually say he's so ambitious he can't afford not to be funny all the time. Look at you. You live your Hi-Jinks brand. He lives his. That's all it is. And at the risk of sounding condescending, don't take it too seriously.'

They all laughed at Kat's comment. Jess supposed Em and Kat had a good point. Humour was Ant's brand, so of course he'd live it.

Then why couldn't Jess shake the odd feeling that, when she looked into Ant's dark eyes, there was so much more than humour there? Goodness, she was definitely overthinking things. He was a *comedian*. And she really needed to run this morning.

'You're still frowning,' Kat pointed out. 'What did we miss?'

Jess smiled. Her friends might be a bit bossy, but they really did care about her. 'The added incentive. The Logies date with Alicia. You didn't tell me about that.'

'Mmm,' Kat said, appearing unimpressed. 'I know. It was very last minute. The producers only sprang it on me before the show the same day. They hadn't told me either. Apparently it had taken a week to convince Alicia to agree to it. There was some back and forth about upcoming appearances on the show to coincide with Alicia's new fashion brand launch.'

'What!' Jess exclaimed. 'So it was a business deal?'

Kat gave Jess a strange look. 'What did you think it was? Alicia isn't exactly going to date him for real.'

They stopped at the edge of the grassed area overlooking the low-lying bushes that bordered the sand.

Jess's thoughts continued to whirl, but she managed to put into words what was bothering her so much. 'It seems kind of unfair, you know, to Ant, if she's not really interested in him.'

'It's how things work though in this modern age of social media. You've built your business on Instagram, you should know that.'

'Yeah, but Jess *is* kind of herself on Instagram,' Em pointed out.

'True,' allowed Kat. 'Seriously, I know this feels a bit off to you because you don't work in the industry, but it's how things are. Alicia gets something out of it and so does Ant—the added exposure for him will take his recognition to another level. He knows how it works.'

'I guess you're right. It just seems so . . .'

'Fake?' Em finished for her. 'Why do you think I'm an academic? But Kat is right. Ant knows what he's in for. And by the time you're finished with him, he'll look great next to Alicia, thanks to you.'

Jess reached out for the wooden fence separating them from the beach and started stretching. 'I'm not some reality TV show. I'm not trying to change Ant. I just want him to give exercise a chance and hopefully like it.'

'If anyone can make a person feel positive about exercise, you can,' Kat told her. 'Now come on. I need my Saturday morning pep talk to get my arse into gear. Off you go.'

Jess grinned in reply. This was what she did best. She pushed all thoughts of Ant to the side and clapped her hands together in readiness for their session. First, they were going to run some lengths of the beach, and then she wanted to show them a few strengthening positions she was working on.

'Alright then,' she said in her best take-charge voice. 'You asked for it. Shoes off, let's go!'

THURSDAY MORNING ANT was down at the beach earlier than required. Not because he was a morning person. Although he had to admit watching the sun come up over the horizon was kind of nice. He lived in the inner city and rarely made it to the beach, so this morning felt surreal, like he was on holiday or a weekend getaway.

The real reason he was here at first light was because he couldn't sleep. He wasn't nervous, not really. That would be kind of stupid seeing as he made a fool out of himself on a regular basis. Hell, the TV station *wanted* him to make a fool of himself during this little publicity stunt to boost ratings.

Ant slipped the sunglasses that had been sitting on top of his head down onto his nose as the sunrise became brighter. He heard a car pull up in the street behind him and twisted to look, his pulse spiking. It returned to normal when he saw a burly guy get out of a white hatchback and retrieve a surfboard from the roof racks. That seemed to be a pretty common occurrence around here at this time of day. Surfers and early morning joggers and walkers were the only ones eager enough to be up and about at this hour. Hey, he wasn't criticising. They definitely looked fitter than he did, so they obviously knew something he didn't.

Ant moved his gaze towards the beach again, which was when he saw her. Her blonde hair glowed in the morning light like a diamond catching the sun as she walked down the hill in the distance. He felt his pulse spike again.

Fine, he *was* nervous, and not because of the stupid show. It was because of her.

Ant didn't need to squint to know it was Jess. Apart from the hair being a dead giveaway, it was the way she walked. With confidence and energy, like she was ready for whatever the day would bring.

Ant wasn't sure he'd ever felt that way.

She waved when she saw him and by then was close enough for him to make out her bright smile. His stomach clenched.

Damn it, Ant. Get a grip. Time to put your game face on.

He stood up from the bench he'd been waiting at and raised a hand to return her greeting.

Oh, holy shit.

Now she was jogging. Not fast, just a light jog, like it took no effort at all—which it probably didn't for a woman that fit.

Ant tore his eyes away from her and focused on the water again. His self-control had to count for something, surely? If he'd kept looking at her, he would have been forced to notice other things, like the way her breasts moved as she ran or the toned shape of her legs.

'Good morning!'

Ant swallowed and turned to face Jess, glad his sunglasses were obscuring his eyes.

'I should have figured you'd be perky at this time of the day,' he replied.

She grinned at him and his stomach clenched tighter.

'Guilty as charged. Have you had a coffee?'

His brow furrowed in confusion. 'Coffee? I thought that wasn't allowed?'

'God, I'm not that much of a task master! You need to ease into this. Come on, there's a place just up the road, and we're early, so we have time before the crew get here.'

Ant made sure to fall into stride beside her. He didn't want her to get ahead of him. Then he'd find himself looking at her inappropriately. When she'd appeared on television, she'd been wearing regular clothes, but Ant guessed Jess usually lived in exercise gear like these skin-tight leggings and fitted top. Unfortunately for him, they fit too well.

'I'm surprised you're here early, to be honest,' Jess said as they walked, giving him a sidelong glance.

He put a hand to his chest. 'You like insulting me, don't you? I enjoy sleeping in as much as the next guy, but this morning we have a job to do.'

'Yeah, *you*,' she joked, and Ant almost tripped on a non-existent bump on the footpath.

He cleared his throat, hoping she hadn't noticed the slight pause as he walked. 'I'm definitely a work in progress.'

She laughed, which was what he'd wanted her to do, but he couldn't remember ever being so satisfied with his ability to make somebody laugh before. He wasn't exactly sure what it was about her laughter. The fact that it sounded like a song? Or the way her eyes danced when she smiled? He didn't have a clue, only that it was addictive.

'We're all works in progress, not just you,' she said when her laughter faded.

Ant bit down on his tongue. Hard. He'd been about to say, "You're not. You're perfect just as you are." Thank God his sense of comedic timing ensured he knew when to speak and when to shut up.

'Here we are,' Jess said when they arrived at a tiny café not far up the road.

Despite the early hour, the café was doing a strong trade. A few locals stood just outside chatting with takeaway coffees in hand while inside there were a group of people waiting for their orders.

'Hey, Jess!' a blond surfer guy called out as they stepped inside. 'Looking great as always. What can I get you?'

'Right back at you, Josh. I'm all good, actually, but my friend here could do with something to start the day.'

Josh studied Ant with interest. He continued to move behind the counter preparing coffees and something that smelled suspiciously of a bacon and egg roll. Ant ignored the way his mouth started to water. He knew he definitely wasn't allowed to have that.

Ant suppressed a groan. He wasn't even exercising yet and this whole thing hurt.

Jess registered his look of pain and reached over and rubbed his arm in sympathy. Ant almost flinched at her touch, but caught himself and hoped he hadn't gone too stiff.

Jesus. She was one of those touchy-feely types, wasn't she? God help him.

'I think Ant needs a coffee or we'll never get through our session,' she explained to Josh.

'Sure thing,' Josh replied. 'How do you like it?'

'Strong, with just a dash of milk, thanks,' Ant replied, already feeling better than he had all morning from the aroma of coffee permeating the air.

'You haven't eaten?' Jess asked.

'No, I thought I wasn't allowed,' Ant said obediently, and Jess shook her head.

'I don't want to starve you! You need something in your system or you won't have the energy to get through the morning.' She returned her attention to Josh. 'Can you do a couple of slices of that seeded bread? To go, thanks.' She touched Ant's arm again. 'Vegemite OK?'

'Sure.'

'I'll bring it out to you,' Josh told them as a couple came through the front door making it difficult for everyone to fit inside.

Ant followed Jess outside and, when she turned back to face him, she caught him frowning.

'Oh gosh, you're not gluten-free or anything like that, are you?' she asked.

'What? No. That would require actual effort and I don't do effort.' He flashed her a grin.

Her blue eyes turned thoughtful. 'I don't believe you.'

Ant blinked. 'Excuse me?'

'I think you put in more effort than you realise. Either that, or you're really good at hiding how much effort you really put in. You don't get to be such a good comedian by not putting in any work.'

Ant stared at her for a moment, his eyes behind his sunglasses wide with shock at her honest and accurate observation. Then he pretended to look away to take in the view of the ocean.

'When you're as funny as I am, it comes naturally.' He meant it as a joke, of course, but hated himself for saying the words as soon as they came out of his mouth. It sounded so arrogant. And it was so far from the truth it wasn't actually funny. Ant had worked hard to get where he was—not that he ever let on that was the case.

He snuck a look at Jess and caught her rolling her eyes, but she was still smiling.

'Well, I'm sorry to say being fit and healthy *does* require some effort.'

'And let me guess,' Ant said, 'you're going to show me?'

She poked him in the ribs, making him jump. 'But you're the one who is going to have to do the hard work.'

Ant mock groaned. 'How far away is that coffee?'

She shook her head at him. 'It won't be long. In the meantime, tell me what sort of things motivate you.'

'Hmm, let me see. That would be food, long sessions on the sofa, and more food.'

Jess rolled her eyes again. 'Can you be serious for one moment?'

'Honestly? No.'

It wasn't strictly true. He *had* kind of been serious when he'd mentioned the long sessions on the sofa. He'd just left out the part about watching showreel after showreel of successful comedians' work to figure out the keys to their success, to see if he could apply them to himself. It wasn't like there was formal training for comedians. Sure, there were basic courses for beginners and open mic stand up nights, but he wasn't a beginner anymore and he wanted to push himself to do better. No, that wasn't true either. He didn't just want to be better. He wanted to be one of the best.

He was distracted from his thoughts by Jess's groan, which sounded more genuine than his. 'Kat told me you'd say that.'

He pushed his sunglasses onto his head. 'Oooh, you've been discussing me with Kat? What juicy gossip did she tell you?'

'For me to know and you to find out.' She finished that worrying statement by poking her tongue out at him. 'Sounds like that's your coffee. And that looks like the crew arriving, too. Come on, we better get a move on.'

'Has anyone told you before that you're bossy?'

'Every single one of my pig-headed brothers, don't worry.'

Ant followed her back into the café, curious about how many "every single one of my pig-headed brothers" numbered. He also sincerely doubted her brothers enjoyed being bossed around by their sister quite so much as Ant knew he was going to.

Chapter Five

JESS ALWAYS LIKED to get to know her one-on-one fitness training clients before launching into their first session. For obvious reasons as well as less obvious ones. Of course she had to have an understanding of their fitness levels so she could tailor a program to suit them, but it also paid to learn a little about them personally, too.

Some clients liked to be pushed, others hated it. Some thrived on achieving a goal they decided on together, whether that be weight loss, strength related or simply being able to complete a session without becoming too puffed.

Ant's profile should have been obvious to her, and on the surface, Jess supposed it was. He was new to exercise, so he needed to start slow and work up to things to make sure he wasn't in too much pain as they progressed. But as for his mindset? Jess found Ant Monticello to be a complete mystery.

He should have been easy to figure out. He came across as an easygoing and straightforward sort of guy. But for the life of her, Jess couldn't figure out what was going to motivate him.

Alicia Travers.

Jess resisted scoffing in distaste. TV program or no TV program, Jess did not bait her clients with ridiculous bribes like that. She'd leave it up to the station to sort that one out. In the meantime, Jess would have to work with Ant over the next few sessions to discover what motivated him—apart from unhealthy food, that was.

By the time the crew was all set up and Ant's and her make-up was done, the sun was high in the sky. Personally, Jess was a little uncomfortable about wearing so much make-up to do a workout, but the producer had insisted on it. They'd even put something suspiciously like bronzer on Ant's olive skin, which Jess didn't think he remotely needed.

'Alright, first up we're going to get some shots of you running along the beach together,' Deb, the producer, explained as a cameraman adjusted his focus next to her.

Ant frowned. 'Run? That's a bit extreme, don't you think? Don't we have to warm up or something first?'

Deb levelled him with a serious look. 'Hon, no amount of warming up is going to save your unfit body from hurting tomorrow.'

Jess bit back a laugh. 'That may be true, but I'm happy to do a few stretches first if that works for you?' she suggested to the producer. There was no point in hurting Ant unnecessarily, although Deb was right—Ant would most likely hurt tomorrow.

'You're too kind, Jess, but sure, some footage of you both stretching will work,' Deb agreed. 'But after a few sessions, you're going to want to inflict pain on him, trust me.'

'Hey!' Ant said. 'What did I ever do to you?'

Deb's expression turned thoughtful. 'Hmm, let me see. There was that time you told the viewers that our crew are terrible at karaoke and you had the footage to prove it.'

Ant's lips flattened, but Jess wasn't sure if he was genuinely contrite or holding back a smile.

'I know, I know,' he said. 'What happens at the Christmas party stays at the Christmas party, I get it. But come on, you've got to admit our make-up team did a fantastic rendition of *Hot Summer Nights* from Grease.'

'It was memorable, I'll give you that,' Deb allowed, then nodded at Jess. 'Start bossing him around and try to forget we're here.'

Jess swallowed, knowing it was pretty unlikely she'd ever be able to forget that there was a camera crew filming her. She caught Ant looking at her.

'Don't worry. I can distract you, I promise,' Ant told her. 'See?'

He started stretching, but not like someone who was a regular exerciser would stretch. More like a comedian would stretch: awkwardly, yet overdone in a way that was sure to attract maximum attention.

She covered her mouth, but a giggle still escaped.

He was dressed in a black T-shirt and matching black running shorts she was pretty sure he'd bought for the occasion. It was the first time she'd seen him without a suit and she was still adjusting to the sight. He actually had nice legs for someone who didn't exercise. The same went for his arms. Because of his Italian heritage he was naturally olive-skinned, and unlike a lot of the guys she trained with who were hairless or mostly hair-free, he most definitely wasn't hairless. Jess knew a lot of guys strived to avoid hair, but in Ant's case it was kind of . . . manly, she decided.

Then she giggled again because Ant's attempts at stretching were both awkward and hilarious.

'How about you copy me?' she told him, then used the nearby outdoor table to brace herself.

Ant watched as Jess demonstrated a leg stretch that involved bending one knee slightly and keeping the other straight.

'I can do that,' he said and mirrored her pose.

'Great, now let's try this.' She ran through a few more basic stretches, which he copied perfectly.

For someone who never exercised, he seemed coordinated enough, which was good. Jess found herself glancing self-consciously back at the camera.

'OK, I think I'm pumped now,' Ant called out. 'Do I look ready to you?'

When Jess returned her gaze to him, she burst out laughing and found she couldn't stop.

Ant was jogging on the spot, lifting his knees high each time a leg left the ground. When she wasn't looking, he'd put a vibrant yellow sweatband around his forehead so that his dark wavy hair flopped over the top of it. He reached over to the table and grabbed Jess's drink bottle, then sprayed himself in the face with water.

Playing it up for the camera, he shook his head back and forth like a model in a hair shampoo commercial, pouting as he did so. Jess noticed the cameraman holding back a laugh too, and the rest of the crew that were further back were laughing quietly as well.

'That's great, Ant,' Deb called out. 'Now we just need to play *What A Feeling* from that movie *Flashdance* when we air that shot.'

Jess couldn't tell if she was serious or being deadpan.

'Phew,' Ant puffed and collapsed onto the seat next to the table. 'Are we done?'

'With our stretches?' Jess said. 'Sure. Now we can jog a length of the beach like Deb suggested.'

Ant leaned over and rested his elbows on his knees. 'You're

kidding, right? I'm spent after that. Can't we just use that footage and pretend I did an exercise session?' Ant asked hopefully.

Deb sighed, and the cameraman turned away, obviously finished shooting for now.

'I can order him to do it,' Deb told her, 'but if you've got a better way to motivate him, he's all yours.'

Jess checked behind her to make sure the camera was definitely off and stepped in closer to Ant. He was still bent over his knees, so she crouched down in front of him and noticed his eyes widen slightly.

'Hey,' she said.

'Hey,' he said.

'You're not really that puffed, are you?'

'Depends on your definition of puffed. I think I'll recover enough to walk back up to that nice café to buy a bacon and egg roll, but I'm much too exhausted for a run.'

Jess heard Deb snort in disgust from behind them.

'Have you ever experienced an endorphin high?' Jess asked him.

'Clearly not from exercise,' Ant joked.

'What about from laughter?' she tried. Laughter was another well-researched form of endorphins.

'Well, yeah. Of course. When you're as funny as I am, you're surfing one continual endorphin high.' He stood up, making Jess shift back onto her hands to look up at him. 'Clearly this exercise thing is a moot point, so I'm all good. Thanks anyway.'

She heard Deb sigh again, and Jess jumped up to bar his way. With four brothers to contend with growing up, she wasn't beat yet. 'How about sex then?'

Ant froze and blinked at her.

She grinned. 'You are familiar with sex, aren't you?' She

knew she was being cheeky, but when Jess was determined about something, she always gave it her best shot. Besides, the cameras were off right now.

Ant cleared his throat and swallowed, making his Adam's apple bob up and down. Then he shoved his fingers through his dark hair and shifted his stance to put a hand on his hip, attempting to look relaxed. 'Naturally.'

Jess couldn't help herself and laughed, then laughed harder when he appeared offended. Appeared being the operative word, because you could never tell with Ant whether he was joking or not—but from what she knew of him so far, he was most probably joking.

'Well, in that case,' Jess went on, 'you'll know about the endorphins you can experience after sex.'

'*All* the time,' Ant drawled, and Jess heard Deb snort again.

Jess didn't turn around. Instead she leaned in close and whispered loudly, 'Exercise is like sex, just in case you were wondering.'

She meant to move back straight away, she really did. But for some reason Jess found herself hovering in Ant's personal space, much too close to be polite. Maybe it was his smell? He smelled *really* nice. Kind of all woody and spicy with a hint of the coffee he'd drunk earlier.

His dark eyes watched her and for the first time Jess saw something other than humour in them, and she jumped back as a frisson of heat flashed through her body.

Seeing as she was way too young to be experiencing hot flashes, it must have been that dark look of his that had created that unexpected reaction. Strange thing was, he wasn't sexy, he was funny, but her body begged to differ.

'I wouldn't know,' he said, his voice sounding gruffer than

usual. He cleared his throat. 'Because, you know, who needs exercise when there's sex?'

'I didn't think you had a partner?' Jess said before she could stop herself.

Ant tipped his head to the side, considering her words. 'This is hardly a polite discussion to be having with a lady, but seeing as you brought it up . . .' His thoughtful expression morphed into a slow smile. 'Let's just say I'm all the partner I need.'

Jess planted a hand over her mouth while one of the crew guffawed behind them.

'Smooth, Ant, real smooth,' Deb called out. 'But I bet Alicia might change your mind on that one. Now, can we just get a move on? We don't have all day.'

Jess clapped her hands together to get Ant's attention. The mention of Alicia had annoyed her for some reason.

'Good point,' she said, keen to forget about her unusual reaction to him and do what they had come here for. 'Let's get going! Follow me.'

Chapter Six

THE FOLLOWING MORNING ANT HURT. Everywhere. Jess and her damn Hi-Jinks manoeuvres. He'd discovered his inability to move properly in the middle of the night when he got up to go to the toilet. It was bad enough that he could barely walk thanks to the beach jogging, but she'd also made him do some sort of weird routine designed to torture and activate muscles he didn't even know he had, like his stomach. Until now Ant had thought of his stomach as something singular. Apparently this wasn't the case at all, because his abdomen hurt in multiple places whenever he shifted or moved. Who knew there were so many muscles down there?

That's why he was still in bed. Thank God he didn't need to be at the studio until later in the day. He'd just lie here until hunger demanded he moved. Which normally wouldn't be that long, but after that stupid healthy eating checklist she'd given him yesterday he'd lost his appetite.

A smoothie for breakfast? Seriously? And the banana and fruit she'd allowed didn't count. That wasn't food . . . it was fruit.

Ant needed carbs. He needed sugar—and no, the sugar in fruit didn't cut it. He craved the refined stuff, and was pretty sure that's what flowed through his veins on a regular basis, so why stop now?

Alicia Travers, that's why.

He huffed, and then groaned because even loud breathing hurt.

Alicia Travers wasn't enough for Ant to put himself through this level of pain for the next three months. Of course she was hot, there was no questioning that. But in Ant's mind, Alicia Travers wasn't quite real. She was like a daydream, not an actual person to him. If he did actually get to meet her at the end of this morbid publicity stunt, Ant didn't expect theirs to be a lasting association. Oh sure, she'd smile for the cameras because that's what she was contracted to do. She'd probably laugh at his jokes, too. But girls like Alicia didn't end up with guys like him. It was one of those invisible law-of-the-universe things. Beautiful people dated beautiful people. Ant was much too busy being funny to try too hard at being beautiful.

Besides, you've been there, tried that.

Ant shook off the little voice in his head. Falling for the popular girl back in high school hadn't been one of his brighter ideas, and he didn't need to dwell on it now.

An image of Jess came into his head. For some insane reason he felt his body relax, which made no sense when she was the reason he was in this amount of pain.

He hadn't been able to get her out of his head since the day before. He rarely remembered his dreams, but he was pretty sure he had dreamed about her last night. She'd been running in his dream, her blonde hair bobbing above her shoulders and her pert little breasts . . .

'Yeah, running away from you,' he said out loud to stop the train of thought, because it was futile.

Even as he said it, another image of her came into his mind. That moment yesterday that had lasted for only a split second when she'd looked at him. Really looked at him. Or maybe his brain was just short circuiting after she'd whispered the word "sex" to him. He could admit he was pathetic enough to let it get him all hot and bothered.

His phone buzzed on the bedside table. After thinking about it for a moment, Ant reached over to retrieve it.

'Kill me,' he muttered as the muscles in his arms, shoulders and chest complained.

He fumbled with the phone when he saw who the message was from and dropped it onto his chest with a dull thud.

'Shit.' He managed to pick it up without too much strain to his poor, injured muscles.

It was from Jess:

Good morning! How are you feeling today?

Ant resisted rolling his eyes. She was even chirpy in her morning texts. It took him longer than usual to reply because while his fingers and hands didn't hurt, they were attached to his arms, which sure as hell did.

I'm man enough to admit it. I hurt.

He sent it then waited while those three dots danced around indicating that she was typing a reply.

You poor thing. Have you eaten? That will help.

His next reply was quicker.

Not hungry.

His phone rang and he answered it.

'You're not hungry?' Jess said, her voice full of concern, and his stupid, stupid body both relaxed and tensed at the sound of her voice. 'Did you drink enough yesterday?'

'If by drink you mean water, yes, I did. If you mean Coke or alcohol, no, I didn't, and my body isn't happy about it, let me tell you.'

'You'll get used to it,' she promised, sounding just as chirpy as her text message greeting. 'And your body *is* happy about it, but you're probably suffering some withdrawal.'

'It has a strange way of showing it.'

'Do you think you can manage our session Sunday morning?'

'Aren't Sundays supposed to be the day of rest?'

'Are you religious?'

'Well, no . . .'

'Great! Then your body isn't either. Seeing as it's the weekend I thought we'd try something different and give your body some variation.'

'So you can inflict pain on other muscles I didn't know I had?' Ant predicted a lot of hobbling around like an old man in his future.

'No, silly. Exercise isn't just about the physical. It's about the mind as well, so getting outside in the fresh air on a weekend should be enjoyable.'

'See, that's the thing. I do plenty of sitting outside at my local pub on the weekend already.'

'You always have a smart reply, don't you?' There was no malice in her tone, just amusement.

'Excellent. My pretty trainer thinks I'm smart,' he joked.

The line fell silent and Ant could have kicked himself, but seeing as that would involve moving his leg, he settled for closing his eyes.

Way to go, Monticello.

Calling her pretty was not going to make her comfortable around him, even if pretty was just the tip of the iceberg. At first glance, some people might say that Jess had an attractive, girl-next-door quality, but Ant knew better. Jess was gorgeous in all the best ways, and if the next three months were going to work, he was going to have to keep a lid on his attraction to her.

He heard Jess clear her throat. 'Anyway, we won't have the camera crew with us for our Sunday session, so I thought I'd surprise you.'

'Seeing as the crew won't be there, we could just forget about it?' Ant suggested.

'Not going to happen, Adonis. For three hours on Sunday morning, you're mine. Deal with it.'

If Ant had been standing up, his head would have lolled back in delight at the words "you're mine", but instead it remained cushioned by the pillow. 'Fine. I can see I'm not going to get out of it.'

'No, you're not. I'll text the details of where I want you to meet me the day before. In the meantime, drink lots of water and try to move around even if it hurts. It will aid recovery.'

'Yes, ma'am. Anything else?'

'Yes, actually. I also rang to say you did good yesterday, when you weren't goofing off, that is.'

Huh. Something like pride swelled in Ant's chest. He went to say, "you think so?" but instead said, 'That's me. I'm a regular ironman.'

Jess laughed, and he let himself enjoy the sound because she couldn't see him. 'If you want to be, you can.'

'You really are the most positive person I know,' he grumbled.

'You don't believe me, do you?'

'What?'

'That you could be fit enough to compete,' she answered.

'The only competition I recall being in was that hot dog eating compet—'

'Ant.'

Whoa. She didn't sound pissed, but she did sound stern. 'Yeah?'

'You're young, with no health issues that I'm aware of. If you decided to eat right and commit to exercise, there is absolutely no reason why you couldn't do something like a triathlon one day.'

For once, Ant kept his mouth shut. She was serious, wasn't she?

'Ant?'

'Yeah?' For once he didn't have a smart remark.

'You may not believe me, but I believe you can do it. Three months with me to get your fitness up. Then an additional three months of training for a triathlon, and in six months you could do it.'

Shit. She meant it. And in six months? That was absurd. He'd almost died jogging that stretch of beach yesterday and it was barely a kilometre.

'Beach jogging is harder than normal jogging,' she told him, reading his mind. 'You'll get used to it.'

'And a triathlon isn't hard?' he scoffed.

'Of course it's hard. That's why you do it.'

He fell silent again. She wasn't chirpy anymore. She was downright serious and determined along with it. It was sexy as hell, even if she was clearly insane.

'Let's just see how I go this Sunday?' he suggested. 'One workout at a time.'

'Definitely,' she agreed. 'But at three workouts a week, you'll be surprised how different you'll feel in a month's time.'

'Better than right now, I hope.'

She laughed. 'I guarantee it. Rest up, but not too much rest, and I'll see you Sunday. Bye, Ant.'

He said goodbye and lay there staring at the phone for a long while.

The girl-next-door type? Hell, no. That was a clever disguise. Ant had a feeling there was a lot more to Jessica Jinks than her cute appearance would have everyone believe. And he couldn't wait to find out more about her on Sunday.

Chapter Seven

ON SATURDAY EVENING on the way to her parents' house, Jess reflected on her conversation with Ant. Why on earth had she suggested he compete in a triathlon? It had been a silly idea and it was bound to scare him off.

Or would it?

Nothing Jess had done in their first session had seemed to motivate him, so she'd thrown it out there in sheer desperation. Sure, he'd scoffed at the idea, but he hadn't told her that she was insane. That was a start, wasn't it?

Maybe Jess was reading too much into those two rare silences of his—they were so unusual, she'd counted—but she actually wondered if he would consider it. At the very least, she felt like he'd heard her. That had to count for something.

Jess sighed as she pulled into her parents' driveway. It was party time. Literally. With four older brothers, when their mother requested a family dinner, it was always going to be a big gathering. Especially now two of them had kids and the other two had steady girlfriends.

Black sheep.

Jess shoved the thought out of her mind. She might be different to the rest of them, but she definitely wasn't a black sheep. They all loved her, and she loved them. So what if they couldn't understand her life choices so far? It didn't make her choices wrong, just different.

With another sigh, she scooped up her handbag from the passenger seat, locked her car, and headed around the back. Her parents' kitchen overlooked their back deck, and she knew that was where she would find everyone.

'Hey, JJ is here! Looking good, sis,' Grant, her oldest brother called out, using her family nickname.

The rest of the family appeared to be inside chatting in the kitchen while Grant and his wife, Susie, were getting some fresh air.

It would have been a perfectly normal greeting except that Grant was holding his toddler son upside down by the legs. The child giggled uncontrollably, squirming around like a wriggly worm. Grant seemed completely at ease having a conversation while juggling his son, but then he'd always been good at multitasking.

'Hey. How's the little guy?' Jess asked, walking over to them and giving Tommy, her nephew, a big grin. She reached over and tickled under his arms and he giggled some more.

'Careful what you start,' Susie warned. She was on the sun lounge nearby, nursing their baby daughter, Mia, who had only been born a few months ago. 'Tommy's having a tough time transitioning from one thing to another.'

'What she means is if you stop *anything* he likes, it's the end of the world,' Grant explained.

'I'd say that's perfectly normal, sweetheart,' Jess crooned, tickling Tommy some more because he was just so adorable and she couldn't resist. 'I've got a client like that at the moment, and he's older than me.'

Grant's dark eyebrows rose. Where Jess was blonde and blue-eyed like their father, Grant had taken after their mother's side. 'Ant Monticello, right?' he asked. 'How's that working out for you?'

He put Tommy down. For a moment, her nephew looked as though he was contemplating a tantrum. But then he spotted their mother's cavoodle curled up by a shrub and off he went. Chester was the equivalent of a teddy bear, so he'd pose no threat to the toddler.

Jess shrugged, although it felt a little forced. 'It's early days, and we've only had one session so far. Half the battle is getting him to take it seriously.'

Susie looked over at them while she stroked the fine hair on Mia's head as she fed. 'Is he as funny in real life?'

Jess considered the question for a moment. 'Funnier,' she admitted. 'I swear he tries to make me laugh to get out of exercising.'

'Uh oh.' Her youngest brother, Nick, stepped outside, joining them on the deck. 'Sounds like you've got an admirer.'

'No,' Jess said immediately. 'It's his *job* to be funny.'

Nick walked over to her and slung an arm around her shoulder, his perpetually messed up blond hair falling forward across his forehead as he did so. He kissed the side of her forehead affectionately.

'Just like it's my job to be your annoying big brother?' he asked.

Jess let herself relax into his hug. She got along with all of her brothers, but Nicky—and she was the only one who was still allowed to call him Nicky—was the one she was closest to. It wasn't only because they were eighteen months apart, although her parents often referred to them as "the twins" because they looked so alike with their blond hair and blue eyes. Nicky had always gotten Jess.

'You looked great during your interview the other week,' Nick said.

Jess screwed up her nose. 'Ugh. I'm trying not to think about it, to be honest. I swear Ant figured out how nervous I was so he made it his mission to make me laugh. It definitely helped.'

Susie and Grant shared a look, and Jess huffed in exasperation.

'Not like that,' she told them.

Why were her family always trying to set her up? Just because they were all paired off happily didn't mean she had to be. Sure, Jess would love to be like them, settled down and having or contemplating kids, but life hadn't turned out that way. Jess's prolonged single status felt like she was betraying the family brand somehow. Her parents had been married almost forty years. They were one of those couples other couples aspired to be like, and her father often said how he loved their mother more with every passing day. If it wasn't so beautiful, it would be sickening.

Nick released Jess as his long-time girlfriend, Chelsea, joined them on the deck.

'Hi there, Jess. Everyone is talking about your new client,' she said, her green eyes rounded in excitement. At first glance Chelsea looked like a supermodel with her long legs and waves of tousled brown hair, but she was actually a very hard-working lawyer. Of all the women her brothers had ended up with, Chelsea seemed to understand Jess's drive for her business to succeed the most.

'Honestly, it's really not that exciting,' Jess said, determined to play it down. 'He's just like any other personal training client.'

Nick let out a loud bark of laughter. 'The TV promo certainly doesn't portray it that way.'

'What do you mean?' Jess asked him.

'The promo is all over the media,' he replied. 'Surely you've seen it?'

Jess paled a bit and shook her head. Chelsea immediately got out her phone.

'Oh my God, is this how people on reality television shows feel?' Jess asked them. 'Does it make me look bad?'

Nick patted her shoulder. 'That would be impossible with Ant around, don't worry. But you're not in this footage, so relax.'

Chelsea handed Jess her phone and hit play on a video. It was a promo for Monday night's *Sydney Tonight*. It started off normal enough with Kat listing off the latest news the show would highlight. And then Ant came on the screen.

Oh.

Jess put a hand to her mouth.

They'd used the footage of Ant doing his running-on-the-spot number complete with the Flashdance music playing in the background. Deb, the producer, hadn't been joking about the soundtrack music. It lasted less than ten seconds, but it was hilarious.

Jess burst out laughing. 'Oh wow,' she said after she caught her breath. 'It's even funnier now I see it played back.'

'Like I said, with that guy in the limelight, your fears are completely unnecessary,' Nick comforted her. 'He'll make you look great.'

'There she is, my gorgeous girl!' Their mother, Joanna, joined them and came straight over to Jess, giving her a big hug.

As much as Jess tried to discourage it, her mother always insisted on calling her their "gorgeous girl". Jess hated the way it made her stand out from her brothers, but whenever Jess brought it up, Joanna waved it off. After four boys she'd given up on a girl, and Jess's unexpected arrival was a blessing they forever thanked their lucky stars for. While it made Jess feel loved, it only served to emphasise the gender divide. And with four extremely overprotective brothers, they didn't need reminding.

Jess pushed the thoughts aside and breathed in the fresh scent of her mother's jasmine perfume, returning the hug. Her mother eased back and cradled Jess's face in her hands. They were about the same height and Jess was in many ways a spitting image of her mother except for the dark colouring. "Light and shade", her father liked to say, and it didn't only apply to their looks. Where Jess was eternally positive, her mother was thoughtful and often serious.

'You're a television star now,' her mother told her.

'Hardly. Can we talk about something else, please? It's really not that big of a deal.'

'It is when it's my daughter.'

'OK, so I'm a television star. What else is new?' Jess asked.

She heard the others laugh.

'Well now, let's see. I saw Jack's mother at the hairdresser the other day . . .'

Oh, please no, not this again. Instead Jess said, 'That's nice. I hope she's well.'

Unfortunately, her ex-boyfriend's mother was best friends with Jess's mother, so whether Jess wanted it or not, she always got an update on the latest about her ex-boyfriend.

'She's better now Jack's on his way home from London—with his *fiancée.*'

Jess tried to hide her shock. She'd known all about Jack's new girlfriend—even if she hadn't wanted to—but news of the engagement was new, as was his return to Australia.

'Oh, that's nice. Is it just for a holiday?' Jess asked casually. God, she hoped so. It was bad enough when Jack was on the other side of the world. She could only imagine the constant news updates if he lived here.

'Apparently, but Jenny is hoping to convince them to settle here long term. She hasn't wanted to say anything to you, as she wasn't sure what you'd think.'

'Mum,' Jess said gently. 'It's fine. We broke up years ago.'

Her mother frowned. 'I know, but you were together for such a long time and everyone thought you were going to—'

'Be the wonderful success that you are today,' Susie said, standing up and coming over to them. 'Here. Mia is all fed. Would you like to hold her?'

'Always,' Jess replied. As her mother stepped back to make room, Jess mouthed "thank you" to her sister-in-law. Susie smiled and put a hand on Joanna's shoulder.

'Can you show me where you keep the salad dressing? I made the salad you asked for, but your dressing always tastes better than mine.'

Joanna smiled, preening a bit. 'Of course. Come inside.'

Jess looked down at Mia's perfect little face. Grant stepped in close while Nick and Chelsea took each other's hands and strolled over to watch their nephew play with the dog.

'I can't take any credit for her,' Grant told Jess. 'It's all her mother's doing.'

Jess elbowed him in the side, careful not to disturb the napping baby. 'You've both done a fine job if her older brother is anything to go by.'

'Thanks,' Grant said, then sighed. 'Mum's upset because Susie mentioned she wants to do some work from home in a few months.'

'You have to do what's right for your family,' Jess told him firmly.

'We're lucky that we don't desperately need the money, but I think Susie needs her sanity.'

'Nothing at all wrong with that. She might need some adult time.'

'Yeah, that's what I think, too,' Grant agreed. He was silent a moment before speaking again. 'Will you talk to Mum for us?'

Jess resisted a sigh, which wasn't that hard while she was cradling Mia's perfect baby goodness. 'Of course I will, if you want me to. Although why everyone thinks I'm the person for the job, I'll never know.'

Grant was the one to elbow Jess this time. 'Oh, I don't know. It might have something to do with that fitness empire you're building.'

'You all have careers,' Jess shot back, but softly, so as not to disturb Mia.

'Yeah, but you're breaking new ground in this family. You're not married with kids or engaged by thirty.'

'Honestly,' Jess muttered. She loved her parents, she really did, but they were very old school. Jess didn't see why she couldn't have both a business and children when the time came. 'It's not like I've got anything against settling down, I just haven't—'

'Met the right person.' Grant put a hand on her shoulder. 'I know. And you hold out until it's the right one, no matter what Mum says, you hear me?'

Jess smiled and rested her head on Grant's shoulder. 'I will. Although I'm pretty sure no one will be the right one to Mum after Jack. Honestly, it's been over three years since we broke up and she still can't accept it's over.'

Grant squeezed her shoulder gently. 'She'll come around when it's the right guy. You'll see.'

'Oh well, she has plenty of time, because it's not like there's anyone on my radar at the moment.'

'Oh, I don't know, Ant Monticello seems like a catch,' Grant joked and they both laughed.

Mia screwed up her face and grizzled in her sleep.

'Whoops, sorry,' Jess whispered, removing her head from Grant's shoulder. 'He's actually a really nice guy,' Jess felt necessary to add. 'And that doesn't mean I like him in that way, I'm just saying.'

'I'm sure he is, but you can do better than a guy who makes a living out of being funny, I'm sure. Come on, everyone else is inside and they'll want to see you.'

Jess let herself be ushered inside, frowning slightly. She was sure her brother hadn't intended his last comment to be an insult, but it came across that way.

Is that what it's like for Ant all the time? she wondered. Because he was a comedian, no one took him seriously? Well, that wasn't right. At least it didn't seem right to Jess. Or fair. Ant was good at what he did. Scratch that, he was exceptional, and Jess had already developed a lot of respect for him in the short time she'd known him.

For some strange reason, her brother's dismissive comment of Ant made Jess more determined than ever to get to know the man behind his public profile.

Chapter Eight

ANT TURNED up at the designated meeting point at eight o'clock on Sunday morning. It felt sacrilegious to be up and out this early on a weekend morning, especially a Sunday. But as Jess had already pointed out, he wasn't religious, so he figured protesting would be futile.

Ant waited by his car in the carpark overlooking the water, feeling more nervous than he cared to admit. She'd wanted him to wear board shorts. Now that he was at the location she'd asked him to meet her at, there was no escaping the fact that whatever they were doing today was going to involve water.

'Good one, Sherlock,' he muttered to himself, turning to survey the view.

The carpark was near the foot of Sydney's Spit Bridge. It was one of the few bridges that still opened regularly to allow boats to traverse Middle Harbour, a major waterway that connected to Sydney Harbour on the northern side of the city.

He had to admit it was a sweet outlook. The marina was packed with boats Ant was pretty sure he'd never be able to afford unless he became the next Billy Connolly. The houses overlooking the water on the other side of the waterway also smacked of executives with big money. Lots of glass and modern architecture perched ostentatiously on leafy, steep cliffs to command the multi-million-dollar views.

'It's gorgeous down here, isn't it?'

Ant had been so preoccupied with the view he hadn't seen Jess approaching.

'Hey,' he greeted her dumbly.

Speaking of gorgeous . . .

Like him, she wore board shorts, but he didn't remember his ever looking quite so good on him. Hers were a cute navy pair that finished well above the knee. They weren't flirtatious —from what he knew of Jess already, she always presented herself professionally. But she'd make even a staid pair of pants look good, he decided.

As for the top . . . He turned back to the view and pretended to gawk at that instead of her. She wore a full length matching blue rash vest to protect her from the sun, but damn it if that didn't suit her as well. She'd left the zip open at the top. It wasn't revealing, it was what it hinted at that made him feel weak at the knees. Jess in a swimsuit . . .

He cleared his throat. Not to mention the tantalising strip of skin across her stomach where the fitted rash vest didn't quite reach her board shorts.

'Aw, did I get you out of bed too early on a Sunday morning?' Jess asked, but not cruelly.

'Careful, I haven't had my coffee yet,' he warned her.

'That's good, because there's a coffee shop near where we're going.'

'Which is?'

'For me to know and you to find out,' she said in a singsong voice that should have been annoying but wasn't in the slightest. She gestured for him to follow her.

'I'm pretty sure it involves water,' he guessed, following her. He caught up to her quickly to make sure he didn't stare at her from behind, although he really, really wanted to.

'You're smarter than you look,' she said and winked at him.

Ant focused on the busy stretch of road with three lanes of traffic flowing in both directions. Something about Jess teasing him affected him in ways he didn't understand. He hadn't been affected by a woman like that since high school.

That wasn't a train of thought he wanted to revisit now. Or ever, really.

'You look worried,' Jess commented.

Ant mentally slapped himself for letting his thoughts get the better of him. 'Me? What could I have to be worried about? An accomplished fitness goddess is about to show me the finer points of staying alive while participating in water sport.'

Jess stopped walking and reached out to grab his arm. 'Oh my God, you can swim, can't you? I didn't think to ask.'

Ant looked down at her hand gripping his arm. She followed his gaze and let go of him, which wasn't actually the result he wanted.

'I can swim,' he said, not joking for once. He was a little offended that she'd thought he couldn't. This was Australia, after all. While plenty of expats and immigrants moving to the country may not know how, Ant had grown up here like Jess.

Jess gave him a smile, but it was a bit uncertain. 'Phew, and good. Sorry, I just assumed you could.'

They started walking again. Jess indicated that they should take the footpath that cut under the main road where the bridge began. It appeared as though it would take them to the other side of the road where a small row of shops was located.

'Actually,' Ant said, 'swimming was one of the few sports I didn't suck at growing up. Don't get me wrong, I never won a race at a swimming carnival or anything like that, but I didn't always come last. And I was able to swim the length of the pool without dying of exhaustion. Just a lot slower than everyone else.'

'Come on, I'm sure you didn't suck at all sports,' Jess said.

Ant had to give her extra fitness trainer points for her positivity. 'Oh, I definitely did. Look at me. I know you might think of me as a big guy because, let's face it, my ego is big enough for both of us, but I'm not overly tall. Or strong. I used to get whipped in any of the contact ball sports. My father held out hope I might excel at soccer because it had less contact and we're Italian, so we had the family's pride at stake. The only thing I defended was the snack cart, much to his disgust.'

'Do you and your dad get along?' Jess asked.

Ant shrugged. 'Occasionally. When he's not having a go at me for not having a real job.'

'You do have a real job!'

They'd reached the other side of the road and Jess turned to look at him, her blue eyes lit with emotion. What emotion, Ant wasn't entirely sure.

'But I don't have a real job,' Ant said. 'It's OK.'

Jess reached over and put her hand on his arm. Her fingers felt like electricity on his bare skin. He was quite happy to suffer the electric shock though.

'Just because you don't work in an office nine to five doesn't mean you don't have a real job,' she said.

'Yeah, but I make people laugh. Think of it this way. At school, when my teachers told me to stop being a smart-arse, the careers counsellor didn't start talking about career pathways for becoming a comedian. They just thought I was a goof-off.'

'Is that what you think of yourself?'

Jess was still staring at him and he stared right back, suddenly mute, and it wasn't because her hand was still on his arm. The honest answer was no, he didn't think of himself as a goof-off, but that's what he wanted the world to think because it suited his image. Most people rarely saw beyond that image, but he was starting to think Jess was different.

'Ant?'

He laughed, more awkwardly than he would have liked. 'That's professional goof-off to you, Miss Jinks.'

She stared at him a moment longer, then finally removed her hand. Ant resisted touching the spot self-consciously.

She nodded for him to follow her again. 'Well, if you don't have a real job, then neither do I.'

'Ah, your Instagram following says otherwise.'

She huffed. 'Sometimes I find it all so . . .'

'Fake?' he guessed.

She stopped again, this time outside a shop with a large number of kayaks stacked everywhere. 'No, not fake because I always try to be myself on social media, as much as that is an oxymoron in this day and age. Just . . . surreal.'

'Well, if you want surreal, try telling jokes for a living. Best. Job. Ever.'

She laughed, and her warm smile was filled with understanding. 'That's why you joke about your career, isn't it? Because you enjoy it so much? There's no need to feel guilty about that. I got over my guilt about my job a long time ago when I realised that what I do helps people. You help people, too. You make them happy. It's the same thing.'

He grinned at her, his heart beating fast enough to make him believe he was doing exercise instead of standing here talking. 'You mean I dumb down the news so it's easier to digest?'

She shook her head at him, amused, but appearing to see right through his jokes. 'Alright. You've probably guessed what we're doing today. Let's go sort out the details and get us out on the water.'

He blinked a few times as she turned to go inside, a little in awe of . . . of everything about her, really. Her ability to cut past the bullshit. Her understanding about what he did for a living. Her unapologetic dedication to being herself. Her sunny outlook on life.

Instead he called out, 'These don't have motors, do they?'

She ignored him and disappeared inside to organise their floatation devices requiring arm strength he was almost certain he didn't have.

Chapter Nine

THE MORE JESS got to know Ant, the more she liked him. There was something so genuine about him, despite him pretending everything was a big joke all the time. He was easy to talk to, and of course he was fun—until exercise was involved, that was.

'I'll wait here until you catch up,' she called back to him, not for the first time.

He was somewhere behind her, bobbing on the water while he rested his arms. She'd lost count of the number of times they'd stopped for a break, but for all his vocalising, Jess had to admit he'd been a good sport.

Eventually, he floated alongside her. 'If I don't look like freakin' Superman after this, I want my money back,' he complained.

'It might take more than one kayaking session for that.'

'See, that's what I don't get. Why can't I just go out, get fit, and then game, set, and match? It's done. I'm fit for life. But, no, it doesn't work that way. First I have to earn my fitness, then I have to keep it up, too.'

'You know, it can be enjoyable when you find something you like. A way of relaxing or letting off steam.'

'If I want to relax, I'll sit at home in front of the television with a beer, and if I want to let off steam, I'll have sex.'

Jess felt herself redden and was glad she was already a rosy colour from the sun's rays. After their initial training session on the beach last week, Jess wasn't going to bring up the subject of sex again. Ant had already proven he could make a big joke out of it, like everything else.

'Of course, letting off steam would definitely be easier if I had a girlfriend,' he said, to prove her point. 'But clearly my fame keeps the women away. Do you find that?' he asked.

'Women are quite comfortable around me, actually,' Jess commented, keeping a straight face. 'I've even had a few hit on me.'

Jess couldn't see Ant's eyes behind his sunglasses, but then she didn't need to because he threw his head back and laughed loudly.

He pointed a finger at her. 'You, Miss Jinks, are deceiving. That killer sense of humour is something else.'

'What? Can't a fitness fanatic have a sense of humour?' She was a little unimpressed that he thought she wouldn't.

'Uh-uh,' he said, waving the oar to indicate that he was ready kayak again. 'That's not just a sense of humour, it's a quick wit. That's a precious thing in my line of work.'

Jess fell into pace beside him, making sure not to go too fast for him. They'd already been out for an hour, and Ant would need a longer rest soon.

'Would you say a sense of humour is something that you're born with?' Jess mused out loud. 'My entire family can all see the funny side of things.'

'Definitely,' Ant agreed. 'Yes, you can learn about comedy. There are classes for everything from how to present yourself to the finer points of telling a good joke. There's a lot more technique involved than many people appreciate. But I tell you what, Robin Williams was born Robin Williams, if you get my meaning.'

'Oh, I definitely do. Did you go to any classes when you were starting out?' Jess asked with interest.

She registered a slight frown on his face. And it was slight, because Ant was the sort of man whose laughter lines were more prominent than his frown lines.

'And don't say you're a natural, we all know you are,' she added. 'I'm curious if it's like working out—the more you exercise, the fitter you become.'

Ant grinned at her, and it was like a punch to the gut. Gosh, he was better looking than he gave himself credit for, particularly when he was smiling. With his reflective sunglasses on, olive skin, and that lock of wavy hair that kept falling over his forehead, he was an odd blend of little boy cheekiness and masculinity.

He didn't seem to notice her momentary loss of speech, and they kept paddling.

'Kind of like exercising your funny bone,' he said. 'Huh. I like that. I guess you could say I taught myself. I tried a class or two, but I never really felt like I fit in.'

'Why ever not?' It was hard to imagine Ant not fitting in around a comedy environment.

He screwed up his nose. 'Lots of mid-life crisis sufferers— not that there's anything wrong with that. I was still in my mid-twenties and wasn't old enough to have a crisis. And there were all these executive dudes that had decided their office jobs were too serious for them.' He shrugged in between oar strokes. 'Even there I was still the goof-off.'

'So what did you do?'

'I went home and started studying all the greats—Steve

Martin, Jerry Seinfeld, Robin Williams, you get the gist. I watched their comedy sketches over and over until I could recite them word for word.'

'And then what did you do?' Jess could easily imagine a younger Ant sitting at home watching those comedians intently.

'I started doing stand-up comedy nights. You know the ones. Free-for-all, open to the public events.'

'And?'

Ant was silent for a moment. The only sounds were the hum of motorboats passing by at a distance and the rush of water against their oars.

'I sucked.'

Jess's jaw dropped open.

'Correction,' he said. 'I worse than sucked. I was so bad, I wanted to throw beer on myself. I actually did one night because I thought it might get some laughs. It didn't, although they did applaud, right before they made me get off.'

'Oh, Ant,' Jess said, genuinely sorry for this younger version of himself. 'That must have been hard.'

He shrugged again. 'Hard isn't the right word. If I had a soul, it would have been destroyed. Fortunately I don't, so I just kept working my crappy job while writing jokes on the side.'

'What sort of job did you have?' Ant had said himself that being a comedian didn't feel like a job, so Jess was curious to know what he'd done to support himself before finding success.

Ant glanced over at her. 'If I tell you, I'll have to kill you.'

'Oh come on, it can't have been that bad.'

'Worse than bad. Your current low opinion of me will seem sky high if I told you.'

'I don't have a low opinion of you! Why would you think that?'

'Hmm, let me see. I'm lazy, I don't exercise, I don't want to exercise, I enjoy eating crap, and I'm shallow enough to be convinced into this PR stunt by the promise of a date with a beautiful woman.'

Jess indicated with her oar that they should head toward the shore. They were nearing Clontarf, a lovely flat harbour beach that was popular with families of young children. Jess thought it would be the perfect spot to take a break and have some lunch.

Once they were heading in the right direction, she resumed the conversation. 'You'd already agreed to the arrangement when the producers announced the Alicia Travers thing.'

'Yes, but they thought I needed to be bribed.'

Jess detected a hint of something that didn't sound like good humour.

'No, they're going for ratings,' Jess told him. 'You know that. And I don't think you're lazy, by the way, just misguided.'

'Uh-oh. You're not one of those fixer uppers, are you?'

Jess shot him a confused look. 'Sorry, a what?'

Ant stopped paddling and rested his oar in front of him, letting the kayak glide along the smooth plane of water. He flicked his hair back and gave her a coy look that was so feminine, Jess put down her oar, too.

'You know, Cheryl, I think he'd just be the perfect man if he'd, hmm, let's see . . .' His usually deep voice was an octave higher. He put a finger to his chin in contemplation. 'If he'd pick up after himself, stop drinking beer with the guys every Friday night, and generally be someone completely different. There! That about covers it!' He clapped his hands together, a fake look of glee on his face.

Jess laughed. 'You know, you make a very good woman. It's scary.'

'So I've been told,' he replied, his voice back to normal.

'So a fixer upper is a woman who wants to change someone?' she asked.

'No, a fixer upper is a woman who seeks out men to change and then plays the martyr when they remain exactly the same.'

'Just because I'm a fitness trainer doesn't make me a fixer upper, you know,' Jess pointed out, interested to note his answer had been serious. It made her wonder if he was speaking from personal experience, which made her want to prove to him that she definitely didn't fall into the category of a fixer upper. 'If anything, my ex-boyfriend would say *I'm* the one who needed fixing, not the other way around.'

Jess snapped her mouth shut. *Whoops.* It wasn't like her to share personal information about herself during a training session, no matter how open her clients may be. This didn't feel like a regular training session, though. Plus, Ant was not her regular type of client. He might not enjoy exercising, but he certainly enjoyed talking, and Jess had let herself get carried away.

Ant's dark eyebrows rose. 'Your ex-boyfriend, did you say?'

'Yes,' she replied, not willing to say any more.

'Then he's an idiot. Any guy who thinks you need to change needs his head read. Or a good, swift kick in the—'

'Look! We're almost at the beach. Did I mention I packed lunch? This looks like the perfect spot to eat it.' Jess's cheeks were flushed pink again, and she was thankful she'd been able to redirect the conversation.

They floated towards the beach together, their kayaks side by side.

'Hmm,' Ant mused. 'So, once we hit the beach, any tips on how to get out of this thing?'

'Oh, sure. Just let me hop out first, then I'll hold your kayak steady while you climb out.'

'You make it sound so easy.'

They were only about ten metres away from the shore now. Jess had it all figured out in her head how they would disembark with the least embarrassment to Ant, whose first-timer status meant that getting out of his kayak was likely to be awkward.

Her plans died a watery death however when, a few metres from the sand, Ant looked around the shallow water and announced, 'It can't be that hard. I've totally got this.'

Then his kayak tipped unceremoniously upside-down and he disappeared along with it.

'Ant, *no!*'

Chapter Ten

'WELL, THAT WENT WELL,' Ant said five minutes later, still dripping with water. He'd taken off his life vest and thrown it onto the sand beside him—fat lot of good it had done him. It turned out it was hard to stay afloat despite wearing a life-saving device when you were trapped underneath a kayak.

He watched Jess drag their kayaks up onto the beach so they wouldn't float away. If he was more of a chauvinist, he would have told her to sit down and he'd do it, but no, he was a new age guy. *#feminist*

Besides, Jess was perfectly capable. Ant was pretty sure she'd be able to lift heavier weights than he could, so the division of labour made good sense. That, and he wasn't on speaking terms with his stupid kayak right now, anyway.

'Is the lunch alright?' Jess called out as she made her way up the beach towards him.

He surveyed the sandwiches Jess had instructed him to pull out of the cooler. 'A bit damp, but they're doing considerably better than me.'

Jess giggled and sat down beside him, unzipping her rash vest as she did so.

Don't look, don't look.

Of course he looked.

Underneath the vest she wore a vibrant pink bikini. Sure, it looked like one of those fitness ones designed not to come off in the surf, but it was still a bikini. And the abs on her stomach would make gym junkies cry.

He diverted his eyes and watched the kids playing in the gentle waves on the shore. 'So, ah, I suppose I should thank you for saving my life back there.'

Jess stretched her tanned legs out in front of her and started unwrapping the sandwiches. 'You're being dramatic. It was shallow water, and you could stand.'

'Yeah, if my feet weren't in that damn kayak. I had moments to live, I'm telling you.'

She handed him a sandwich, and Ant noted it was the driest of the two. Sweet and caring as well as fit and beautiful. Would Jess's perfection ever end?

He accepted it gratefully and was just about to bite into when he paused. 'Wait just a minute. What has this got on it? Are you about to introduce me to kale?'

He eased the sandwich away from his mouth like it was a ticking time bomb while Jess shook her head at him.

'I wouldn't dream of sneaking kale into your sandwich without your full knowledge. There's no kale in there, I promise. It is vegetarian, though.'

Ant put his free hand to his dripping chest. 'You're killing me.'

'Just try it, drama queen, then tell me what you think.'

He did as he was told because, well, she was cute, and he didn't want to disappoint her despite the way his stomach recoiled in horror at the word "vegetarian".

'Damn,' he said between mouthfuls. 'This is *good*.'

'See, I told you,' Jess said, not without a hint of pride.

'What's in it?'

'Grilled vegetables, mainly. Eggplant, tomatoes, and zucchini, with my secret salsa.'

'Does that mean you salsa around the house when no one can see you while you're making it?' he asked hopefully, secretly loving the image it conjured in his mind.

'No, not quite. But I do like listening to loud music while I'm cooking.'

'Define music,' he demanded.

She shrugged. 'Taylor Swift.'

He choked on his food, and she patted him on the back.

'Got you. But I do listen to her in group classes because people want upbeat, modern tunes. At home I'm more partial to the classics—Led Zeppelin, Fleetwood Mac, Crowded House.'

He managed to swallow his mouthful. 'You almost lost your perfect woman status there for a second,' he told her. Then started to choke again.

She didn't pat him on the back this time.

'Is that what you think?' she asked, her eyes wide and her complexion a pretty shade of pink. She quickly looked away. 'Oh, crap. That's not what I meant. I wasn't fishing. You know what? Forget it.'

They fell silent, and it was awkward—definitely awkward. What was it about Jessica Jinks that made him lose the one brain cell he actually had? His words were usually so carefully chosen and timed to perfection. Not around her they weren't. It took him back to his younger years, and there was a place he definitely didn't want to revisit, so he blurted out something equally stupid.

'I used to work as a car salesman.'

Jess stopped and swallowed her mouthful, then turned to face him with a big grin on her face. 'You used to be a car salesman?'

'Don't judge me, alright? It's a family business. My uncle's dealership, in fact. After being such a continuous disappointment to my father, I figured I'd try to build my credibility by working there.'

'Did you enjoy it?'

He finished off the sandwich and brushed the crumbs from his hands. It had actually been edible.

'Enjoy? That's too strong a word. But once I figured out I could test my jokes on the customers, it got more interesting.'

'You didn't!'

He pushed his sunglasses up onto his head and levelled her with a serious look. 'You bet I did.'

Jess put a hand to her mouth to cover her laughter. 'Oh wow, I wish I could have seen it. Were you yourself or did you play at being a creepy car salesman?'

Ant was impressed with the direction of Jess's thoughts, so he answered her honestly. 'At first I was just myself. After a while, when customers started laughing at my well-timed humour, I began trying out different characters—'

'You did not!'

'Did too. That's how Giovanni was born.'

'*The* Giovanni? The smooth-talking creepy guy?'

Ant's Giovanni character had earned him nationwide recognition after being featured on a comedy sketch show. Sleazy, creepy, slimy—Giovanni was the ultimate greasy car salesman, and the truth was Ant still missed playing him. He didn't have much opportunity to these days when he was co-hosting *Sydney Tonight*. Sure, he was able to make plenty of jokes, but he had to be himself.

'Maybe it's time Giovanni made a comeback,' Ant

pondered, then gave Jess a salacious grin. 'Why, hello there, pretty lady. Have I got a deal for you . . .'

Ant shifted his body so that he was sitting shoulder to shoulder with Jess, then put an arm around her.

'Picture this,' he said, and waved his free hand in the air like he was conjuring an image. 'You, me, a bottle of wine, in that sexy yacht over there . . .'

Jess shuddered and moved out of his arms. 'Oh my God, that is so creepy! You do that far too well.'

Ant knew it was Giovanni that Jess was creeped out by, but he still wished she hadn't moved away.

'Would you believe it sold cars?' he said.

'Actually, knowing you, yes, I can believe it.'

'I committed to playing Giovanni for one entire month. Best sales I had all year. Then my uncle found out what was going on and almost fired me.'

Jess cringed. 'Ouch. I bet he regrets that reaction now.'

'Kind of. My comedy success isn't really a big thing in our family.'

Jess moved closer to Ant again. 'But why? My parents didn't really understand my chosen profession at first, but now they're my biggest supporters.'

Ant shrugged. 'Think about it. No parent thinks to themselves when their kid is growing up that they see a bright future for them in comedy. We've been through this—it's not a reliable, responsible job.'

'Well, it's a career you're damn good at, and if I was your parent, I'd be proud. You've mentioned your father. What about your mother?'

Ant preened a little, he couldn't help it. 'Yeah, she's proud. I can't deny it.' He tried not to think about his father. 'But then I'm her only child, so she hasn't got a choice.'

'You're an only child?'

He shrugged again. 'You say it like it's a bad thing. I don't mind. Besides, it means everything is all about me.'

Jess cracked a smile at his last comment. 'It's hard to imagine from my perspective. I grew up with four brothers.'

'*Four?*' Wow. Ant had often wondered what one sibling would have been like. But four? That was overkill.

Jess's smile turned to laughter. 'Yep, last time I counted anyway. And I do kind of need to count these days, seeing as they're all either engaged or having kids. When the family gets together, it's rather busy. But come on. You're of Italian heritage, aren't you? Surely there's a big extended family you're hiding somewhere?'

Ant blew out a breath. 'No, sorry to disappoint you. I'm sure the generalisation is true for a reason, but not because of our family. Dad left his extended family behind in Italy. Mum was born here, but her parents passed away a long time ago, and she only has one brother who never married.'

'Have you met your Italian relatives?' Jess asked.

'No, we're not close.'

'Huh,' Jess murmured, like she was trying to imagine it for herself.

'Do you like being part of a big family?' Ant asked in return because he was curious.

Jess tilted her head to one side, considering his question. 'Most of the time, yes. The over-involvement in each other's lives I could do without from time to time, but I can't imagine it any other way.'

They settled into a companionable silence, much different to their earlier awkwardness. After a few minutes, Ant held out hope that she wouldn't feel compelled to continue with the exercise routine. Perhaps the warming sunshine and the view of the water had lulled Jess into a state of relaxation?

'Right,' Jess announced, clapping her hands together and making Ant jump.

'Is that a fitness trainer thing?'

'Probably.' She stood up and stretched her arms above her head. Ant was treated to an eyeful of her taut stomach before he diverted his gaze.

'Ready to head back?' she asked.

'If you mean to the marina I can see from over here, absolutely,' he agreed, relieved the exertion part of the day was almost over.

'Oh, that would be cheating,' she told him. 'I thought I'd take you via—'

She stopped when Ant put his head in his hands.

'Oh, come on. It won't be that bad. It's a beautiful day and we might as well make the most of it. You've been doing really well so far.'

'It's tomorrow I'm worried about when I won't be able to lift my arms.'

She stood over him, looking down at him. 'Trust me. You can do this. I wouldn't suggest it if you weren't capable of it.'

He made a show of groaning loudly as he got up. 'My body is also capable of a great amount of pain.'

She stepped in close to him and put her arms on his shoulders. Ant's lack of height meant they were basically eye to eye.

'Stop telling yourself you can't and maybe you'll discover you can,' she told him.

He tried to bite back his smile, he really did. But it was no good.

'Did you get that inspirational comment from one of the posters at your local gym?' he teased. 'I'm sure if I Googled it, I'd find it online.'

Jess sighed and dropped her hands. 'I was trying to motivate you.'

'I'll concede that it was a valiant attempt, but I'm not your average guy, unfortunately.'

'Yeah, I got that,' Jess called back as she made her way across the sand to their waiting kayaks. 'And I'm holding your kayak while you get in, whether you like it or not.'

He held up his hands. 'Not arguing after I saw my life flash before my eyes earlier.'

She waited for him to put his life vest back on and held the kayak still while he slipped his legs in and sat down.

'You know, Nicky, my brother, thought he'd never have what it took to compete in a triathlon,' she said. 'If I can convince him, I still think I can convince you. Although his resistance was less out of laziness and more to do with not wanting me to be right.'

Ant watched as Jess hopped easily into the kayak beside his, then he asked, 'So is he some sort of elite athlete?'

They floated away from the shore together, watching for swimmers as they went.

'He placed in the top twenty of his last triathlon.'

'*Right*. So, let me guess, he wasn't new to the whole exercise thing?'

'He loves team sports. He played rugby growing up, basketball, cricket—anything that involved a team, basically.'

'I'm pretty sure I'd hate him.'

Jess looked alarmed. 'Why would you say that? You've never met him.'

'I know the type, that's all.'

'So anyone who is fit, healthy and committed to exercise is someone you don't want to know?' she pressed.

'No, not exactly. I'll admit I don't mind you.'

'I'm flattered, really. You know, I used to hate exercise when I was a teenager,' she said.

Ant stopped rowing momentarily. 'Get out.'

'I thought you already knew,' she said. 'You can find inter-views online when I've spoken about it. I was a nerd at school. A shy, bookworm type.'

'Uh-uh. No way. You don't decide to become Jessica Jinks, fitness goddess, one day and just turn into her. You were born that way, I'm telling you.'

'Have you heard anything I've said this last week or two?' Her voice held a note of exasperation. 'My brand of fitness is all about the everyday person. It's accessible to everyone. I'm not targeting gym addicts. I'm targeting you, Ant, whether you believe me or not.'

'Alright, so enlighten me then, Miss Closet Nerd. How did your transformation come about?'

Jess screwed up her nose. 'The mean girls at high school.'

Huh. So maybe they had more in common than he first thought.

'Go on,' he prompted.

She sighed. 'I had a falling out with my bestie. I would have been around fifteen, I think. Anyway, she turned on me, and all the girls I thought were my friends didn't talk to me. And we're not just talking about for a week. It went on for months.'

'Bitches,' Ant agreed.

Jess's lips curved in a ghost of a smile. 'Something like that. I was feeling pretty low, I guess you'd say. So low that my family was worried about me. Nicky, who's closest in age to me, encouraged me to get out of the house and stop moping. At first, it was just walking. Then he suggested I start jogging. Oh my goodness, I was so bad in the beginning!'

'You?' Ant interjected. 'Couldn't run?'

'Totally. In fact, I could barely run a few hundred metres without losing my breath, and I'd always failed big time at school athletics. But slowly, that started to change. Eventually, I was running five kilometres at a time. Meanwhile, my mum had insisted on dragging me to her Pilates class on a Saturday morning. I won't lie—it was all the mother hen attention I was getting from her girlfriends that got me there in the beginning. They made me feel loved and special at a time when I needed it. Then one day, I decided to try some equipment in the gym where the Pilates classes were held. The guys at the gym were so encouraging.'

'I bet they were,' Ant muttered.

'No, not like that, silly,' Jess admonished. 'Most of them were my brother's mates, so they were looking out for me. Then, later that year when I'd been exercising for around four months, I looked in the mirror and saw someone else.'

'That would have been terrifying.'

Jess laughed. 'I mean, it was me, but not me, you know? I saw this young woman who looked fit, healthy and capable. It was then that I realised I didn't give a fuck—and pardon the swear word, but that's how I felt—about those girls at school anymore. That's when everything started to turn around for me.'

'Did those girls come crawling back to you?' Ant asked, hoping that if he didn't have any positive high school memories, maybe Jess did.

'Mmm. Not straight away, and not all of them. But by then I really didn't care. I made new friends when I went to the sports teacher and asked if we could organise Pilates classes once a week during lunchtime for anyone who was interested. To my surprise, it attracted a lot of kids. I ended up meeting some great new friends, some of them now lifelong, not just from my year but from other years as well. By the start of the next school year, I wasn't that shy, bookish girl anymore.'

'You were Jessica Jinks . . .' Ant raised his oar and tried to manoeuvre it around like lightsaber, but failed miserably. 'Slayer of mean girls and champion of the nerds.'

Jess laughed again. 'So there you go. That's why, when I tell you anyone can exercise, I mean it.'

Ant lowered his oar and looked at her. 'You know, for someone so inspirational, I might just try kale someday.'

She pointed her oar at him. 'I'm going to hold you to that. On Wednesday at my place. I'm going to show you how to cook real food. I didn't tell you, but the network wants me to host some cooking sessions with you and take lots of snapshots on our phones to share on social media. They were afraid if we went in too hard, too fast, you'd get cold feet.'

Ant looked down at his now dry body. 'My feet are still a little damp, I'll admit. But alright, JJ, for you I'll put my stomach on the line.'

A cute little furrow appeared between her brow. 'How did you know my nickname is JJ?' she asked.

'I didn't. But it suits you. And every fitness hero needs a moniker.'

She grinned at him. 'So what's yours?'

'Ant is short for Antony.'

'That's boring.'

'Well, seeing as I'm boring you, can we please, please head back now? My arms are going numb.'

'If you insist . . . *Adonis*.'

With that, Jess used her oar to turn her kayak around in a few swift paddles. Ant did the same—only a lot less elegantly and he lost count of the number of strokes.

He didn't mind, because he was too busy thinking about the subject of nicknames. As far as he was concerned, the nickname of Adonis had a nice ring to it. Now he just had to live up to it.

Chapter Eleven

JESS PACED the hallway outside Kat's apartment door.

It was late, and she was being stupid. She should just return downstairs to her own apartment. But she kept pacing and glanced at her watch.

Ten-thirty at night. Kat was usually home after the evening broadcast of *Sydney Tonight* by now.

Jess stopped and listened. Nothing. It was quiet on the landing and she couldn't hear any noise coming from the apartment inside.

Right. She'd just return to her place then. Finally having made a decision, even if it did involve chickening out and retreating, Jess headed back towards the lift.

She let out a squeak as the lift doors opened.

Kat stepped out, giving her a strange expression. 'Hey, Jess. Sorry to scare you. Are you looking for me?'

'No. I mean, yes. Actually, you know what? It's not really all that important and it's late. I'll catch you another time.' She went to step into the lift, but Kat caught her arm.

'Spill it, Jinks. You're here for a reason.'

Jess sighed and let the lift doors close behind them. 'Can't I just be wanting to catch up with my favourite neighbour?'

Kat indicated Jess should follow her. 'You're usually in bed by now, so it must be important.'

When your favourite neighbour was a news journalist, nothing got by her. Jess waited while Kat dug her keys out of her bag, considering how best to word her next sentence.

When Kat opened the front door, another thought occurred to Jess.

'Oh, Matt's not home, is he? I don't want to intrude.'

Kat rolled her eyes. 'No, he's at the hospital for an emergency delivery. And would you get to the point already?'

Damn. Kat's fiancé was an obstetrician and often worked odd hours. Jess would just have to come out with it, then.

'Have you seen this?' Jess blurted and shoved her iPhone in Kat's face.

Kat took a step back and frowned at the image on Jess's phone.

'Well, yeah,' Kat said after a moment. 'The subject warranted significant discussion on the show tonight.'

'Oh,' Jess said. She hadn't seen the show earlier as she'd been instructing a Hi-Jinks class.

Kat narrowed her eyes. 'What do you mean, "Oh"? And come inside, would you?'

Jess followed Kat into her apartment, stopping so Kat could kick off her heels and put her handbag down.

While she waited, Jess studied the image on Instagram for the hundredth time that evening. It had been posted by a stranger, and it was of Ant and Jess on the beach the day before. Ant was still dripping wet after his kayak malfunction. Jess was sitting beside him, smiling. If Jess remembered correctly, that was when Ant had been reliving his near-death experience.

The caption below read, "Looks like @antmonticello is serious about getting fit. Although I'd get fit for @hijinks too. Looking great, Jess!"

'I told you the unpaid publicity on this would be amazing,' Kat told her as they headed down the hall. 'The first progress session hasn't even aired yet and strangers are spreading the word.'

The weirdness factor aside, Jess had to admit it was pretty cool. But that wasn't what she'd come here for tonight. Jess was worried about Ant, but it would seem strange asking him outright if he was all right. That was something you asked a friend, not so much a client. Kat was Jess's friend *and* worked with Ant, so she figured that was the next best thing.

'But what about Ant? How does he feel about it?' Jess asked, trying to sound casual.

Kat went into her open-plan kitchen and got out a glass. 'Water?' After Jess shook her head, Kat answered, 'You know Ant, he loves being the centre of attention.'

'But did he read the comments?' Jess pressed. While a lot of them had been complimentary towards Jess, some hadn't been so nice about Ant.

'You mean the trolls?' Kat said. 'Comes with the territory. Ant knows that.'

'But some of them were so nasty,' Jess persisted. Her phone screen had turned off, but she could still recall the worst of the comments from memory.

No amount of exercise will transform a nose that ugly.

I'd turn lesbian for Jess, she's so hot.

One look at Ant, and I'd turn lesbian, too.

There's no way Ant has what it takes to get fit. Such a joke. #publicitystunt

'Water off a duck's back, I can assure you,' Kat reassured

Jess. 'Ant's used to it, don't worry. He's made of tougher stuff and won't let a few loser trolls bother him.'

'I hope so. I'm really worried it's going to put him off the whole thing.'

Kat took a sip of her water. 'He's contracted to do it, don't worry.'

Jess threw her hands up in the air. 'That's not what I care about! I actually *want* him to want to exercise. It's not just about the publicity for me.'

Kat regarded her friend thoughtfully. 'You really are the nicest person I know, you know that? That, and you live your brand.' She put her glass on the island bench and stepped towards Jess. 'Ant is going to be fine, trust me. Especially after Alicia's post. Ant forgot about the mean comments the second he saw it.'

'What are you talking about?'

Kat's eyebrows rose. 'You didn't see it? Huh. I guess she didn't tag you. Here. Pass me your phone.'

Jess did as instructed and waited while Kat entered something into the search bar of Instagram, then handed it back to her.

It held a photo of Alicia standing by a treadmill at the gym in all her statuesque model glory. Her long, perfectly straight, dark hair fell to just above her waist. And if Alicia's glossy hair wasn't sickening enough, she was beautifully made up, too. Her dark eyes were outlined in kohl and her big, pouty lips— Jess was almost one hundred percent sure they were fake— were upturned in a coy smile.

Jess couldn't help herself and snorted. Kat raised a questioning eyebrow.

'Oh, come on!' Jess cried. 'She's not working out! No one who works out looks like that. There's no sign of exertion, no flushed face, no sweat. Not to mention her hair. Who exercises with their hair out, for God's sake? It's all so staged.'

'Finished?' Kat asked.

Jess huffed. 'I suppose.'

'Read the text below.'

Jess did so, and then surprised herself when a growl slipped out. Kat bit back a laugh.

Jess read the caption again, imagining a "throwing-up face" emoji this time.

Birds of a feather @antmonticello. Looking good on the beach yesterday. Maybe we should work out together sometime. #exercisedaily #exerciseforlife #fitnessgoals

'Jealous, much?' Kat teased.

'I'm not jealous,' Jess shot back instantly. 'It's all so . . . *fake*.'

'Welcome to the world of entertainment,' Kat said dryly.

'Why would you think I'm jealous?' Jess asked. 'Trust me. I have no desire to be anything approaching what Alicia Travers represents.'

'Oh, I wasn't talking about Alicia. I meant Ant.'

'Me?' Jess squeaked. 'Jealous of Ant? But he's my client.'

'Oh, come on. Don't tell me you haven't noticed the way he looks at you. The times I've witnessed it, I think you've kind of liked it.'

Jess cleared her throat and turned around to stare out Kat's floor-to-ceiling balcony windows. Outside the ocean was dark and restful, unlike her mind which was whirling.

'Jess?'

'I *might* have noticed him notice me,' Jess hedged.

Kat scoffed. 'He's not very secret about it.'

Jess turned back to face Kat, feeling like she needed to defend Ant. 'Oh, but he's polite. I've never caught him leering at me or anything like that.'

'I didn't mean that,' Kat said. 'Jokes aside, Ant is actually a gentleman when all is said and done. That's why you like him.'

'Of course I like him. As you said, he's a nice guy. And funny. But I don't *like like* him,' she clarified, so there was no confusion.

Kat crossed her arms. 'Then explain your reaction to Alicia's post.'

Jess resisted rolling her eyes. Kat was like a dog with a bone when she got her teeth into something. Her award-winning interview skills didn't help.

'OK, so I like Ant enough to feel protective of him. I don't want him to get hurt or to be taken advantage of,' Jess explained. 'But he's a client,' she added firmly. 'I don't let myself *like like* clients.'

How two women in their early thirties had come to be having a conversation this teenage, Jess wasn't entirely sure.

'And if he wasn't a client?'

'I'm sure he'd make a good friend,' she replied brightly. 'But seeing as he's going to be a client for the next three months and my business reputation is on the line, why are we even discussing it?'

Kat shrugged. 'I don't know. You were the one who came to see me. I thought maybe you cared about him more than you were letting on.'

'No. Nothing like that.'

'Just a dedicated fitness trainer, huh?'

'That's me,' Jess agreed. 'Anyway, I better let you wind down after work. It's late. Sorry to bug you.'

They began walking down the hall towards the front door.

'Anytime, Jess. And hey, I think Ant would be touched that you care so much.'

Jess stopped, her sneakers squeaking on the tiled floor. 'Please don't tell him about this, will you?' At Kat's amused expression, Jess added, 'If he does kind of *like like* me, then I don't want him to get the wrong idea. Our arrangement needs to be strictly professional.' Jess inwardly cringed at her overuse of the word "like" again.

Kat mimed zipping her lips with her fingers. 'I won't say a word. Besides, Ant's ego is inflated enough as it is. I don't want to add to it any further, believe me.'

They said goodnight and Jess made her way to the lift. Inside, she reflected on Kat's last words. That was the thing. Jess didn't really believe Ant's ego was that big, not in reality. He pretended it was, definitely. But deep down, something told her Ant was sweet, but insecure. Maybe it was the way he agreed too readily about the mean girls at school when she'd told him her story the day before. Or the way he always jokingly put himself down. Yes, it was his style of comedy, but perhaps there was a hint of truth to it as well.

No amount of exercise will transform a nose that ugly.

'Ugh,' Jess muttered. What sort of horrible person left a comment like that? Ant's nose certainly wasn't small, but it wasn't ugly. More like prominent. Plus, it suited him because of his Italian heritage. Didn't they call it a Roman nose? Jess thought it gave him character.

The lift dinged for her floor and Jess got out, walking distractedly towards her front door, still deep in thought.

And what on earth had made Kat think Jess liked Ant in that way? Just because Ant had a bit of a crush on Jess—and she was pretty sure that was all it was—didn't mean Jess felt the same way.

Don't you?

Jess pulled out her keys and shook off the rogue thought. No, she most definitely didn't have a crush on Ant Monticello. She'd meant what she'd said to Kat—it was a point of pride that Jess always kept things professional with her clients.

Jess sighed and opened the door. But yeah, she did like Ant genuinely as a person, especially the more she got to know him. He always made her laugh, but it was more than that. When it had just been the two of them yesterday, it was as if the walls had come down and she'd gotten to know the Ant behind the public persona.

And it was the first time in as long as Jess could remember—since her break-up with Jack—that she'd found a man so interesting.

Oh shit.

Jess shoved opened the door and slammed it closed behind her.

Maybe she did *like like* him, after all.

Chapter Twelve

JESS MANAGED to ward off any unwanted thoughts about Ant by keeping busy. This proved relatively easy because there was never a time in her life lately when she wasn't busy.

On Wednesday morning Ant was due to arrive at Jess's apartment for their cooking session, and she'd just finished taking some snapshots of the raw ingredients when the buzzer rang. They'd agreed late morning for lunch would be best, seeing as Ant needed to be at the studio by mid-afternoon.

'Good morning,' she greeted him, overdoing her enthusiasm slightly.

Ant's eyebrows rose. 'You didn't tell me you were the other half when you gave me your address.'

'Huh?'

'As in, you're how the other half live. Sweet location over-looking the beach. It's awesome how you've been able to make the fitness goddess thing work for you.'

Jess ushered him in. 'It does now, but it didn't always. And it's not just my place. My brothers own a share in it, too.'

He followed her down the hallway. 'Brothers plural?' He

whistled and put his hands on his hips when they stepped into the open-plan living and kitchen area. He walked over to take in the view of the Pacific Ocean from the floor-to-ceiling windows that led to a glass-enclosed balcony.

'All of them,' Jess said, waiting while he got his bearings.

And she most definitely did not have a crush on him, she decided. It wasn't like her heart fluttered or her pulse raced at the sight of him. He was just Ant, a guy she found likeable.

He turned to face her. 'Is that wise? Investing with family like that?'

Jess smiled. 'It is in my family, don't worry. All the boys wanted to invest in property, and in typical fashion, they loved the idea of helping their little sister out. I also think they figured I wouldn't be here forever, and we could hold on to it for a few years then sell it for a tidy profit. They're always hoping I'll settle down and start a family, and this isn't exactly a family home.'

'Will you?'

'Settle down?' She shrugged. 'I'd like to one day. But you kind of need to find the right person for that to happen.'

'See, you're smarter than me—not that that would be hard,' Ant told her. 'You're waiting for the right person.'

She gave him a strange look. 'That's the idea, isn't it?'

She walked over to the large island bench and pulled out one of the stools for Ant. 'I've already taken some before photos, so we might as well get straight into it.'

Ant joined her and sat down. 'I'll comment on this unusual array of food in a minute. So you never found the right person?'

'Not quite.'

Jess busied herself getting out utensils while Kat's words from the other night rang in her ears.

Don't tell me you haven't noticed the way he looks at you.

Ant picked up a passionfruit and inspected it like he'd never seen one before.

'Quite?' he said. 'That implies you came close. Me? I settled.'

Jess closed the drawer and looked at him properly. 'Oh?' She didn't want to sound too interested, but she definitely was.

'Yep. Divorced by thirty-one. Another proud moment for my parents.'

She handed him a knife. 'Here. Can you chop up some pineapple for me? I didn't realise you'd been married.'

Ant sighed. 'And you know the worst thing? I'm not even allowed to make bad jokes about it.'

'What do you mean?'

'Because my ex-wife would have my balls on a platter, that's why. Divorcing her was the best thing I ever did, and it pains me that I can't tell the whole world about it.'

Jess stopped peeling the mango she was working on. 'Wow, I think that's the most serious thing I've ever heard you say.'

He grimaced. 'So many jokes, trust me. It physically pains me to bite my tongue.'

'In that case, here. Something to sweeten the bad memories.' She picked up a square of mango and popped it in his mouth before she realised what she was doing.

Her finger brushed his lip, and she snatched her hand back quickly, watching for his reaction. Ant went very still, his dark eyes wide. Not taking his eyes off her, he slowly chewed and swallowed the mango.

'I'm sorry. I didn't even ask if you like mango,' she blurted.

'I like it,' he said, and his voice sounded lower than usual.

She forced a smile onto her face. 'That's good, because we're using half of one in the smoothie I'm about to show you. Here, you can have the other half if you like.' With that, she plonked the plate with the rest of the mango in front of him and turned around to wash her hands at the sink behind her.

The cold water rinsed off the stickiness of the mango, but it didn't get rid of the tingling in her fingers. Why were her fingers tingling like that? She'd just brushed Ant's lips for the briefest second.

He had nice lips, she noted. They were full, and her hand had grazed his permanent five o'clock shadow. The memory of it sent a shiver through her.

Stop tingling, she willed herself. This was Ant, for God's sake. Her *client*.

By the time she turned around again, Ant had chopped the pineapple into neat squares.

'Hey, you're not bad at that. I thought you said you don't like cooking,' she said, almost feeling back to normal again.

'No, it's cooking that doesn't like me. No matter how well I do in the preparation part, it always ends up a disaster.'

'Not today,' Jess promised him. 'The things I'm going to show you can't be messed up.'

Ant pointed at the blender. 'Oh, I don't know. I foresee a multitude of ways I can mess that up. I can leave the lid off by accident and give your kitchen ceiling a health-kick. Or I could get my hand caught in the blender. Or I could drop something into the blender that shouldn't be there, like a knife. Or—'

Jess held up her hands and laughed. 'Alright. I get the picture. How about I operate the blender?'

'That would be the safest option. So what disgustingly healthy concoction are we preparing today?'

Jess started popping ingredients into the glass container. 'I call this one "The Hulk".'

'I like the sound of that,' Ant said.

'It's not just sweet, it's packed with iron too, from the spinach and—'

'Wait right there, JJ. What did you just say?' Ant looked paler than he had a second ago.

Jess bit her lip. 'What colour is the Hulk?' she asked instead.

Ant's eyes narrowed. 'Green.' Then he dropped his hands onto the bench with a loud thwack and stood up. 'I knew it! I knew this wasn't going to go well. At least it's not kale, but it's still *green*.'

'Spinach is filled with nutrients,' Jess began.

'And it's a *vegetable*. Vegetables don't belong in smoothies.'

'That's not true. Plenty of people have carrot juice or—'

'But I'm not plenty of people!' He sat back down in defeat. 'Fine. I'll try it because I don't really have a choice, and I have to give you points for not trying to sneak in kale.'

'It's really tasty. As well as spinach, it's got banana, mango and pineapple. It's the perfect early morning smoothie for before an exercise session. A lot of people find it unpleasant to exercise straight after a meal, but I recommend always having something in your system, particularly after a long sleep. This smoothie is a great option.'

'That's quite the sales pitch, JJ, but I'm still not buying it. If I want something in my system after a long sleep, the perfect early morning solution is leftover pizza.'

Jess screwed her nose up in disgust. 'My brothers used to do that when they were teenagers.'

'Are you implying I have the maturity of a teenage boy?' He shrugged. 'I'll own that.'

Jess decided not to make any further comment. She put the lid on the blender, then hit the green button.

While the blender hummed, Ant stood up and walked over to the wall of photographs near Jess's sofa.

'I take it these are your brothers,' Ant said when she'd hit stop on the blender. 'Either that, or you're into reverse harems.'

Jess let out a loud cough-laugh that ended with her covering her mouth with her hand. When she recovered, she shot him an unimpressed look. 'Yes, those are all my brothers.'

'And your folks,' Ant said, looking at another framed picture. 'Don't take this the wrong way, but they sort of look like the parents from a sitcom. Are they that perfect in real life?'

Jess walked over to view the picture Ant was talking about. She loved that one. It had been taken on their fortieth wedding anniversary.

'They kind of are, actually. I'm really lucky,' she said.

'Figures,' Ant said. 'The apple doesn't fall too far from the tree, huh?'

Jess shoved him on the arm lightly. 'Come on. You need to try the smoothie while I take pictures of you.'

'Not just yet.' Ant grabbed her wrist before she could step away.

Jess's lungs constricted. His touch was light, but his thumb was pressed against the soft skin of her wrist. It felt so good it hurt, and part of Jess wanted to snatch her hand away. Another part of her didn't.

What was wrong with her?

Relief came a second later when Ant dropped her hand and pointed at someone in a group photo.

'Who's this? He doesn't look like a brother, and I count five, so that's not right.'

Jess cleared her throat, and the flush that she'd felt working its way up her neck just moments ago vanished like someone had thrown cold water all over her.

'That's my ex,' Jess said, and this time she did turn away and return to the kitchen bench.

Ant studied the photo more closely. 'God, even he's perfect. Why is he still on display?' Ant turned to face her and grimaced. 'Ugh. Sorry. You could have broken up with him yesterday for all I know. I'll remove my foot from my mouth now.'

Jess gestured for him to sit down again. 'No, that's alright. It's been over three years, don't worry. I guess I've always liked that photo, and it seemed like a shame to take it down just because of him.' She carefully poured the green liquid into two tall glasses. 'That, and my mother,' she muttered, and instantly regretted it.

'Ooh, do tell. Was she a fan of the perfect ex?'

Jess picked up her phone. She really needed to stop having this conversation right now. It wasn't professional to be talking so freely like this with a client. But then this was the first time she'd ever invited a client into her a home for a meeting. The whole situation just felt strange to her. Not wrong. Just strange.

Instead of answering him, she started snapping photos of the two glasses from various different positions.

'Whatever angle you take that from, it's still green,' Ant pointed out.

Jess sighed. It couldn't hurt to answer his question. Besides, Ant was Kat's co-host, and Kat considered him a good friend and an excellent colleague.

Jess lowered her phone. 'I think my mother loved Jack more than I did.'

Ant put a hand to his heart. 'Ah. The one that got away, huh?'

'Not exactly. I was the one who dumped him.'

Ant rested his elbows on the bench and regarded the green drink suspiciously. 'You know, a coffee would be ideal to enjoy over this juicy sort of gossip. Not *that*.'

'Just try it.'

Ant reached out and picked up the drink. With his other hand he covered his eyes, then brought the glass to his lips. He took the tiniest of sips, then set the glass down.

'Holy hell. It's nowhere near as bad as I thought!'

'Can I use that as a testimonial when I post the recipe online?'

'Feel free. So I've done my bit, now you have to tell me about your sordid love life.'

She pointed at him. 'Only if you drink it while I take photos of you enjoying it.'

'Enjoying it? That might be going too far.'

'OK. No gossip, then.'

Ant picked up the drink again with a sigh and plastered a fake smile onto his face. Jess took a shot of him.

'Now drink it,' she instructed.

'Mmm,' Ant said unconvincingly, while Jess continued to take photos.

They were pictures, not audio, so it would have to do.

'OK. Now some selfies,' Jess said.

She came around to his side of the bench and held up her glass next to his. Just as she hit the button to take the photo, he pretended to be crying.

Jess didn't want to encourage him, but couldn't help herself and laughed. Then she had an idea.

Jess put the glass down, and still with the camera on them, picked up his glass.

'Hold your nose,' she told him, smiling.

He gave her a questioning look but did as he was told, and Jess tipped the glass like she was trying to pour the green liquid down his throat against his will.

He grabbed the phone when she'd taken the shot and let out a loud bark of laughter.

'Yes! That's awesome,' he said, a big grin on his face. 'You're on to something.'

Well, at least Ant had forgotten about the subject of her love life. That was something.

Then her mouth dropped open as he poured the green liquid all over the front of his T-shirt.

'What are you doing!' she cried.

Jess rushed around the bench to get some paper towel to clean up the mess, which was steadily travelling toward his jeans.

'Wait,' Ant ordered. Then he lifted the phone and took a selfie, pretending like he'd thrown up all over himself.

'We can't use that!' Jess protested.

'Why not? Come over here and look distressed.'

'That won't be hard,' she muttered.

'Hands in the air like you're surprised and dismayed,' he told her.

He snapped off another photo of them both, then held the image up to show her.

She giggled. OK, it was actually very funny.

Ant stood up. 'Right. Now your turn.'

Jess shot him a confused look, then narrowed her eyes when she registered his evil grin.

'No,' she said, edging backward. 'No. No, no. NO.'

He stepped towards her, holding the half-full glass with the other hand.

'Oh, yes,' he replied.

Jess shook her head. 'No way are you going to pour that on me. I'm wearing a white T-shirt.'

He took another step closer, his dark eyes wicked. 'That's the whole point.'

He lunged for her and Jess screamed, darting out of his

grasp while the green smoothie sloshed dangerously close to the top of the glass.

Jess scampered around the bench, putting it between them.

'I can't believe you just tried to do that,' she said, slightly puffed. But not so much from the exertion. More from surprise. And possibly from the way those dark eyes gleamed at her with playfulness.

'Believe it,' he said.

Then he threw the green smoothie all over her from across the bench.

Jess screamed. A proper scream of surprise and indignation.

Ant was a good shot. The liquid covered the front of her T-shirt as well as the white countertop in front of her.

Jess raised her hands, which were dripping, and surveyed her T-shirt with dismay. When she looked up, Ant was still grinning at her.

'Smile,' he said, then took a photo of her.

Jess's eyes widened. Right. That was it. The last straw. Her gaze narrowed.

'You forget I grew up with four older brothers,' she said, her voice low.

He wriggled his eyebrows like they were laughing at her. 'Do your worst, JJ. It can't be worse than a green smoothie.'

Jess could have picked up the other glass and attempted to throw that on him, but she had an even better idea.

She turned around and opened the fridge, then smiled, a manic, sinister smile, when she spotted what she wanted in the crisper. She snatched it out and rounded on him.

'*Kale!*'

His brown eyes widened in genuine horror, and he took a step back.

'Time to eat it, smart-arse.' It wasn't a threat. It was a promise.

She bounded around the island bench towards him. He hesitated for only a second, then sprinted away from her up the hall.

It didn't matter. Jess was fitter and faster, and a moment ago she would have said she was furious. But it occurred to her as she dashed after him that she hadn't had this much fun in as long as she could remember.

And now Adonis was going to pay.

Chapter Thirteen

ANT HEARD Jess chasing him up the hall, her sneakers squeaking on the tiles.

Far out, she was quick.

Not surprisingly, he found himself outpaced and outsmarted. When he reached the end of the hall like one of those victims in a thriller movie who found themselves cornered in an alley, he looked around wildly. There was a bedroom off either side.

He picked the nearest one and darted inside. He could have escaped out the front door, but while he didn't want Jess to catch him, he didn't actually want to run away from her either.

He stopped at the foot of a bed. Jess's bed. Christ. Bad choice. The room was neat, but lived in, with a bright cover on the bed and several books piled on the bedside table. He hadn't meant to invade her privacy. He turned to leave the room and yelped.

'Huh! Got you,' cried Jess, her gorgeous blue eyes so intense they appeared to glow.

He took a step backward and raised his hands. 'Yep, got me. Look, I'm sorry but—'

'Time to eat your punishment,' she growled in a voice that sent shivers down his spine.

Good shivers. The best kind.

She stepped in close and shoved the kale in his face, and he instinctively reeled back, which was when he discovered he had nowhere to go. The back of his calves pressed against the end of the bed. He probably should have just opened his mouth and tried the damn kale, but self-preservation prevailed and he lost his balance.

He fell backwards, right onto Jess's bed. And oh heck, she was coming with him.

Her high-pitched cry had him grabbing for her—another instinct—and by the time they both hit the bed, his hands were holding on to her hips. She obviously had good instincts too, and her free hand reached out to grip his shoulder to break her fall.

Unfortunately, her other hand still held the kale, and it brushed against his nose as she waved it in front of him.

'Eat it,' she demanded.

Ant kept his mouth sealed shut. Hell, he was too distracted by her taut body pressed against his to worry about the kale right in front of his face. That stretch of hard stomach against his softer, much less toned stomach. And those pert little breasts pressing into his chest. Made even worse—or was that better?—by the fact both of their T-shirts were covered in green goo from the damn smoothie. It was like a vegan's version of mud wrestling and he didn't think he'd ever experienced anything sexier.

Jess appeared unmoved and pushed the kale against his mouth.

'It's really not that bad,' she told him with a grin so evil it made him want to curl his toes.

'No, I guess it's not,' he replied softly, and in that moment, he saw it.

The recognition sparking in her eyes. They flared with surprise and then something even more unexpected. Heat.

She froze on top of him. He saw her considering everything he had a second ago. He didn't dare to move because he didn't want to scare her away.

He had no idea what she was thinking. A part of him expected her to jump off him immediately, but when she didn't, another part of him held out a sliver of hope that she felt it, too. He wondered what his eyes were saying.

Stay.

She blinked at him, then removed the kale from his face.

'Oh my God, I'm so sorry,' she breathed. 'This is just so ridiculous. I got carried away and I shouldn't have—'

He caught her wrist. 'I thought it was quite fun, actually.'

She froze again, and he waited with bated breath for her reaction. Surely she'd jump off him now?

Please don't go.

Instead, she threw her head back and laughed so hard, tears started streaming down her face. She dropped the kale on the bed beside them and used her hands to shift herself up, but was laughing so hard she couldn't get off him.

'Oh . . . my . . . God,' she managed between gasps of laughter. 'I can't believe you threw the smoothie on me. And then I just saw red and . . .' She dissolved into fits of giggles again and collapsed on top of him.

Ant blissed out for a moment. He was convinced that he hadn't seen anything more beautiful in his life. Jessica Jinks covered in "The Hulk", her face flushed pink and with a smile big enough to light up the entire world was a sight to behold. And now she was lying on him.

Predictably, he went and ruined it.

Without thinking, he reached over and brushed the side of her face with the back of his hand. Another instinct—not a good one. But she was just so goddamn beautiful it hurt.

Her smile vanished instantly and she eased herself up, looking down at him while blinking again.

'Just so you know, I'd only eat kale for you,' he said.

Another mistake.

This time she did jump off him and shoved a hand through her blonde hair, not realising she'd just smeared green smoothie through it. Of course, it looked good on her. Like it was part of her fitness goddess brand.

'That was so unprofessional of me,' she said more to herself than him while pacing the room. 'I don't usually act like this.' Her eyes darted to meet his, and his heart broke a little at the regret in them.

He forced himself to stand up, delicious delusions of what could have happened a moment ago still running wild in his head.

'Hey, this isn't a negative reflection of you. I started it and I'm a bad influence. Ask pretty much all of my schoolteachers.'

She stopped pacing and looked at him, her expression still concerned. 'Yes, but you're my *client*.'

'Yep, and your worst client at that. Seriously, don't worry about it. I'm not going to judge you for it or mention it to anyone. Although, I will think twice about challenging you in the future. You're scary when you're determined.'

He earned a twitch of the lips for that. 'Blame my stupid brothers.'

'And if you want me to try the kale, I'll do it. It started as a joke, but I know I'm being childish about it.'

Jess shook her head and took a step towards him, then hesitated like she was unsure about how close she should get. 'No, I've been stupid about it. Let's forget about the kale for now. I won't force it on you anymore. How about this instead? If you wake up one day and discover you genuinely *want* to exercise—I'll eat kale in every single meal for an entire week. How about that?'

It pained Ant to stop himself from reaching up and brushing a strand of her blonde-green hair away from her face, but he really, really wanted to. 'You'd eat kale for an entire week? Because of me? Wow.'

She shrugged a shoulder. 'It's not that bad, and I can be creative. I might even come up with some new recipes.'

'You're a unique woman, JJ.'

She dropped her gaze, and his words hung in the air between them. When would he learn to keep his thoughts to himself around her? But that was the thing. When he was around her, he felt compelled to shower her with compliments. On some level, that was a good thing, right? Surely it made him a nice person? Not a creepy one, who was crushing pointlessly on his fitness trainer.

Pointlessly?

Until today, he never would have dreamed Jess would remotely entertain the idea of someone like him, but now he wasn't so sure. Or he was delusional. Definitely delusional.

She met his eyes again and he tried not to suck in a sharp breath. Uncertainty. Jess was feeling uncertain around him. Because she'd felt something for him?

No, because she just did something unprofessional when she was supposed to be working, you idiot.

She smiled, but he could tell it was forced.

'Mind helping me clean up?' she asked.

He nodded quickly. 'Sure thing.'

'And I'll see if I can find you a fresh T-shirt,' she continued. 'I think I might have one of my brother's in the spare room.'

With that she left the room, leaving him standing there. He caught a glimpse of himself in the full-length mirror near the wardrobe and shook his head at himself. He looked like he'd just done several rounds with the Hulk and come off second best.

He made a promise to himself then. No more goofing off around Jess Jinks. OK, that wasn't true. He'd still joke occasionally, because she seemed to enjoy it. But no more stupid attempts to distract them from their sessions. He was going to take this exercise thing seriously from now on. And try to eat right.

Jess's business reputation depended on it.

Chapter Fourteen

JESS KEPT things one hundred percent professional with Ant after the smoothie incident.

It made it less awkward that their next session was being filmed, so there were production and camera crew present. Ant acted predictably funny, but Jess noticed a difference in him, too. She might have been wrong, but he seemed to be taking the exercise seriously for a change. He did everything she asked without complaint. A part of her almost missed his humorous protestations. The only time he really goofed off was when it was obviously for the cameras and the sake of ratings.

'You don't seem your usual happy self,' Em commented on a Friday night a couple of weeks later.

They were sitting on her penthouse balcony enjoying the view of the Pacific Ocean drinking cocktails. Jess's was a mocktail, because she chose not to drink alcohol.

'Oh, I'm happy enough,' Jess replied, wishing Kat could have joined them.

They'd messaged her earlier, but Kat had replied that she had a work function on in the city. A charity dinner or something like that.

'Could have fooled me.' Em topped up their glasses with the pineapple juice to make their drinks last longer.

Jess sighed. Em was refreshingly honest—it was one of the things Jess liked about her neighbour.

'I'm sorry, it's nothing important, really.' Jess took another sip, enjoying the tart freshness of the fruit in her mouth. Since things with Ant had settled into a predictable routine, it wasn't a cause for concern anymore.

Em waited.

'Oh, alright,' Jess relented. 'You really are very good at getting things out of people, you know that?'

Em put down her glass on the small side table sitting between them and raised her hands. 'I didn't say a word.'

'I know, that's just it! You wait people out!'

Em laughed lightly, her auburn waves bobbing. 'Blame my father. World's stubbornest man. I learned not to fight with him, but to be patient.'

'Did it work?' Jess asked.

'Sort of. He's more stubborn than me. Usually after waiting him out on whatever we were in a disagreement about, I'd do something worse to distract him from the original point of contention. It was a valuable life lesson in dealing with people.'

'I'm sorry,' Jess blurted, then regretted it, because it came across as condescending.

She couldn't imagine being at odds with either of her parents, though. Several things Em had said during the time Jess had known her indicated that Em's relationship with her father wasn't easy.

Em shrugged. 'Don't be. We still love each other, don't get me wrong. We just disagree about some things.' Then she added, 'Most things.'

They laughed.

'Anyway, we weren't talking about me,' Em went on. 'Nice try, by the way. We were talking about you.'

Jess sighed again. 'It's just a family thing. Nothing major. More annoying.'

'I've had a lot of experience at dealing with annoying family things, if it's not already obvious.'

That made Jess smile. 'Well, in this case, it's not my father. It's my mother.'

'You've mentioned you get along, but you're quite different,' Em commented.

'Definitely. She's, how shall I say? Traditional.'

Em sat up in her seat. 'Oh, don't tell me! She wants grandchildren. I'm barely twenty-six and my father thinks I'm "on the shelf".'

'My mother would prefer marriage first. And it's not so much that I'm on the shelf, it's that she was devastated when I broke up with my long-term boyfriend. I swear she was more upset about it than I was.'

Em sat back in her seat and studied her wine. 'Oh. That's rough. I've never had a boyfriend long-term enough that my father could get excited about it.'

Jess's lips quirked. 'Yeah, I kinda got that.'

In the time that she'd lived there, Jess had witnessed Em date a steady stream of guys—and there were plenty she probably hadn't witnessed, too.

Em shrugged. 'It works for me. I get to enjoy a man in my life and stop my father from setting me up with someone, which he is always desperate to do. Instead I can say, "Sorry

Dad, I'm seeing someone". Who cares if it's a different someone from one week to the next? So why'd you destroy your mum's hopes and dreams for your future?'

Jess's smile turned into a laugh. 'It was all really boring, actually. There wasn't a lot of angst involved, unless you count my mother. Basically Jack wanted to go and work overseas, and I didn't. He works in banking, and I suspect he earns a ton of money by now. Even when he was young, he was always executive material. So he thought that the next step in climbing the corporate ladder was to take a position in London.'

Em tapped her glass with her fingernail thoughtfully. 'Don't take this the wrong way, but I can't see you with executive material.'

'Oh, he was super-fit as well,' Jess said, not sure why she was defending her ex-boyfriend. 'We had a lot in common.'

'Yes, but you're so . . . full of life. I can't imagine you settling for a corporate type.'

'Well, I didn't in the end. Jack went off to London and that was it. A decade-long relationship over.'

Em whistled. 'Wow, a decade? You practically *were* married then. How old were you when you started going out?'

'We were high school sweethearts. We started dating in our final year.'

'Wow, that's a seriously long time. And a seriously serious relationship.'

'You've really never had a long-term relationship?' Jess asked with interest.

Em grimaced. 'No way. I think the longest I've lasted is six months.'

Jess let out a small gasp. 'Sorry. That was rude.'

'No. Not rude. Just honest. I'm fully prepared to be a

middle-aged spinster who lives for my work. With the occasional fling on the side, of course.'

'Of course,' Jess agreed.

'So are you looking for another long-term thing?' Em asked.

Jess considered Em's question. 'Definitely. But only with the right person. Whoever that is.'

'So what wasn't right about Jack?'

'You know, for the longest time he *was* right for me. We grew up together and I always saw us settling down at some stage. But in those couple of years before we broke up, we started growing apart in small ways. When push came to shove and Jack said he was going overseas with or without me, I realised all those little things added up.'

'You didn't want to try the long-distance thing?'

'We discussed it. But Jack's really driven, and he wanted to do the overseas thing his way. And that meant me coming with him or we break up. He ignored or argued against all my objections.'

'Like?'

'Like I was just starting my business up here in Australia. So he told me I could do the same thing overseas. It didn't matter that the United Kingdom is a completely different market or that I wanted to build my business here. I also didn't want to be away from my family. His response was predictable —that I was being close-minded and the experience would be good for me.' Jess shrugged. 'Living overseas is something I've never felt driven to do.'

Em winced. 'Ouch. Harsh.'

'My family are all really close,' Jess started to explain.

'Oh, don't worry, I get it. I don't want to be so close to my family, but it's not a choice. We just are.'

'See! You get it. He never did.'

'Did Jack like your family?' Em asked.

'Oh, he loved them, don't get me wrong. He just didn't understand our level of closeness, I suppose. He has one older brother who he talks to maybe every other month. They get along, but they're distant. I'm on the phone to a member of my family most days.'

'Maybe he thought you'd gain more independence from them overseas?' Em wondered.

'I didn't want to! I can't imagine not being able to call my brother when my sink gets blocked, or see my toddler nephew or my gorgeous baby niece whenever I want. It's who I am, I guess.'

'Then one day you'll find someone who gets that, I'm sure. But I've got to ask, why is Jack so top of mind now? Didn't you say you broke up several years ago?'

Jess stared at her glass for a moment, thinking it was a shame she didn't drink alcohol after all. Then, without further hesitation, she finished it in one gulp. Em watched on in amusement.

'Jack's just returned from London. With his English fiancée. And they're coming to dinner at my parents' house. His mum and my mum are best friends and catch up regularly.'

Em observed the expression on Jess's face. 'Ah. I see why your mum was hoping for marriage if she's close to Jack's mum. And I'm guessing you're invited to this dinner, too?'

'Exactly. It's going to be so awkward.'

'So why not invite someone along?'

Jess frowned. 'Who? I'm so busy with work these days, I haven't even tried dating in the last eighteen months.'

'You don't have a male friend who would agree to go with you?'

'And pretend to be my partner? No way. My brothers would pick up the lie in a second.'

'OK. Fair point. It's just me that stoops to lying to my family, obviously.' Em's light blue eyes reflected the ocean as she looked out at the view. A second later, they sparked with excitement. 'Oh, I know! I've got it.' She turned to face Jess in her seat. 'You invite Ant along!'

Jess's mouth fell open.

Before she had a chance to protest, Em rushed on. 'I don't mean as your partner. As your friend. If anyone can take the pressure off you, he can. The man's a comic genius. Everyone will be so busy laughing, they'll all be like, "Jack who?"'

Jess thought about it for approximately one second, then she shook her head. 'No. It would be really weird. Besides, he's my client, not my friend.'

Em arched an eyebrow. 'Really? Kat says you get on really well with each other. It's not an offence to become friends with a client, surely?'

Maybe. Maybe not. Jess wasn't sure being friends with each other was what either of them had been thinking when they were on Jess's bed the other day covered in green goo. But Em didn't know about that, and Jess had no intention of telling her.

'Jess?'

'Yes?'

'Is it really that bad of an idea?'

No, it wasn't a bad idea necessarily. After the PR exercise was over, maybe Jess could imagine being friends with Ant. But right now? It wasn't professional.

But that was the thing. Ever since the smoothie incident, Ant *had* been professional. Maybe the possibility of having a respectful friendship with him wasn't so far-fetched.

Jess tried to imagine Ant around her family and smiled in

spite of herself. She had a feeling he'd love the audience, and her brothers would enjoy trying to get the better of him—in a friendly way, of course. Something told Jess it was a challenge Ant would relish.

'I can't just invite him to dinner at my parents place out of the blue,' Jess said to Em. 'It would be weird. And how would I explain Jack?'

'Just tell him what you told me, only a simpler version. I think he'd be honoured to be asked.'

Jess fell silent and watched the ocean. It was calm tonight and the sky was an inky black, which made the stars even brighter.

Jess supposed Ant already did know about Jack as he'd seen that photo in her apartment the other week. So it wasn't like she'd have to explain everything from scratch . . . but no. Jess couldn't even believe she was considering it.

'I can hear the cogs whirring in your head,' Em said, breaking the silence. 'It's really not as big of a deal as you think it is. It might seem like it because you had a relationship that lasted ten years, but in my world I take guys along to family gatherings all the time. It's almost expected of me. The surprise would be if my family saw the same guy twice.'

Jess giggled. 'When you put it that way . . . God, how do I even ask him, though? In person?'

'Seriously, just message the guy. Say you need a wingman for an awkward family dinner and his humour is required. And that your family would love to meet your latest famous client. If he's not keen, he won't be put on the spot and can just say no, he's busy.'

Em did have a point. And the thought of not attending the dinner alone would come as a relief. Jess was used to being the only solo one on account of her brothers all having partners, but this was different. Very different.

'I'll think about it,' Jess relented.

Em smiled. 'Just don't overthink it, alright?'

Jess laughed. 'I'll try.'

'Good. Now let's order takeaway. I'm starving.'

That sounded good to Jess, and with that she pushed the subject from her mind for the time being.

Chapter Fifteen

ON THE WEEKEND Ant decided to review his wardrobe. Not the physical wardrobe itself, of course, although he had to admit that it was kind of ugly. It was one of those mirrored glass numbers with gold edging from the nineties. He'd slowly been renovating his terrace house in the city's inner suburbs since he'd bought it a couple of years ago. But the dated wardrobe had always seemed less important than other projects, like the salmon puke bathroom tiles.

Now he found himself wishing he had taken the time and money to replace it with something a lot less reflective. He stood in front of it wearing his favourite pair of jeans and no shirt. How was it possible his jeans were now loose, but his belly was as soft as ever?

He poked at his stomach. There had to be a six-pack in there somewhere, surely?

Yeah, in an alternate universe where Jess wanted to kiss him, and Alicia Travers was actually keen to go on a date with him.

Ant sighed and reached for his T-shirt lying on the bed. Obviously his stomach was as stubborn as he was when it came to exercise. Much like his chest hair. He occasionally wondered about getting laser hair removal—a lot of guys did these days—but the thought of him being hairless weirded him out. Besides, with guys like Aidan Turner from that *Poldark* show making chest hair sexy again, maybe Ant would be back in fashion before too long.

'You've never been in fashion, you idiot,' he muttered, and pulled his T-shirt over his head.

Ant knew that if Jess heard that he'd lost some weight since the PR stunt began, she'd be ecstatic for him. She'd say something ultra-positive like, "It's only been three weeks and you've already lost three kilos? That's amazing!"

He smiled at her imagined response. He supposed it was kind of cool that he'd shed a few kilos. He was also genuinely trying to eat better, too. He only allowed himself beer on the weekend—he wasn't a saint, he was human. And the same went for takeout. He only let himself order out once a week, and even then he'd select healthier options like sushi.

Ant supposed he did feel pretty good, when all was said and done. Instead of dragging himself out of bed in the morning for their triweekly exercise sessions, two of which were filmed, he found himself getting up with a spring in his step.

Because of Jess.

Well, duh. Of course because of Jess, but Ant was finding he was actually enjoying most of the exercises they were doing. He liked some more than others. Ant wasn't a big fan of anything that resembled intensity training. Frankly, that was going too far in his opinion. But to his surprise, Ant genuinely liked running, and they'd tried bike riding last week too, which had been fun. He seemed to enjoy the activities that allowed his body to get into a rhythm. When that happened, Ant found it was good for his mental health, too.

Often he'd find himself reflecting on his day, which jokes had worked, which hadn't, and sometimes new jokes would come to mind out of the blue, which was a bonus. It was like the exercise was giving his brain space to work through things, and he liked it.

'Maybe I should try swimming sometime,' he wondered out loud.

He stopped sliding the wardrobe door closed and froze.

'Holy crap. Jess is right. I'm starting to *want* to exercise. What is happening to me?'

And now he was having a conversation with himself out loud, which was equally worrying. But then again, what was so bad about fitting some exercise into his week if it made him feel better physically as well as mentally?

Ant finished closing the wardrobe and turned to collect the pile of clothes on his bed that needed washing. He scooped them up and headed to the laundry off his kitchen.

He wouldn't tell Jess about his desire to exercise just yet. Right now it was a sort of mini desire. More like a curiosity thing. He wasn't going to make Jess eat kale for a week straight unless he was hooked on exercise—and Ant still couldn't imagine that happening.

This was more like he and exercise were speed dating. Some running here. Some Hi-Jinks moves there. So maybe he'd throw some swimming into the mix and see how that went. Ant knew himself well enough to know that he had a short attention span. He might think running was OK this week, but next week he could be back on the sofa binge-watching a Netflix series while eating takeout. He wasn't going to get too hasty about the way things were going.

Maybe when he had some actual muscle definition Ant would believe that this exercise thing was paying off. For now, he'd treat all motivating thoughts on the subject with suspicion. Maybe part of Jess's strategy was brainwashing him and he didn't know it.

Blow him away with drop-dead gorgeous looks, talk to him in a voice that was more like a song, then laugh in all the right places at his jokes, and he was anybody's. Preferably hers.

'Bad train of thought,' he said, and closed the washing machine door.

Jessica Jinks was never going to be his. Even if he did discover he was the owner of a ripped six-pack, girls like Jess didn't end up with guys like him. He'd learned that lesson the hard way many years ago, and he wasn't going to make it again.

He needed to be realistic. Do the PR stunt, get fit, maybe even stay fit for a few months after if he was lucky. During that time, he could try to date again while he looked good. Not girls like Jess, of course. Just regular girls. Nice girls that wouldn't mind if he weighed a few extra kilos one day. Which he inevitably would.

Not that Jess wasn't nice, but someone in her line of work deserved to be with someone who fit her brand.

She hadn't ended up with Mr. Perfection, which was food for thought. That was how Ant was thinking of Jess's ex-boyfriend after seeing that picture of him. Ant was dying to know why things hadn't worked out, because as far as appearances went, Mr. Perfection fit the mould. Ant wasn't surprised Jess's mum was disappointed. They'd have made beautiful grandbabies for her.

That was yet another reason Ant would never end up with a girl like Jess. He had no plans for giving his parents grandchildren. Marriage wasn't something he was keen to revisit either. And Jess was the sort of girl that deserved a happily ever after. Like she said, she was waiting for the right person.

Ant doubted he'd ever be someone's right person. He definitely wasn't like the prince in a fairytale, ready to give the heroine a happily ever after. The thought was laughable. Ant as a prince? More like a court jester.

Pushing all thoughts of Jess and fairytales aside, Ant turned and surveyed the kitchen. He needed to get some food supplies today. He began entering a list of essentials on his phone. While he could remember a joke from five years ago, in the time it took him to leave home and arrive at the supermarket he'd completely forget what he was there for if he didn't make a list.

A message flashed onto his screen as he typed. He caught a glimpse of it before he disappeared.

'Holy shit.'

He had definitely read the message incorrectly. It was from Jess and said something about "dinner" and "family". Something that clearly didn't involve Ant.

He opened the messaging app on his phone and read it properly.

Hey Ant. I need to ask a favour, but don't feel obliged. My family is hosting a dinner that I can't get out of and you came to mind.

Ant preened a bit, then kept reading.

My ex-boyfriend's parents will be there (my parents are good friends with them) and guess who else they invited? My ex-boyfriend and his new fiancée. I'd feel way more comfortable with a friend there. Someone who always knows what to say and will help me keep my foot out of my mouth ;) It's this Sunday evening. Like I said, don't feel obliged! JJ.

Ant stared at the message for a long moment. Reread it. Reread it again.

'Hell, yes,' he said, and then began typing his reply.

Chapter Sixteen

CONSIDERING Ant was never in fashion, he spent way too long on Sunday afternoon deciding what to wear. In the end, he settled on a black pair of jeans and a simple black shirt, because black was slimming, wasn't it?

When he turned up at Jess's front door his palms felt sweaty.

It's not a date, it's not a date, it's not a date.

This was just one friend helping out another. The fact that she considered him anything approaching a friend was enough to make his heart race, which he knew was pathetic. Still, he'd settle for Jess as a friend any day.

'Hey, Ant!' Jess greeted him when she opened the front door. They'd agreed it was easier to meet at her place and then drive together to her parents' house, which was nearby.

'Hey, Jess.' And that was about all he was capable of saying.

She wore a little black dress, not the going-out-to-a-night-club kind. This one was sweet and sexy at the same time, with spaghetti straps and a sort of frilly neckline. Below that the dress was fitted and showed off her great curves before it flared just above the knees.

Jess caught him looking at her, because basically he was staring.

She grimaced. 'Is it too much? I wasn't sure what to wear. What is someone supposed to wear when they're going to catch up with their ex-boyfriend?'

'It's fine,' he said, then could have slapped himself in the face. It was more than fine, it was stunning. 'I mean, it's hot without throwing it in his face that you're hot.' And now he was calling her hot. He stopped talking.

Jess giggled. 'You read my mind then. I wanted to turn up looking nice, but not too nice.'

'Just the right amount of nice,' Ant said, then thought, *and the best kind of sexy*. But he kept that to himself.

'And look, we match,' Jess exclaimed, then turned to get her bag off the hall stand. 'I'm driving by the way, since I don't drink.'

'Oh, so you'll let me get drunk. Sacrificial lamb, huh?'

Jess grinned and ushered him out the door. 'It's for a good cause.'

Ant wasn't going to disagree because anything involving Jess was a good cause as far as he was concerned.

They headed towards the lift in the hallway.

'So, I'd better give you the rundown before we get there,' she told him. 'My parents will both be there obviously, as well as my oldest brother Grant, his wife Susie, and my adorable niece and nephew. My other brother, Nick, and his partner, Chelsea, will be there, too. And of course, Jack, his fiancée Poppy, as well as Nick's parents, Sandra and John.'

The lift doors opened, and they stepped inside.

'Hang on a minute, did you say Poppy?' Ant asked.

Jess hit the button for the basement, presumably where her

car was parked, and gave him a sideways look. 'Yes, I know. I thought that, too.'

Ant shot her an innocent look. 'Thought what?'

'*Poppy,*' Jess said in a pretty good imitation of a Cockney accent.

Ant cracked a smile, which turned into a grin. 'Now you don't know if she's that sort of Poppy. She could be a Gwyneth Poppy.'

'A what?'

The lift dinged and the doors opened. Ant followed her towards a cute white Mercedes hatch that Ant thought suited Jess perfectly.

The lights flashed as Jess unlocked the doors and Ant got in the passenger side. It was only when they were both inside that it occurred to him that being in her car felt intimate some-how. He shook the thought off, and as was his way, opted for humour.

'She could be some crusty, snobbish type who follows all the latest fashion trends including Gwyneth Paltrow's Goop,' he said, then added 'Poppy' in his best upper-crust British accent.

Jess started the car, her eyes twinkling. 'Oooh, you're so right. She could totally be rich and have enough money to think steaming her vagina is a legitimate thing to do.'

Ant coughed. Then coughed again.

Jess turned to back out of the parking spot and flashed him a devastatingly wicked grin that made Ant's heart flip-flop in his chest.

'See?' she said. 'This is why you're here. I'll definitely say something inappropriate otherwise.'

'So I'm in charge of the inappropriate humour?' he replied when he was able to talk again.

'With my full permission.'

Jess waited until the security garage door opened and then drove outside.

'Are you absolutely sure about that?' Ant asked.

'Oh, I'm certain. Jack always thought my sense of humour was too wacky, and there were times I'd embarrass him. My mother has a tendency to agree with him. I need to be on my best behaviour tonight, but think of this as an opportunity to be wacky on my behalf.'

'Mission accepted.'

Damn. Tonight was getting better and better and they hadn't even arrived yet.

First of all, Ant got to spend time with Jess—that was a bonus in itself. Next, he was getting the opportunity to meet some of her family, which he was really curious about. And lastly, he had permission to toy with her ex-boyfriend.

Ant was pretty sure life didn't get any better than this.

WHEN THEY ARRIVED AT HER PARENTS' house fifteen minutes later, Jess's nerves started to get the better of her. She hadn't seen Jack since they'd broken up three years ago, and the strangeness of the situation suddenly hit her.

Pulling on the handbrake and shutting off the engine, she snuck a look at Ant.

Having him here was another level of weird, too. It had taken her hours to make her mind up about sending that text, and when she finally had she felt impossibly stupid. Fortunately, Ant's reply had put her at ease.

Obliged I am not, but I'd never pass up an opportunity to put my foot in my mouth. Send me further details. I'm flexing my legs to ensure my feet have maximum reach.

Jess smiled at the memory. OK, so maybe it wasn't that weird having him here. They'd chatted easily the entire journey, and not just about her stupid ex-boyfriend either. Everything from the latest news to a Netflix series that was rating well to Ant making random funny comments about people walking down the street.

'You don't need to be nervous, Jess,' Ant said, reading her expression. 'Once they see me come through the door they'll forget all about you, trust me.'

'Is that a promise?'

'It's an Ant Monticello guarantee—maximum laughs or your money back.'

Jess let herself smile, and for the first time that night she felt grateful that Ant had said yes. He went to open the door and Jess found herself reaching across to grab his arm.

He turned back to her and she dropped her hand awkwardly.

'Thanks, by the way, for coming tonight. I know it's a bit weird.'

He gave her his best television smile. 'Weird is what I do best.'

He turned away again and got out of the car, leaving Jess staring after him. Gosh, when he smiled like that, it did something funny to Jess's insides.

She shook off the thought and forced herself to get out of the car. Ant was waiting on the footpath for her, and when she came to his side, he held his elbow out for her.

'Showtime?' he asked.

'Showtime,' she agreed, and linked her arm through his, ready to face whatever lay ahead inside.

Chapter Seventeen

JESS'S PARENTS' house was a large two-storey suburban home with well-established gardens and French windows. When they stepped in the front door, Ant couldn't help but notice the fashionable decor and finishes. Yet it still had a lived-in, inviting family feel.

'Nice place,' Ant said quietly as they entered. 'Did you grow up here?'

'Yep. Mum and Dad have been here thirty years now, and Mum's just finished driving Dad nuts renovating it. Come through.'

They headed towards the sound of voices and laughter, presumably in the direction of the kitchen. When they stepped into a large, modern living area at the back of the house, the conversation immediately stopped.

Well, hi there, everyone, Ant thought as all eyes focused on them. And it was "all eyes". He and Jess must have been the last to arrive judging by the number of people already there, some inside and others out on the back deck.

Jess cast a nervous glance at Ant and raised a hand in greeting. 'Hi everyone. This is—'

'I'm no one. Carry on as you were. Don't mind me,' Ant finished for her.

There were a few lukewarm laughs, mainly from the women outside. They resumed their conversations. That was all right. It was still warm-up time as far as Ant was concerned. He needed to read the room some more before he laid on the jokes too thick anyway.

A brother stepped forward—and Ant would bet his life it was a brother, because the guy had the same blond, blue-eyed features as Jess—and held out his hand.

Ant took it and they shook. It was firm, but not unfriendly.

'Nice to meet you, Ant. Hey, you're looking good, now I see you in person. Jess's regimen been paying off for you already?'

Jess smiled at her brother. 'This is Nick.'

'Let me guess,' Ant said, 'the ironman brother? Good to meet you.'

Nick's eyebrows rose. 'Ironman? I don't know about that—'

'Come on, you're being humble.' Another brother stepped forward—the tall, dark-haired one that Ant recognised from Jess's photograph. 'I don't do triathlons, so in this family that makes Nick the ironman. I'm Grant.'

More shaking hands, and suddenly Ant was grateful only two of Jess's brothers were here tonight. Grant may not have been an ironman like Nick, but both brothers were big and burly, and Ant got the distinct impression they viewed Jess as a valuable treasure worth protecting.

'Where's Jack? Is he here?' Jess whispered to Nick, and Ant noticed her gaze move towards the group outside chatting on the deck.

Nick nodded in that direction. 'Yep. And his fiancée, *Poppy*.'

Ant and Jess shared a look, then they both cracked up. Jess's brothers stared at them, confused.

'Sorry,' Jess apologised. 'We had a similar joke going in the car on the way over here,' she told her brothers quietly. 'We were trying to imagine what someone called Poppy looks like.'

Grant, the dark-haired brother, crossed his arms. 'And what did you figure?'

Ant spoke up. 'Rough London East Ender or Gwyneth Paltrow sophisticate—you know, fashionable but clueless.'

'She's neither,' said Nick, leaving Ant more intrigued than ever.

At that moment, a woman with waist-length red hair broke free of the group outside. When she saw them standing inside, her eyes lit up. Even from their position indoors, Ant could make out their striking green colour.

'Prepare yourself,' Nick said under his breath. 'The Flower Child is coming this way.'

"Flower Child" was an accurate description, and based on Nick's comment, Ant had the distinct impression this woman wasn't one of their wives.

Poppy.

'Jessica!' The woman's breathy voice somehow floated magically above the sound of the conversation. 'I'm so excited to meet you. I'm Poppy.'

Jess shot Ant a panicked look, then plastered a smile onto her face. 'Hi.'

Poppy wafted into the living area—waft being the operative word. The room filled with the scent of sandalwood or something distinctly woody as soon as she stepped inside. Ant was pretty sure he hadn't seen a woman dressed in clothes like that since the seventies. Or maybe his last trip to Byron Bay.

Her full-length floral skirt clashed terribly with her loose floral shirt. What she lacked in fashion sense, Ant had to admit she made up for in looks—if you liked the free love type.

The woman went straight over to Jess and embraced her in a hug. Jess stood still for a second, then stiffly raised a hand to pat Poppy on the back of the shoulder while mouthing "help me" to the rest of them.

Her brothers grinned unhelpfully, while Ant did a better job of hiding his amusement.

Well, he hadn't seen this one coming.

Poppy released Jess and smiled serenely at her. 'When I did your cards, I just knew we'd get along.'

'My cards? You did?' Jess replied weakly.

'Oh, yes. Absolutely. Your vitality for life and my affinity with the natural world—we're a natural fit.'

Ant didn't see the fit himself and could only assume "my cards" meant tarot cards or something equally screwy. Judging by the deer-in-the-headlights look currently on Jess's face, this was his cue.

Ant stepped forward and shot them his best showbusiness smile. 'I bet you didn't see me coming, though, did you?'

They all laughed—Jess in relief—except for Poppy.

Her green eyes locked on to Ant's and he felt uncomfortable all of a sudden.

'Ah, yes,' she said. 'The Fool.'

'Damn. My reputation precedes me again,' Ant shot back.

Jess's brothers cracked up, while Ant looked over at Jess quickly. She appeared more relaxed now, thankfully.

'No, The Fool means lasting happiness,' Poppy corrected him. 'It was positioned near the Two of Cups, indicating a strong bond of some kind—all very auspicious for Jess. Although whether you're the bond the cards speak of, I couldn't say.'

Ant didn't put any stock in tarot readings, but an illogical part of him desperately wanted to be the person that lasting bond spoke of.

Instead, he said, 'Well, I have been known to linger like a bad smell, so that could be it.'

More laughter, but still Poppy didn't smile. Man, for all the Earth Mother vibes she was giving off, she was a bit too serious for Ant's tastes.

Poppy turned her attention back to Jess. 'Now, you must come and say hi to Jack and his parents. I know this will be weird for you, but please don't let it be. Think of it as an opportunity to exhale the past so that you're ready to inhale the future.'

Before Jess could protest, Poppy did that wafting thing again and swept Jess off along with her.

'Holy shit,' muttered Ant. 'I don't know about the future, but she's definitely been inhaling something good.'

Jess's brothers laughed again, and Grant slapped Ant on the back.

'I'll say. Consider yourself lucky. I bet you thought you were going to be the weird one here tonight.'

'I'm feeling upstaged, actually,' Ant admitted.

Nick grinned. 'Don't worry. We'll be laughing with you, not at you like her.'

Ant decided he liked Jess's brothers, despite their annoying manly good looks and the protective vibes they gave out. Who could really blame them? Jess was worth protecting.

'So, the PR exercise going well so far?' Grant asked.

Ant snuck another look outside. He didn't want to be rude to Jess's brothers, but he really felt like he should be out there alongside Jess protecting her from Poppy and the ex-boyfriend —who he was still keen to meet.

Ant grinned. 'Jess is fit and inspiring. I'm a lazy comedian. It's a natural fit,' he quipped.

'I meant what I said earlier,' Nick said. 'About it looking like it's paying off.'

'Hey, thanks mate,' Ant said, meaning it. 'I feel like it's too soon to tell, although my jeans have been a bit looser. I just put it down to my need to buy new clothes, not anything I've done.'

'Keep it up. You'll see,' Nick promised.

Ant narrowed his eyes. 'Is this a family thing? The whole exercise-is-for-life mentality? Did Jess brainwash you all?'

'Well and truly, I'm afraid,' Grant said. 'She's done training plans for all of us. Even Mum and Dad. You wait. She'll convert you.'

'I'm doing my best to resist, but your sister has some pretty special superpowers,' Ant told them.

Nick's lips quirked. 'And what would those be?'

Oh, shit. Had Ant just implied Jess was having an effect on him, and not only when it came to exercise?

Foot. Mouth. And not the way he had planned tonight.

'Anyway, talking of special powers, I think Jess might need some help with the dark forces over there. I'm back-up tonight in case you were wondering. My speciality is distraction.'

Grant patted him on the back again. 'Yep, you do that. It's gotta be hard for Jess seeing Jack end up with someone so . . .'

'Alternative,' Nick finished. 'Not that there's anything wrong with that, of course. It's just that Jack used to say Jess was a bit out there. He's super corporate and Jess isn't.'

'Well, if Jess is out there, Poppy is an alternate universe,' Ant told them. He leaned in and whispered behind his hand. 'Come on. Tell me the truth. Were you happy or unhappy when things with Jess and Jack ended?'

Ugh. Jess and Jack. Jack and Jess. It was doomed just on that sickening basis in Ant's opinion.

Grant gazed thoughtfully outside. 'They were right in a lot of ways. And I've always really liked Jack. But it turned out they were wrong in the areas that counted the most.'

'Yeah,' Nick agreed. 'Turns out our Jess wasn't alternative enough after all.'

They all laughed again, and Ant took that as his cue to leave and find Jess.

Ant wasn't sure if humour was considered a special power. But tonight, he was willing to give it a shot.

Chapter Eighteen

JESS WAS at the point of excusing herself to get a drink—anything to extract herself from Poppy's clutches—when Ant appeared at her side.

Thank God.

'Hi there, everyone. I seem to have lost something,' he said smoothly, nodding at Jess.

A round of introductions followed. Jess's parents, Jack's parents, and of course, Jack. Jess's parents excused themselves to organise the food, and Jess was somewhat relieved. She didn't need an audience for this awkward reunion.

Jack hadn't changed one bit. If anything, his smooth executive charm had only intensified. He wore a pair of linen trousers and an off-white shirt—both designer label. Jess remembered the expensive suits he wore to work. With his solemn grey eyes and slicked-back brown hair, it didn't surprise her that he was still good looking. But Jess was glad there was no pang of recognition when she set eyes on him. No pull. Nothing.

It seemed odd to her that she could spend ten years with someone and then feel nothing.

It was probably just as well they hadn't gotten married then.

Jess watched Jack and Ant shake hands. She could have been wrong, but Ant's warm brown eyes weren't as warm as usual. Jack's certainly held a hard glint.

'I didn't realise you had a new partner, Jess,' Jack said, looking between them with interest.

'Oh, we're not,' Jess said immediately. 'Ant is . . .'

Actually, Jess wasn't sure what Ant was. It occurred to her belatedly that she really should have come up with a better plan before introducing him.

'I'm a friend and co-worker,' Ant finished for her. 'Of sorts. We're doing a public relations exercise for the television network.'

Jack's eyebrows shot up. 'Television?'

Jack's mother, Sandra, sighed. 'Yes, Jack. I did tell you about this, remember? Ant's the comedian on the prime-time news show.' Sandra gave them an apologetic look. 'I'm sorry, Jessica, darling. He's been very preoccupied with work of late.'

'And plans for our nuptials,' Poppy broke in, smiling serenely.

Ugh, Jess thought, not for the first time since meeting Poppy. What sort of person their age referred to wedding plans as nuptials?

Jack's gaze fell on his fiancée and it softened. 'Yes, I'm afraid I've had a lot going on. Work is busy, but Poppy is also very distracting.'

OK, strike that. Jess did feel something when it came to her ex-boyfriend. Distaste.

'When are you getting married?' Ant asked.

Jess felt thankful once again for his presence. Ant's ability to read a crowd seemed to translate into an ability to conduct small talk, too.

Poppy waved a hand in the air. 'Mid-summer next year, of course. It's the best time.'

Jess didn't dare ask why it was the best time, because she suspected it would have something to do with a waxing or waning moon or some other such nonsense.

Instead she said, 'So you're getting married in the UK, then?'

Jack and Poppy both nodded, while Jack's mum Sandra frowned. Jess knew that look. The wedding's location was obviously a point of contention between them.

'I have a large family,' Poppy explained. 'And it seemed like the most practical option.'

Jess resisted a snort, which she knew wasn't very mature of her. Nothing Poppy had said so far had indicated that she was in any way practical.

'Well, I wouldn't say that,' Sandra said, joining the conversation. 'It's still long enough way that nothing's been finalised.'

Jack gave his mother a pointed look and turned his attention to Ant. 'So you're a comedian, Ant?' Jack asked with interest.

'That's what I'm told they pay me for.' Then he leaned in and whispered loudly, 'But I'd do it for free if we're being honest.'

The comment was met with laughter.

'So what's a comedian got to do with Jess's business?' Jack asked.

Jess found herself silencing a groan. She hadn't forgotten just how business-minded Jack was. Business always came first in his world.

Ant grinned. 'Jess is going to make me look good.'

'No,' Jess interrupted. 'I'm going to help you get fit. This isn't about looks, remember?'

'Hey, I need all the help I can get,' Ant joked, and everyone laughed again.

Everyone except Jess.

Jess found herself wishing he wouldn't poke fun at himself so much. Sure, he could do with being fitter, but there was nothing wrong with how he looked. Yes, he was on the short side and had strong Roman features, but it was those striking features that made him look good on camera.

'Television coverage won't do your business any harm,' Jack commented with a thoughtful frown. 'Are you prepared with a business plan for when things ramp up as a result?'

Jess opened her mouth and then closed it again. She'd been about to say yes, when really the answer was no. Jess felt herself redden. Jack had always been like this. Picking holes in all her plans, like she had no hope of creating anything lasting.

Ant bumped his shoulder against hers. 'That's all top secret with the network, of course, and Jess is sworn to silence. We wouldn't have agreed to it otherwise.'

Jack nodded and appeared to accept Ant's answer. 'I'm impressed, Jess. It's great to see you growing something of your own.'

Ant patted his belly lightly. 'Just so long as this doesn't grow any further for the next few months, the plan is on track. Jess already mentioned you're in banking, Jack. How about you, Poppy?'

Jess knew her mum had probably wanted to fill her in on all of this, but whenever the subject came up Jess was quick to change the subject.

'I'm a counsellor specialising in relationship and family counselling,' Poppy replied.

'We work in the same building,' Jack explained. 'We kept bumping into each other at the coffee shop.'

Poppy smiled that annoying smile that seemed to imply she knew something everyone else didn't. 'It was obviously meant to be.'

'Huh,' said Ant. 'Where were you when my ex-wife and I needed you?'

'Did you try counselling?' replied Poppy seriously, despite Ant's joke.

'Not worth it, trust me. We're better off apart.'

'Not always,' Poppy said. 'Counselling often results in a favourable resolution for many clients.'

'Well, if you count not being married anymore as a favourable resolution, I'm good.'

Poppy frowned. 'That's not the sort of resolution I was referring to.'

Ant shrugged. 'I got to keep my comic book collection, the sofa, the flat screen television, my car, and my balls. That was enough for me.'

Poppy's frown deepened, and Jess wondered if maybe the calming Flower Child persona was all part of Poppy's job. Jess couldn't imagine picking through people's relationships for a living.

'Well, if you're ever in need of a good counsellor, I have many contacts in Sydney,' Poppy told Ant.

'Nope, it was over years ago now. I'm good,' Ant said. 'Marriage isn't on the cards for me again—unless your cards know something I don't.'

'It's not?' Jess asked, then wanted to slap a hand over her mouth. What was she doing asking that sort of personal question in front of everyone? Let alone at all. It was Ant's business.

Ant shrugged. 'I'm not against another relationship, but

my last marriage cured me of the institution for life.' Ant gestured around them. 'You've been lucky, Jess, growing up in this environment.'

'I thought your parents are still together?' Jess asked.

'If you count tolerating each other as being together, then I guess they're together. I bet you see that a lot, hey, Poppy?'

Poppy nodded, her serene smile nowhere to be seen. 'Sadly.' Then the smile re-appeared, and she put an arm around Jack's hips. 'That's why I waited until I knew I'd found the right person.'

'But we're still drawing up a prenup,' Jack added with a grin.

'Of course,' Poppy agreed.

Of course, Jess thought. How unromantic. Maybe Jack and his Flower Child partner were more suited than Jess had first thought. She wondered if Poppy wore outfits like that to work. Come to think of it, Jess could imagine Poppy in smart navy trousers and a matching jacket with one of those floaty floral tops underneath. Professional yet approachable.

Jess glanced over at Ant, still a little surprised by his earlier answer about marriage, as well as feeling a bit sad for him. For all the family pressure for Jess to settle down and get married, Jess still held out hope she'd find the right person one day. And hopefully that wouldn't involve the need for a business-style arrangement in regard to their partnership. Or maybe Jess was just being naive? But Jess knew for a fact that her brothers didn't have prenups, and they all seemed perfectly happy.

'Hey, do I smell food?' said Ant. 'Don't mind me, will you?'

Thank goodness. Jess wasn't sure if it was deliberate on Ant's part, but she wasn't going to lose the opportunity to escape.

'I'd better go with him,' she said, pretending to be apologetic. 'He's liable to reverse all our hard work and eat something he shouldn't if I'm not watching.'

Ant rolled his eyes in mock disappointment, but waited for Jess.

And with that, they made their exit.

Chapter Nineteen

THE REST of the night went well as far as Ant could tell. Well, as far as sharing dinner with your ex went, he supposed.

Jess and Ant had a good laugh about it in the car on the way home. They wondered how an educated woman like Poppy, who insisted on a prenup, could take any stock in tarot cards.

'I bet she secretly reads the cards for each prospective client,' Jess said as they waited at a set of traffic lights. 'If she doesn't see a fortuitous ending, she won't take them on. Maybe she's a witch?'

'No, the lawyer that my ex had was a witch, I can assure you. I'm pretty sure Poppy is just weird.'

The light went green and Ant mistook Jess's silence for concentration until she spoke again.

'I'm sorry about your divorce,' she said. 'It sounds like it was kind of horrible.'

'No,' Ant said. 'The marriage was horrible. The divorce was just an extension of that.'

'I could be wrong, but I feel like you're not joking for a change.'

Ant grinned at her. 'You'll never know, will you?'

Jess reached over and brushed her fingers against his leg. 'You don't have to joke all the time, you know. At least not when we're off camera, anyway.'

Ant's chest constricted and he suddenly felt short of breath. He knew Jess was a touchy-feely person, but then why had her touch felt so intimate just now?

He swallowed and looked out the window. 'If I didn't joke, it would be boring.'

Ant expected her to reply with something typically nice or complimentary, as he was learning was Jess's way, but her next words took him off guard.

'What was she like? Your ex-wife? And don't say scary.'

Ant studied his hands in his lap for a long moment, debating how to answer Jess's question. Then he figured, to hell with it. She'd welcomed him into her family home tonight. The least he could do was be honest.

'Enid liked to be in control of everything. It had the unfortunate effect of making me behave like a two-year-old.'

'You mean more than normal?'

At Jess's cheeky grin, Ant found himself sharing more.

'Way more than normal. I became a man-child she had to order around. The more she tried to control me, the worse I got. It wasn't pretty. Think pizza boxes left out for days and a complete inability to clean up after myself.'

The funny thing was, now he was living alone, he kept his place neat.

'How did you end up together?' Jess asked.

'She told me she wanted to go out with me, and I did what I was told.'

'What!' Jess exclaimed as they pulled into her street. 'You don't go out with someone because they tell you to.'

'What can I say? I was desperate, and she'd never admit it but she was desperate, too. Just a lot bossier than me. So I went along with it.'

'You must have found her attractive at least,' Jess commented, as they waited for the garage door to open.

Ant grimaced. 'Not really,' he admitted, still not quite believing he was saying this shit out loud.

Jess twisted in her seat to face him. 'Really?'

Ant sighed as they pulled into Jess's garage. He'd told her this much, he might as well tell her the entire sorry story now.

'Enid is an academic. The serious, hard-working type. She looks like an academic in that "I could be a lesbian" way, except no one is really sure if she is or not. I was with her for five years and I'm still not sure, to tell you the truth.'

Jess laughed, but in a disbelieving sort of way.

Ant felt the need to explain further. 'Looking back, I think we both wanted someone to keep each other company. I wanted someone to come home to and she wanted a plus one to take to all of her faculty functions. The problem was we didn't have much in common.'

'Opposites can attract.'

'Like I said, there wasn't a lot of attraction going on.'

Ant was pretty sure he'd said way too much, so he got out of the car once Jess had killed the engine and prepared to say goodbye for the night. Hopefully by the time they had their next fitness session, Jess would have relegated this weird discussion to him having one too many wines. Never mind he still felt quite sober.

Jess closed the driver's door and blipped the button for the alarm, then came around to where he was standing.

'Come on,' she said. 'Let's go for a walk.'

Ant stared at her. It was his turn to say, 'What?'

'It's a beautiful night. And I don't know about you, but I could do with some fresh air to work off the weird vibes from seeing Jack and his fiancée.'

'OK,' Ant said uncertainly.

Jess put a hand on her hip and studied him with a small smile. 'Or am I being too bossy?'

'You are *nothing* like Enid,' Ant blurted, then snapped his mouth shut.

Jess smiled again, and her eyes were kind. 'Come on,' she said again, and gestured towards an emergency exit Ant hadn't noticed before which led outside to the front drive.

'It's almost a full moon,' she said. 'Perfect for a beach walk.'

Ant shot her a suspicious look. 'By walk, you don't mean run, do you?'

Jess's laughter floated on the night air like a song. 'No, silly. Just a walk, I promise.'

They headed up the street together, not talking for the first hundred or so metres.

Jess was the one to break the silence. 'I know I've said it already, but thanks again for coming tonight. It made it so much easier for me.'

'I'm glad you didn't end up with him.' OK, maybe Ant had had more to drink that he realised.

She cocked an eyebrow at him as they walked. 'You know, seeing him again tonight, I'm really glad I didn't end up with him either. He's so boring. Oh, and thanks for stepping in when he asked about my business plan. That really freaked me out.'

'Why?' Ant asked.

Jess huffed. 'Because he's right. I don't really have a business plan. Not an updated one at any rate. I'm really just making it up as I go, and now things are gaining momentum I really should work on a revised one. I'm at the point where I should get a business advisor or someone like that to run things past, but I wouldn't know where to find one. At least my accountant is quite good with the money side of things.'

'I can help you,' Ant offered without thinking.

Jess skidded to a halt on the footpath and stared at him dumbly. 'You can?' Then she winced. 'Oh my God, that sounded horrible! I can't believe I just said that.'

Ant gave her a crooked grin. 'Entirely justified. But I actually can. Enid's area of academia was business and economics. She taught MBAs and the like. When we were together, she made me work on a business plan. Like I said, I did what I was told.'

'You have a business plan for your comedy?' Jess asked, a hint of amazement in her voice.

'Sure.' Ant shrugged. 'Everyone needs a plan, particularly if you're self-employed or you have a public profile. As much as I complain about Enid, if not for her pushing me to do one, I don't think I'd be working somewhere like *Sydney Tonight*. Getting a regular television gig was part of my plan.'

'Wow,' Jess said, a note of respect in her voice that did strange things to Ant's stomach. 'That's really cool. I still find it hard to think of myself as a brand, though.'

'Your brand isn't who you are in real life. You know that, right?' Ant said. 'It's a business concept.'

They started walking again in silence, and Jess appeared to be pondering what he'd said. Once again, he wondered if he'd said too much. Ant usually kept his business plans to himself. Not because he was embarrassed by them. Mainly because he'd never really had anyone to talk to about it. While Enid had encouraged him to be serious about his career, she hadn't really been all that interested. Comedy wasn't her thing. She'd preferred bingeing on Netflix drama series or science fiction. Whenever he'd tried his jokes out on her, the most he'd gotten was a half-smile. He eventually figured out that meant it was funny, but it wasn't really the level of enthusiasm he was aiming for.

'So what sort of plans do you have outside of *Sydney Tonight*?' Jess asked. They were almost at the beach and headed in the direction of the empty table and chairs overlooking the horizon.

Ant considered her question before answering. 'The usual —a twelve-month, three-year and five-year plan. Some possible book ideas. A few show ideas that I'll pitch one day if I ever get the chance. More character ideas, too. And always more jokes. My phone is full of ideas I've dictated or notes I've made when something strikes me out of the blue.'

They stopped near one of the tables and Ant followed Jess's lead when she sat on one, resting her feet on the bench seat below.

'Do you want to know something interesting?' Jess said, her eyes scanning the horizon. 'I'm still trying to figure out which parts of you are your brand, and which parts are the real you.'

Ant didn't know how to reply to that, so he did what he always did—joked. 'Then I'm better at this branding thing than I thought.'

'No.' Jess twisted to face him. 'I think you use it as a protective mechanism.'

'I think you give me credit for being smarter than I am,' was his immediate reply.

'Stop it.' Jess's brow furrowed. 'Why do you put yourself down all the time?'

'For laughs?'

Jess sighed. 'You don't have to be the butt of the joke every time.'

Ant raised his hands in an offhand gesture. 'Hey, when it works, it works—'

Jess grabbed the hand that was closest to her. 'Ant,' she said, then stopped.

They both looked down at her hand holding his.

'I really shouldn't say this, since you're currently my client,' she said softly. 'But I think you need to stop making fun of yourself all the time, because I think you're amazing.'

Her eyes met his and Ant became transfixed by the way they shimmered in the moonlight.

He opened his mouth to say something. He wasn't sure what, most likely another joke because that was his default reaction to everything. But he was silenced by Jess placing a finger on his lips.

Ant felt all the breath leave him.

'Don't,' she told him seriously, 'you dare tell me another joke. Anything but that.'

'Anything?' Ant managed to say.

Then he did possibly the stupidest thing he could think of. He reached over and cupped Jess's face in his palm, and he kissed her.

Chapter Twenty

JESS'S first thought when Ant's hand touched her face was, *oh*. Not a surprised *oh*, although there was an element of that. No, this was more like her body was remembering the contact with Ant when they'd had that stupid green smoothie fight, and she just sort of blissed out completely.

Before she could get a handle on her reaction, Ant's lips were on hers.

Her next thought was, *oh no*, and then immediately after that, *oh yes*.

His lips were soft and tentative, as though he was scared she might vanish in a puff of smoke if he kissed her too hard. Like she was some sort of daydream he knew wasn't real.

Jess knew it wasn't a daydream, and the impulsive part of her decided to prove it.

She reached up behind his head, burying her hands in his hair—hair that she'd always wondered what running her fingers through would feel like. Then she directed him closer and deepened the kiss.

His groan of response sent tingles to all the best parts of

her body and she shifted closer. What was it about this man? Gosh, he smelled so good. He tasted good, too. Spicy, warm and delicious. But it wasn't only that. It was how he made Jess feel. Whenever she was around him, she felt happy. Now she didn't just feel happy, she felt downright sexy. He made her feel that way. Like she was full of light and life and that she shone brighter when he was near.

His other hand came up to cradle her face. His thumb stroked her cheek as they kissed, then travelled a lazy journey down her jawbone to her neck.

Jess shuddered in response, imagining other places that lazy thumb of his could travel.

With Jack, his touch had been deliberate. A kiss here. A stroke there. Always with a purpose in mind.

This? This was playful in the best sort of way. Kissing just because. Kissing because it felt good. It tasted good.

Then his hands were on her hips, and still that lazy thumb was stroking her hipbone, making Jess sigh. She wished she wasn't wearing a dress so she could feel his hands on her bare skin.

Jess was just about to shift even closer when a pair of bright headlights lit them up as a car swung around on the road behind them.

It was enough to startle Jess out of her heady reverie.

She scrambled backwards on the table and stared at him.

He stared back, his dark eyes wide. Darker than she'd ever seen them, which sent another pulse of lust through her belly.

Jess shook her head to clear her thoughts and raised her fingers to her lips.

Oh, my God. What had she just done? This was Ant. Ant Monticello. Her client. The co-host of *Sydney Tonight*. And here they were sitting outside kissing for all the world to see. How could she have been so stupid? If anyone saw them it would be all over the papers, the internet. Everywhere. And their little PR exercise would be considered a farce, damaging her brand and *Sydney Tonight*'s in the process.

'Jess?' Ant said softly.

Despite her mortification at what she'd just done, his deep voice was like a caress.

She jumped down off the table to put some distance between them.

'I'm so sorry,' she began. 'I shouldn't have done that. That was so wrong of me.'

'Was it?' Ant asked.

'Yes! Of course it was! We're contracted for another two months. You're my client,' she finished, breathing heavily.

Ant got down slowly from the table. He stepped towards her, but Jess took a step back, keeping some space between them, so Ant stopped and stayed where he was.

'I was the one that kissed you,' he said. 'So it's my fault. But—'

'It doesn't matter,' Jess rushed on. 'As long as we agree it was wrong.'

'I'm sorry, but I'm not going to apologise for that,' he replied gruffly. 'There was absolutely nothing wrong with that kiss.'

They fell quiet and stared at each other some more. Jess thought he had a point, but wasn't about to say it. He was right. Everything about that kiss had been amazing, yet . . .

'Ant,' she said gently. 'We can't get involved. You know that.'

'Because of the show?'

She nodded. 'We have to do what we're contracted to do.'

Ant nodded slowly, then turned away to look out at the ocean. The moon was high in the sky and it cast a silver glow on the waves as they crashed onto the shore. Jess felt a bit like she'd been tossed about in the surf herself.

'Can I ask a question, then?' he said, still not looking at her.

'Of course.'

'What about when it's over? How about then? Or am I imagining this?'

Jess hesitated. 'You're not imagining this. But I don't think it's a good idea.'

When Ant went to speak, she held up a hand.

'Let me finish. I like you. A lot. But I think we're too different.'

'Is this because I don't exercise?' he asked in disbelief, turning back to face her.

'No. Although you know how important that sort of lifestyle is to me. You said something tonight. About not wanting to get married again.'

'And you do?'

Jess threw her hands up in the air. 'Yes! I do. I know that makes me sound old fashioned, but I do believe in love that can be lasting. My parents are a great example of that. And as cliché as it is to say, I want that, too. I want to find The One to settle down with. Have kids with. Grow old with. I like you Ant, but I don't think that's what you're looking for.'

Ant pushed a hand through his already unruly hair and swore. 'Me and my big mouth.'

'It's not what you want, is it?' she pressed.

'No,' he said darkly. 'It's not. I'm just not sure I'm that kind of guy. Being The One involves a lot of pressure. Not only that, can you imagine me as a family man? I'd end up being just another one of the kids for God's sake.'

Jess stepped in closer again. 'You don't want kids?'

Ant didn't hesitate and gave her a lopsided grin. 'Seriously? Would you want kids with me?'

'I am being serious, and you haven't answered the question.'

Ant huffed. 'I've never seen myself having kids, no.'

Jess nodded, and Ant sighed.

'That's not the answer you wanted to hear, is it?' he asked.

'No. But don't blame this on yourself. We are who we are, and we both deserve someone special. Like I said earlier, opposites can attract. Just because we're attracted to one another doesn't mean we're each other's someone special, though.'

Ant reached over and grabbed her hips, pulling her close. 'You're so damn special it makes my heart hurt, Jess.'

Jess swallowed a small whimper of surprise. Ant when he was earnest and not joking was pretty damn special, too.

Jess stood on tiptoes and placed a soft kiss on his forehead, and Ant's shoulders fell in response.

'You're friend-zoning me, aren't you?' he muttered.

Jess lowered herself back to her feet again. 'I think so.'

Ant was still holding on to her hips and didn't let go. 'We could do friends with benefits?'

Jess laughed. 'That's a tempting offer, but I'm not that sort of girl.'

'Damn it. I thought as much. You can't blame me for trying though. Just so you know, the offer stands if you change your mind.'

Jess laughed again, but the sound disappeared when Ant reached up and caressed her cheek.

'What would it take for a girl like you to be with a guy like me?' he whispered.

'By the sounds of it, for us to be two different people, not to mention a different past for you. And we can't change that.

We also can't change that we want different things. Let's not beat ourselves up about it, hey?'

'Maybe just a bit,' complained Ant.

She linked her arm through his. 'Let's head home.'

They walked back up the road together, and Jess silently hoped she hadn't ruined things with Ant. Or that the remaining months of training weren't going to be awkward now. They'd been getting along so well until she'd had that moment of weakness and kissed him back. She should have known better.

She'd known for a while he was sweet on her—even Kat had noticed. And Jess couldn't deny she was curious when it came to Ant. She'd admitted to herself that she did kind of *like like* him. But she'd meant what she said about them being too different and wanting different things. It was wrong of her to mess with his feelings with that kiss.

But as they walked home, a part of Jess couldn't bring herself to regret the kiss as much as she should have. Because whether they were well-suited or not, it had been the nicest kiss she'd had in . . .

It had been the nicest kiss she'd ever had.

Chapter Twenty-One

ANT DIDN'T SLEEP well that night and woke early—too early. He wasn't a morning person as a general rule given his workday started later than most. It was so early he didn't feel hungry, so he made a damn smoothie. It didn't have anything green in it. At least it would stop him from eating something bad later on when he was tempted to snack.

Not that there was much in his house that was unhealthy now. His pantry was usually poorly stocked on account of his tendency to order takeaway food for dinner. He'd gotten into the habit the last few weeks of picking up fresh fruit and some of that grainy bread Jess had recommended. It didn't actually taste half bad with Vegemite—thankfully that was still allowed.

And Ant was still thinking about Jess.

She was all he'd thought about the entire night.

Those sweet lips and that sexy way she'd invited him to taste more . . .

'God, Ant! Stop it!' He banged the empty smoothie glass onto the counter with a loud crack.

Jessica Jinks was not for him. She never would be, no matter how many nights he lay awake imagining the possibility of it.

Ant glanced around his apartment desperately. His closest mates would be at work, because unlike him they had sensible day jobs. Not that he planned on telling any of them about his useless crush on a woman way out of his league. He might regularly make himself the butt of his jokes, but he wasn't about to make a complete fool of himself.

'Fuck it,' Ant muttered, and headed to his bedroom.

He went straight to his wardrobe and slid open the door. He started rifling through his clothes. His swimmers had to be in here somewhere. He'd used them last summer when he'd gone to the beach on a few of those really hot days, but he'd always worn boardshorts over the top.

With a satisfied grunt, he pulled the Speedos from the back of the shelf where they had been stuffed.

He held them up and looked at them. They dangled from his fingers. Was it possible for a piece of clothing to be taunting him?

Ordinarily Ant wouldn't be caught dead wearing nothing but a pair of Speedos, which were basically glorified underwear. But it's what men wore when they swam laps, and that's exactly what he was going to do this morning.

It wasn't that he wanted to exercise. Oh, no. This wasn't cause for Ant to lose Jess's bet about him genuinely wanting to exercise. There was no genuine about it. Because right now Ant needed to do something—*anything*—to take his mind off a certain beautiful fitness goddess.

And sitting around home bingeing on Netflix just wasn't going to cut it. Ant needed something to release his pent-up frustration—or was that desperation?—before he showed up at work later.

So he put on the stupid Speedos and threw on shorts and a T-shirt. Then he packed a bag with a towel and a water bottle. He didn't have any goggles, but he was certain the pool would sell him some overpriced ones at the front counter when he got there. It didn't matter. He could afford it.

What he couldn't afford was to become obsessed with someone he couldn't have. He'd already done that once before in his life, in a time long before Enid. It was a period of his life he was careful to keep in the past and one he didn't plan on revisiting. Ever. Nor would he make the same mistake twice.

He had two more months of contact with Jess, and he needed to be on his best behaviour. But right now it was more important that he clear his head, so he picked up his bag and drove to the pool.

WHEN HE HOPPED into the pool with the impossibly tight swimming cap and goggles the sales assistant had helpfully sold him, Ant scanned the pool casually. Surely the other swimmers would figure out that he was an imposter? But none of the people in the other lanes paid any attention to Ant. To his surprise, he didn't look that out of place. Sure, there was that university student in the far lane with the washboard stomach, but the kid seemed to be in his own world. He'd probably been swimming laps since he was five-years-old judging by the easy way his muscled arms ploughed through the water.

But everyone else looked unexpectedly normal. And by normal, Ant meant average-looking like him. There were a couple of middle-aged women doing laps together, stopping now and then to chat. They weren't overweight, but they weren't ripped either. It kind of rang true with what Jess kept telling him—that being fit and healthy wasn't about how you looked, it was about how you felt.

At this time of day, the pool also seemed to be the place to be for the retirement set. An aqua aerobics class was going on down in the far end and the old dears seemed to be having the time of their lives. In the lanes closest to him there were a couple of older guys that were slow but steady. Ant thought it was pretty cool that dudes their age could swim lap after lap without stopping. It was actually something to aspire to.

Ant didn't even feel too self-conscious about his bare chest either. No one blinked at his dark chest hair. And judging by the old guy with the generous tufts of hair on his shoulder blades, Ant had a long way to go before needing to worry about getting himself waxed.

So Ant tried swimming a lap of freestyle and was secretly amazed, and even a little proud, when he was able to do it without stopping. He noticed some of the lap swimmers swimming continuously, but many stopped regularly, so he wouldn't be out of place taking frequent breaks.

He surprised himself by not needing as many breaks as he'd expected. Jess's fitness regimen was obviously paying off. Ant even decided that next time he came, he'd work towards swimming a kilometre and a half. Not that having the intention of a next time meant that he *wanted* to exercise. It was more of a mental health thing for him to relieve his frustration and stop him from lying around the house being unhealthy.

It's not like he was going to post his trip to the pool all over social media or anything. The good thing about the goggles and cap were that they obscured his identity—not that he was *that* famous. And Ant doubted anyone who followed him online would look for him in a place like this anyway.

No, Ant would keep the pool thing to himself for now. Besides, he might grow bored with it in a week or so. A lot of people considered swimming laps boring, although that hadn't been Ant's experience today. To him it felt like a relaxing way to exercise. Finding a rhythm with your body and breathing, and then just allowing yourself to go with the flow.

An hour later Ant returned to his car feeling tired but strangely satisfied. He wondered how much he would hurt tomorrow after swimming more than a kilometre. He couldn't quite believe he'd done it.

Ant was smiling as he put the keys in the ignition and then remembered he hadn't checked his messages. He scrolled through them. One from his mum. An email from the producer with the run sheet ready for their production meeting this afternoon. And a message on Instagram. It was probably another smart-arse troll, or a random person trying to connect. Ant got them from time to time and usually ignored them.

He went into the messages section of the app.

'Huh.'

It was a message from Alicia Travers. It read:

Hi, Funny Man. Can I ask a favour? I'm launching a new fashion line for men and women, which I'll be talking about on your show in a few weeks. My publicist had the great idea to ask you to wear some of my creations. They're intended for the everyday man and woman—I don't want to be another one of those models pushing couture. I ran it by your producers and they're cool with the idea. Can we meet for coffee sometime? I can show you some of my designs and we can discuss. You're doing good with Jess btw, looking great! Cheers, Alicia x

Ant sat with the engine running, looking at the message. Then he reread it.

He wouldn't read anything into the kiss in the sign-off—he

had a feeling that's how a glamazon like Alicia signed off every message. But him wearing her fashion? That was out of left field. Ant had never considered himself an everyday man, whatever that was. He was certain it wasn't him.

What the hell, he thought, putting the phone in the hands-free cradle. This wasn't personal. It was business. He'd hoped he might get the opportunity for some extra exposure if he was deemed worthy of being Alicia's Logies date at the end of the PR stunt. This could be just as good, maybe even better.

Who knew getting fit would provide opportunities like this?

Maybe it was time to revise his business plan.

Chapter Twenty-Two

AFTER THEIR KISS, the fitness sessions with Ant weren't so much awkward as strange. It was like after the green smoothie incident, only worse. They were both professional with each other, and Ant was predictably as funny as usual, but it all felt wrong somehow. Like Jess couldn't talk to Ant the way she used to. That they couldn't joke around or be friends— because that's what they'd become, wasn't it?

Jess was dying to discuss the situation with someone, but she still hadn't figured out who.

It certainly couldn't be Kat, because Ant was her co-host. And her whole "let's keep things professional" policy wouldn't be professional anymore if Jess let slip to Ant's colleague that she had kissed him. Or that Ant had kissed her. Jess wasn't sure which. Ant had definitely started it, but Jess had kissed him back.

Jess considered talking to Em, and she still hadn't ruled it out. With Em's casual approach to men, she wouldn't judge Jess and would probably even understand, but something stopped Jess from telling her.

In the meantime, Jess proceeded to overthink everything. Could she still ask Ant for help with her business plan, for instance? Or would that be too weird? She definitely needed someone to help her with it.

One night about a week and a half later, Jess was on social media. It was part of her regular routine after a busy day of classes and one-on-one Hi-Jinks sessions. It was when she took the time to reply to her followers. But this time she found herself scrolling aimlessly through her feed. At first, she almost scrolled past it.

'What the?' she whispered.

She scrolled back and looked at the post from Ant—she'd been sure to follow him before they'd started working together.

'Oh my God,' she breathed.

There was an image of Ant sitting in a café with Alicia Travers, both of them smiling at the camera. Her hand was on his arm and their shoulders were touching. Jess would say Ant was beaming, except he didn't so much beam when he smiled, but grin. And this was a really big grin.

Jess read the caption:

Turns out getting fit pays off. @Aliciacatwalk has asked me to model for her new clothing line and she's promised there's no waxing involved. #hotstuff #fitnessmotivation #pinchme #catwalkmodel

Jess set the phone down with a frown. The image had been posted three days ago, and she'd trained with Ant since then. It had been with a camera crew present, but Jess was surprised Ant hadn't said anything. It struck Jess as the sort of thing he'd want to gloat about. Or that friends would tell one another.

Her phone buzzed and Jess eyed it suspiciously, like someone had known what she'd been looking at. Not that what she'd been looking at was cause for suspicion.

'Oh, stop it,' she told herself, and picked up the phone again.

It was a message from her brother, Nick:

Hey, JJ. Do you still need me to look at your kitchen tap? Chelsea and I just finished having dinner with some friends in the area and we can pop over if you like?

Jess typed a quick reply:

That would be great. See you soon x

With that, Jess hopped up off the lounge and did a quick tidy of her apartment. Not that she was untidy. But her weeks were usually busy, and things like washing had a way of piling up. She'd just finished loading the machine with some of her workout gear when the buzzer sounded.

A minute later she opened the door and let them in. Both Nick and Chelsea gave her a quick peck on the cheek as they entered, then her brother strode up the hall with a toolbox in hand. Jess found herself smiling at the sight.

'Have toolbox, will travel,' whispered Chelsea to Jess, matching her smile.

When her brother was younger he'd apprenticed as a plumber, but for the last five years he'd run his own home handyman service doing whatever clients needed. He claimed it was better than unblocking toilets for a living, although he occasionally still used his plumbing expertise when the situation called for it. Like now.

Chelsea often joked that business was booming because all the older ladies enjoyed having Nick call on them. As well as being super easygoing, Nick was easy on the eyes.

'How was dinner?' Jess asked, as she followed Chelsea and Nick into the kitchen.

'A bit dull,' Chelsea replied. 'It was a work thing of mine. Lots of lawyers and their partners. Nick was the most exciting partner there if you ask me,' she finished with a wink in his direction.

'I'm not that exciting,' he said as he opened the cupboard below the kitchen sink. 'Now if Jack had been there with Poppy, that would have been interesting.'

Chelsea rolled her eyes. 'Poppy is one of a kind.'

Jess tended to agree. 'She'd definitely make an impression.'

'I hope you haven't been thinking about Jack and Poppy too much,' Nick said before his head disappeared under the sink.

'Oh, no. Not at all,' Jess said honestly. 'I've been too busy.'

Chelsea waggled her eyebrows. 'With Ant?'

Jess blinked. 'Well, partly. We've had a few more sessions, which have gone well and—'

'I don't think Chelsea meant that kind of busy,' Nick called out, his voice muffled as he worked underneath the sink.

Jess reddened, glad her brother couldn't see her. Unfortunately, Chelsea still could, and her sister-in-law grinned at her.

'Oh, no. Nothing like that,' Jess said quickly. 'Like I said the other week, we're just friends. And he's my client.'

Chelsea crossed her arms. 'Grant and Susie met at work.'

That was true, Jess supposed. Her oldest brother ran a real estate agency and Susie had been one of his agents until they'd started their family and she'd taken maternity leave.

'Yes, well, that's different,' Jess told them. 'It's Grant's business, and he's the boss.'

'You're the boss of your company,' Chelsea pointed out.

'This is different. I'm on national television and have an arrangement with the station. Ant isn't my employee.'

'But if he was your employee?' Chelsea asked with a gleam in her eye.

Sometimes it really sucked to have a sister-in-law who was a lawyer. She was far too good at asking the right questions.

'We're *friends*. And just because you're happily married doesn't mean you have to try to set me up with everyone.'

Usually her mother was the worst culprit at trying to set her up with eligible men, but her brothers and their partners weren't above it either.

'Not everyone,' Chelsea corrected. 'Just Ant. I like him.'

Nick's head popped up over the bench. 'Mum and Dad really liked him too, by the way.'

Jess sighed. She'd gotten that impression during phone calls with her mother lately. *Funny, a great conversationalist, not egotistical in any way*, were the words she'd used to describe Ant.

Jess had put the compliments down to her parents being surprised that someone who worked on television could be a normal person, but no such luck.

'Mum probably just feels sorry for me because Jack's engaged, so she wants to see me paired up with someone,' Jess told them.

Nick straightened and started undoing the tap. 'While we want to see you happy, we're not going to encourage you to be with just anyone, JJ.'

'What? And you think Ant is the right person?' Jess asked in disbelief.

'Why not? You seem to get along.'

'I get along with my neighbours too, that doesn't mean I want to marry them!'

Nick shrugged, and Chelsea stepped forward and touched Jess's arm.

'We're not trying to be pushy, Jess. We just got the impression that he liked you.'

Jess opened her mouth to say something, then shut it again. It was true, Ant did like her. But she didn't really want to tell them that, because then she'd have to explain the other reasons she'd friend-zoned him, and she wasn't sure she had the energy for it.

Instead, she pulled out her phone and brought up the image of Ant and Alicia, then shoved it at Chelsea.

'I'm pretty sure Ant likes her, too. So I wouldn't read too much into it.'

Chelsea studied the image, then raised her eyes to look at Jess. When Jess crossed her arms, Chelsea handed the phone to Nick.

'Sweet,' Nick said. 'And of course he likes her, she's Alicia Travers.'

Chelsea retrieved the phone from Nick and handed it back to Jess with a thoughtful expression. 'Do you really think Ant's into Alicia?'

'Like Nick said, she's Alicia Travers,' replied Jess.

Chelsea shrugged. 'Then good on him. If you're not interested, and Alicia Travers is, then he's a lucky guy.'

Jess glanced at the image again, then pressed the button to make the phone go blank.

'Do you think Ant stands a chance?' Jess asked, then rushed on because that sounded mean to Ant. 'I mean, she is one of Australia's best-known supermodels.'

That was the diplomatic way of putting it. Jess didn't want to say in front of anyone else that Ant had a low opinion of himself. But he'd seemed unsurprised when Jess had declined any hope of a romantic relationship between them. Jess still felt bad about it, even though she had stressed to him that her decision was due to them not being compatible. Jess still couldn't shake the feeling Ant thought he wasn't good enough for her—which was absolute rubbish.

'It's called punching above your weight, JJ,' Nick said, setting the disassembled tap down on the bench. He nodded at

Chelsea. 'Look at us. I didn't think a high school dropout like me would stand a chance with her.'

Chelsea threw her husband a fond look. 'I just keep you around for your good looks.'

'I know my place,' Nick agreed.

Chelsea returned her focus to Jess. 'So in answer to your question, yes, I don't think it's outside the realm of possibility that Alicia could be interested in Ant. He's a funny guy, and women love men with a sense of humour. Looks aren't everything, despite what your brother may say.'

'Damn. And I thought I'd fooled you,' Nick told his wife. 'But seriously, Jess, Chelsea's right. Ant's got a lot going for him. A successful career, a great personality, and now he's getting fit thanks to you. I'd say that would make him quite a catch for someone like Alicia who is in the public eye like he is. Sure, he's not Chris Hemsworth, but who is? He's a decent looking guy. If I were you, next time he brings it up, I'd tell him to go for it.'

Jess nodded and went over to the kettle to turn it on. She needed a coffee. A strong one.

'Yes, I think you're right,' Jess said weakly.

Chapter Twenty-Three

JESS WAITED until the end of the next exercise session with Ant to bring up the subject of Alicia. Not that she was entirely sure it was any of her business. But she knew if she didn't raise it, then she'd be left wondering . . .

Wondering what, exactly?

Well, just wondering.

Today's session had been held down at Freshwater beach near Jess's again. Jess had to admit she was looking forward to seeing this week's footage. Ant was now running up and down the beach like a pro, and his jokes weren't aimed at his lack of fitness anymore.

This week he'd gotten laughs from bystanders by showing off his newfound skills. He'd drawn a crowd of onlookers while doing a sequence of Hi-Jinks manoeuvres dressed in tight shorts, a bandana, and sweatbands. To complete the look, he'd brought along a boom box Jess was sure was a relic from the eighties, then proceeded to play *Eye Of The Tiger* at maximum volume.

On the beach he'd pretended to try to pick up a few of the

female beachgoers, and they'd all responded with smiles and waves. Not laughter. It had been two months now, and the changes were subtle, but Jess could see definition forming in his arms and legs. He'd also noticeably lost weight, and Ant seemed lighter and quicker on his feet. The women he'd run past seemed to notice, too.

'So, ah, I hear you're going to be a fashion model,' Jess said casually after they'd finished filming.

They were standing near the entrance to the beach, drinking from water bottles one of the sponsors had provided while the crew packed up.

Ant wiped his mouth with the back of his hand and winked at her. 'Stalking me on social media, are you?'

The mouthful of water felt like it got stuck in her throat, and Jess forced herself to swallow. 'No. Remember I'm on Instagram all the time? I saw your post with Alicia.'

'Oh, that. Pretty cool, hey?' Ant raised one of his arms and flexed his bicep. 'Maybe I should get some tatts? Then I could become the next David Beckham.'

'Um, OK.' Jess had been about to make a comment about how he didn't need tattoos. Jess generally didn't like them, but it occurred to her that Ant might actually look quite hot with a few tattoos on his arms. She cleared her throat, pushing the thought aside. 'Anyway, I wanted to say congratulations. It's really exciting.'

'Thanks.' Ant tossed his empty bottle into a nearby recycling bin. 'Between you and me, it doesn't feel quite real. But I'm going with it. Alicia's been really enthusiastic about the whole thing. Maybe this exercise thing has its benefits after all.'

I bet she has, thought Jess. But she said, 'When will we get to see the photos?'

'The week before our Logies date when Alicia comes on the show to talk about her new fashion label. The concept behind it is really clever,' Ant went on, and continued talking about how great Alicia's new fashion label was.

Jess didn't mean to, but she found herself tuning out.

The week before the Logies was a few weeks from now, she mused. In four more weeks, Jess wouldn't have anything to do with Ant anymore. Jess threw her own bottle in the bin, still only half listening to how great and talented and fantastic Alicia was.

Blah, blah, blah.

It also occurred to her that she needed to ask him for help with her business plan sooner rather than later or she'd lose her chance.

Plus, with the continued exposure on *Sydney Tonight*, her class enquiries had gone up tenfold. Jess was finding it hard to keep up. She'd even had a few enquiries from personal trainers asking if they could be trained in Hi-Jinks to teach their own clients. It had definitely gotten Jess thinking about the best ways to expand her business model.

Em had also suggested to Jess more than once that she should create her own merchandise, in particular exercise equipment. Something like that would definitely make sense if Jess wanted to expand, and it would be another opportunity for revenue, too.

'Earth to Jess.' Ant's voice broke through her thoughts. 'Are you listening? Or is my stratospheric success boring you?'

'What? Oh, no, of course not. It's fantastic.' Jess tried to sound enthusiastic. 'And you've got a guaranteed date for the Logies, too.'

Ant's eyebrows shot up. 'Guaranteed, you say? I thought you had to give final approval on my results in a few weeks' time?'

'Well, yes, I do, but if you keep doing what you're doing and don't slack off, I'd say it's likely.'

'You should come, too.'

Jess paused. She'd been about to pick up her sweat towel hanging on a nearby fence. 'Where? To the Logies? I don't think so.'

'Why not?' Ant asked. 'You're practically a household name now. I'm sure your followers would love to see you all glammed up in an evening dress.'

'Oh, I don't know. It's a bit beyond my brand, really. And you don't just turn up to the Logies, you need to be invited.'

Actually, Jess had no idea who was in charge of the invitations, but she definitely knew she wasn't on the list. Nor did she have any desire to go. Being on television was scary enough, let alone getting "glammed up" as Ant put it. Not to mention being on the red carpet with all those other celebrities, like Alicia. Jess wasn't stupid. She was good at Hi-Jinks, not being a supermodel.

'I'm sure I could get you an invite,' Ant said, interrupting her thoughts again.

'Don't be silly. That's not necessary.'

'Jess, think about it. It would be a great opportunity for your business.'

Well, when he put it like that . . .

'I'm just not sure I'd feel comfortable going.' Or going alone. Jess didn't have a plus one or a celebrity partner like most of the other attendees. It would be nerve-wracking at best, terrifying at worst.

'Just think about it, and I'll see what I can find out. I'm sure Kat will have some contacts.'

Jess was about to protest again and potentially ask him about helping with her business plan when Ant's phone buzzed in his pocket. He retrieved it, then shot her an apologetic look.

'Sorry. It's my mum. I've got to take this.'

Ant turned away to take the call, so Jess set about gathering her things ready for the walk home. She had a rare free morning and didn't have a class until late in the day. She decided to stop in at Josh's café on the way back to grab a coffee.

Jess said her goodbyes to the crew, who all knew her by now, and waved at Ant, who was still talking on the phone with his mum. She saw him shove a hand roughly through his dark hair and hoped that everything was OK.

She averted her eyes and set off towards the café. The conversation was obviously private and she didn't want to intrude, although she had to admit she was curious about Ant's parents. Was his mother the classic overbearing Italian mama? And what was his father like? Jess wondered if he was as stern and humourless as Ant made out.

Jess enjoyed her coffee sitting at one of the tables over-looking the beach, and ten minutes later she set off in the direction of her apartment. She frowned when she saw Ant further up the hill, standing beside a small white Volkswagen hatch, talking animatedly into his phone.

When she reached him, she waited for him to finish his call. Jess wasn't sure who he was talking to, but judging from phrases like "that long?", "it won't start", and "can't you get here sooner?", she surmised it was something to do with his car.

'Oh, hey, Jess,' he said, appearing unusually flustered. 'I didn't see you there.'

'Do you need a lift somewhere?' she asked.

'Yes.' Then his eyes darkened, and he added, 'No. It's fine.'

'Doesn't sound fine. Have you got somewhere you need to go?'

'I'll just call an Uber. It's fine.'

'It's OK. I'm free until later today. I can take you.'

'You are *not* driving me to my parents' house,' Ant snapped, then looked away.

Jess stared at him. This was the first time she'd seen him anything but happy. Not only that, he was angry. Really angry.

'Why?' she replied lightly. 'Do they bite?'

Ant threw her another one of those dark looks. 'They're not like your picture-perfect family, I'll tell you that much.'

'My perfect family aren't so perfect when you get to know them, trust me. Come on. I'll drive you.'

Ant didn't move and started scrolling through his phone for something, presumably an Uber. 'My day's already ruined, I'm not going to ruin yours,' he muttered.

Jess sighed. 'Ant, you're not going to ruin my day, I promise.'

But he was ignoring her, still looking intently at his phone. He swiped at the screen with his thumb several times, then his eyes grew wide.

'Half an hour?' he muttered. 'The nearest car is half an hour away! You've got to be kidding me.'

He appeared to be ranting to himself, and Jess watched on in fascination, feeling a little rude for doing so. But seeing him angry and emotional was like watching an entirely different Ant from the one she already knew.

'I can't leave Dad lying on the floor for an hour. I'll never hear the end of it,' he growled, and cast a desperate look towards the ocean as if it held the answer.

'What did you just say?' Jess demanded in a loud voice.

Ant froze. Obviously he'd forgotten she was there. He shoved his hand through his hair, which Jess was beginning to understand was a gesture of frustration.

'Nothing. Forget about it.'

'Stay right there,' she told him. 'I'll run up the road and get my car. I'm driving you there whether you like it or not.'

Ant opened his mouth to speak and Jess shot him what she hoped was a firm look.

'Don't make me tackle you and force you into my car,' she threatened. 'You know who would win.'

For the briefest second his mouth twitched and his eyes lit with amusement, then they turned dark again. 'Fine. I know when I'm beat. But I'm telling you now, you'll regret this.'

'Let me make my own mind up about that,' she said. 'Now stay right there and I'll be back as quick as I can.'

Then she set off at a brisk run up the steep hill.

Chapter Twenty-Four

ANT STARED after Jess in dismay and a touch of awe.

Wow, the woman could run. Her legs ate up the incline like it was effortless to her. Which it probably was.

Shit. What had he just done? He couldn't have Jess drive him to his parents' house. It would be so many levels of awkward that it would make the aftermath of their kiss not feel embarrassing. Ant had been working hard to act like everything was normal between them, which it mostly was, except for the sharp pang he got whenever he looked at her.

Every. Single. Time.

He shook away the thoughts of Jess as more than a friend. She'd made the situation clear, and he respected her honesty, even if it wasn't what he'd wanted to hear. It was only a few more weeks and then he wouldn't have to see her regularly anymore—and didn't that just set off an entirely different sort of painful pang?

'It doesn't matter,' he muttered to himself.

One visit to his dysfunctional family home and she wouldn't want anything to do with him anyway.

'Far out,' he said, louder this time.

Jess was already driving down the hill in her shiny Mercedes. A moment later she pulled up beside him, and he got in.

'Address?' she asked.

He gave her his parents' inner-city address and she typed it into her sat nav.

She shot him a worried look. 'It's saying it will take thirty-five minutes. Is that too long?'

'Not for someone as stubborn as my father,' he replied sourly. He should have held his tongue, but it felt good to vent.

'Is he hurt? Should your mother call an ambulance?' Jess persisted.

Her concern was valid, and he wouldn't expect anything less of someone as caring as Jess.

Ant sighed. 'He's fine from what my mum tells me. It's just the usual hit to his pride.'

'Want to give me some background?' she asked, then added, 'But you don't have to if you don't want to.'

Ant sighed again. 'Dad's not in the greatest health. He's got arthritis and bad hips. He had a hip operation a couple of years ago, and don't ask me why, but it seemed to make things worse.'

'Did he have rehabilitation? I've worked with a few clients who were recovering from hip operations.'

'Oh, he had rehabilitation alright, not that it did him any good, the grumpy old bastard. He scared away four physio-therapists and refused to do any of the exercises.'

'Oh, I'm so sorry. That must have been hard. How's his mental health?'

'Grumpy is his permanent state of being.'

'Gosh, are you sure he's your father?'

Ant's mouth twisted into a half-smile. 'Yeah, I've often

wondered the same thing. I even asked Mama if she'd ever taken a liking to the postman, but no such luck.'

Jess's mouth dropped open. 'You did not!' She thwacked him on the arm with the back of her hand.

Ant smiled properly. How could he not? Having Jess touch him, even just a good-natured swat, improved his mood immeasurably.

'So I take it this isn't his first fall?' Jess asked gently as she expertly zipped through the morning traffic.

Not speeding, Ant noted. Just swift and determined like everything else she did.

'I've lost count, to be honest. That sounds really bad, doesn't it? Mama called the ambulance the first few times, but then she worried that there were more serious emergencies, so she usually calls me first instead. I tried suggesting they move elsewhere, to a place without steps or an assisted living facility, but Dad didn't speak to me for a week after that. It was kind of nice actually.'

'Is your mum in good health?'

'Strong as an ox, both mentally and physically, but she's still not able to lift Dad when he has these falls. It takes the two of us to get him up again. So I'm on call, I guess you'd say.'

'You're a good son,' Jess told him.

Ant released a sharp laugh. 'You give me too much credit.'

Jess reached over and brushed his arm. 'You can't choose your family.'

'Some of us are luckier than others,' Ant grumbled.

They fell silent. Jess seemed content to focus on driving, and for once Ant didn't feel the need to fill the silence like he usually would. He supposed if anyone had to meet his father under these circumstances, Jess was the obvious candidate. Not only was she kind and caring, she also wasn't the type to judge.

The rest of the journey was made in silence, and when Jess

pulled up in front of his parents' compact terrace house, her eyes lit up.

'It's gorgeous!'

'You can stay here,' Ant replied seriously. She'd have a much more enjoyable experience if she stayed outside.

'Don't be ridiculous, I'll come and help.'

'No, that's not—'

He'd been about to say "necessary", but his mother flung open the passenger door.

'Mama!' Ant yelped. 'What the hell! How did you even know I was in here? This isn't even my car. What if you'd surprised a stranger?'

'Nothing wrong with my eyes.' She ushered him out of the car. 'Hurry, hurry. If I have to listen to your father for much longer, I'll finally kill him.'

Ant closed his eyes and let his mother tug him from the car. Like he'd told Jess, despite her small size, she was deceptively strong.

He glanced back inside the car and noticed Jess staring at them, her blue eyes wide.

'You stay—'

'Kettle's on in the kitchen, Jessica,' his mother called out. 'You come in, too. I've been dying to meet you.'

Sweet Mother Mary, could this day get any worse?

Ant didn't look back again, but he heard a car door close behind him.

Well, this was going to be a barrel of laughs.

JESS FOLLOWED Ant and his mother quickly inside the cute little terrace house. If Jess didn't like living near the beach so much, she'd always wondered about living somewhere like this.

The small garden was filled with beautiful roses and other bushes, and Jess could imagine Ant's petite mother out here carefully tending to her garden.

In the brief moment Jess had seen her, Ant's mother struck Jess as capable, no nonsense, and surprisingly young and beautiful. Jess had expected someone a lot older. Not the woman that she'd seen with barely wrinkled olive skin and dark raven hair drawn back in a neat bun with only a few flecks of grey in it.

Jess kept up with Ant. The terrace was compact with a long hall and a couple of bedrooms off to one side. Towards the back of the house there was a cosy kitchen with a step down into what appeared to be a sunroom. It was all a bit dated but very homely.

They found Ant's father lying on his back just inside the sunroom, his eyes closed and face contorted in pain or frustration, Jess couldn't tell which.

Ant and his mother rushed over to him and crouched down together.

'On three,' Ant told his mum, but Jess spoke up.

'No, please let me, Mrs Monticello. Why don't you sit down?'

Ant shot her a warning look while his mother straightened.

'It's Abi, and I'm stronger than I look,' she replied, her dark brown eyes—so much like Ant's—filled with determination.

'Oh, Ant told me that already,' Jess said. 'I just thought it might be nice to have someone else do the heavy lifting for a change.'

Mrs Monticello frowned, but only slightly. She appeared to be considering Jess's words while Ant's father blinked up at them from his position on the floor.

'Who are you?' he demanded.

'I'm Jessi—'

Abi turned back towards her husband and shot him an angry look. 'Jessica Jinks, you fool. You know, the lovely woman who is helping our son get fit and healthy, unlike you. Or are your eyes going on you, too?'

Jess bit her lip. Ant shrugged as if to say, "I told you so."

Jess found her voice. 'Hi, Mr Monticello. Ant's car wouldn't start so I gave him a lift here—'

'How many times have I told you to go and see your damn uncle about a new car, Antony?' his father bellowed. 'You have the money now. There's no excuse for driving around in that rust bucket.'

Jess wondered if anyone in this family ever managed to finish a full sentence, but decided to try again.

'How about we have this conversation once you're off the floor, Mr Monticello?' Jess asked brightly.

They all stopped and looked at her.

'She has a point, Stefano,' Abi said. 'Much as I'd like to leave you there so you can learn your lesson about not doing your exercises, I couldn't stand the complaining.'

Jess stepped forward, and Abi moved away with a nod.

'Alright, I won't say no to the help,' Abi said, 'but I am going to make you a drink to say thank you. Mainly so I can find out if my Antony has been behaving himself.'

Jess squatted down, and together she and Ant helped his father sit up from the floor with Ant supporting his father's head.

Stefano groaned, but didn't resist.

'How's your head?' Jess enquired, worried that he might have given himself a concussion when he'd fallen.

Stefano gave her a dark look. 'There's nothing wrong with my head.'

'That's because his backside took the brunt of the fall,' Abi called out from behind them in the kitchen where she was boiling the kettle. 'One day I hope it's his head, because it might finally knock some sense into him.'

Jess couldn't imagine her mother talking to her father that way, but she kept the thought to herself.

'Ready?' Ant asked.

Once again, they worked together to help Stefano into a standing position. They held on to make sure he was steady, and he shook them off.

'I can stand!'

Stefano stomped away unsteadily, leaning on the wall as he took the single step up into the kitchen. Once there, he shuffled over to the dining table and sat down slowly.

It occurred to Jess that Ant's father was a lot older than his mother. Again, she kept that thought to herself.

'Coffee or tea, bella ragazza?' Abi said.

Ant stood up and nodded at Jess. 'She's asking what you'd like.'

'Oh! Oh, of course. Tea, please. No sugar, and milk if you have it.'

'What are you doing here?' Stefano's voice said from behind her.

Jess turned and looked at him, surprised. She'd just answered that a moment ago, hadn't she? Maybe Ant's father had hit his head after all.

Abi stepped in beside her, putting a cup on the bench in front of Jess.

'Alzheimer's. He's only recently been diagnosed, I'm afraid. The only good thing about it is that I can insult him all I want and he doesn't remember.'

Despite the attempt at a joke, Abi's eyes didn't hold any hint of mischief. They were filled with so much pain that Jess had to stop herself from reaching out to her.

'I'm so sorry,' Jess whispered. 'I didn't know.'

Abi eyed the men on the other side of the kitchen. Ant appeared to be checking his father for bruises or any injuries they might have missed.

Abi turned her attention back to Jess. 'Ant doesn't like to talk about it. They've never gotten along well, but I think Ant always held out hope that one day things might improve. It's getting harder to believe that will ever happen due to Stefano's state of health.'

'Oh,' Jess breathed, her heart breaking for Ant and his mother, and for Stefano, too. Then the more practical part made her speak up again. 'Is Stefano seeing anyone at the moment? For his exercises or physiotherapy?'

'No,' Abi said. 'I'm the only one who can bear to put up with him.' But it was said with fondness and Jess realised it wasn't just Stefano fighting to remain at home. His wife genuinely wanted him there, too.

'I could try to put together some physical therapy sessions for him,' Jess suggested without thinking.

She heard Ant suck in a sharp breath from behind her. 'You can't do that.'

Jess turned to face him. 'And why not?'

'Because you're a personal trainer, not a physiotherapist or a rehabilitation specialist.'

'I trained as an occupational therapist,' Jess told him.

Ant gaped at her. 'You what?'

Jess put her hands on her hips. 'You heard me.'

Ant's mouth opened and shut a few times. Out of the corner of her eye, Jess saw Abi take a sip of tea, her dark eyes dancing with humour.

Ant took a step forward. 'You're an occupational therapist?'

'Was,' Jess corrected. 'It wasn't for me in the end. But I still apply the knowledge I learned on a daily basis.' Ant was still staring at her with such a dumbfounded expression that Jess retorted, 'How else do you think I came up with such an in-depth approach to exercise?'

'I don't know,' Ant said quietly. 'I guess I thought it was from your personal training experience.'

'Some,' Jess replied lightly. 'But you know how I go on and on about exercise needing to be accessible to all people? That's the OT speaking.'

Ant walked over and his mother handed him a coffee. He regarded Jess thoughtfully as he took a mouthful.

'So, not only are you gorgeous, successful and fit, you're university educated, too?'

'Antony!' His mother backhanded him lightly. 'I brought you up to believe women can be anything.'

'Oh, I know, Mama. I just didn't realise Jess was *every* capable woman all rolled into one.'

Jess dropped her gaze to her drink, as if burned. The look in Ant's dark eyes had been . . . electrifying. Jack had never looked at her with such respect. Or awe. And Jess didn't know what to think about it, so she changed the subject again.

'So I am qualified to help your father if you want,' she told them.

Abi smiled a sad smile. 'It's not what I want, bella ragazza. It's what he wants.'

'And unfortunately he doesn't want to exercise,' Ant finished.

'Oh, I don't know,' Jess said, hiding a grin behind her mug. 'I seem to recall another Monticello man with that attitude as well, and I managed to convince him.'

Abi threw her head back and laughed, a loud, warm sound, and Jess found herself smiling, too.

'She's got your measure, Antony,' Abi said when she'd

finished laughing. She reached over and squeezed his bicep. 'And look at you, my dashing son. So fit and healthy. It's a miracle.'

'Hey, I wouldn't say it's a miracle,' Ant said. 'I wasn't that bad.'

His mother shook with laughter again and nodded at Jess. 'Be my guest, Jessica. You are welcome to try to convince my husband. Anything you can do to help him and make his life more comfortable.'

Again, Jess witnessed that mournful look, and she rethought her earlier assessment about Ant's family being mean to one another. Like Ant, his mother liked to joke—albeit those jokes were painfully close to the truth sometimes. But this woman loved her husband above all else.

'When he was younger, what sort of things did Stefano like to do?' Jess asked.

Stefano had turned on a small flat screen television sitting opposite the kitchen table and appeared to be absorbed in the morning news report.

Abi thought for a moment and her sad expression was replaced with joy.

'Oh, you should have seen my Stefano. So handsome. So virile.'

'*Mum*,' Ant complained.

Abi ignored him and leaned in closer to Jess. 'I was the younger woman, you know.'

Jess's eyebrows rose involuntarily. 'You were?'

'Stefano lured me away from all the younger suitors with his poise and sophistication.'

Ant rolled his eyes. 'Seriously, Mum? Must you tell this story to every new person you meet?'

'I want to hear it,' Jess told him, also ignoring Ant.

'I'd trained in administration and was just starting out, and

Stefano ran his own business. He was very confident and assured. Back in those days, he rowed regularly and he enjoyed cycling, too.'

Jess stored this information in her brain, making a mental note that both of those things were supported activities that didn't put undue strain on the body.

'Unlike the other young men, Stefano treated me with respect—and I don't mean the sort of respect every woman deserves. He treated me like an equal. That was something in those days.'

Ant reached over and rubbed his mum's shoulder. 'That's because you are his equal in every way. And you're special.'

Jess blinked at the open affection between them and felt her heart twist a little.

'And he didn't just expect me to get married and start having babies either. Before Antony arrived, I ran the office—it was *our* business, he always told me. And then afterwards, when Antony was little, I continued to do some work from home. Then later on, I'd work school days. He always made me feel a part of the business in every way until we sold it a few years ago.'

'That's such a wonderful story, Mrs Monticello,' Jess said genuinely.

'Please call me Abi. We all need an equal. That's what my life with Stefano has taught me. Someone who believes in us, lifts us up when we need it, and is there to support us even when we may not want the support.' She looked at her husband meaningfully over Jess's shoulder. 'He lost a big part of himself when the business closed, I'm afraid.'

'Well, I'm more than happy to see if I can help him redis-cover some of his motivation again. Physical therapy is great for that,' Jess explained.

'You won't be happy after a few sessions with him,' Ant muttered.

'Oh, be quiet, Ant. I put up with you, don't I?' Jess shot back, then snapped her mouth shut, wondering if she'd gone too far. She and Jack had never really bantered with one another. He'd always been too serious. But it came naturally to Jess on account of her four big brothers.

Abi nudged her son. 'I like Jessica. She gets you.'

Ant gave his mother a strange look. 'How is a woman telling me to be quiet "getting me"?'

'Because you like the sound of your own voice and she knows it. She also knows when it's good for you to be quiet.'

Jess hid a smile behind her mug. She was really looking forward to seeing if she could help Ant's father and mother out.

Whether she would have any success remained to be seen.

Chapter Twenty-Five

ANT DID his very best in the following days to discourage Jess from helping his father. At first he ignored her messages, all of which were asking practical but very worrying questions like "would his father attend a gym?" and "does he like listening to music?"

In his defence, he was slightly distracted on account of making his debut as a fashion icon.

'Excellent!' Alicia's million-dollar smile lit up her perfect face—and Ant suspected that smile was literally worth a million dollars whenever she starred in a photo shoot. 'That's a wrap.'

Thank God.

Ant stopped sucking in his stomach and relaxed. Not that he had much of a stomach these days. It was more of a gentle rise on an otherwise flat torso. It wasn't even that soft anymore. If Ant didn't know himself better, he'd almost suggest there might really be a six-pack in there somewhere.

Alicia walked over to where Ant was standing in front of the photographer.

'Well done, you. Very impressive for a first-time model.'

Ant preened a bit—not all of it put on. 'Why, thank you. I've just been waiting for the right time to make my debut.'

'Now is definitely the right time,' Alicia told him, her eyes looking him up and down.

It sent tingles down Ant's spine, but he also couldn't shake the feeling of being assessed, like his body was separate to his personality. Was this what models felt like on a regular basis?

'You're looking very manly now you've gotten fit. The camera loves those dark, brooding looks of yours,' Alicia commented, continuing to contemplate him.

Ant's dark looks had never been described as brooding before—more like goofy—but he wasn't going to disagree with her.

She put a finger to her lips as though deep in thought. 'You know, I think we should go out to dinner sometime.'

'*You what?*'

The photographer smiled and discreetly turned away to pack up his things, giving them their space.

Alicia strolled closer, still looking thoughtful and ran a finger across Ant's shoulders. He tried not to shiver. He kind of felt like Alicia was a sleek leopard and he was some sort of prey—probably something defenceless like a gazelle.

She stopped and tilted her head. 'What do you think? Dinner Saturday night? Tetsuya's is one of my favourites.'

Of course it was. It was only one of the most expensive restaurants in Sydney. Ant had never eaten there because he couldn't quite get his head around the idea of a degustation menu. While having multiple courses sounded good in theory, in reality you were paying a lot for tiny morsels of food.

'Sure,' he replied, already hating himself for agreeing to eat at a restaurant he'd never go to otherwise.

But this was *Alicia Travers*.

'Wonderful.' She shot him another one of those show-stopping smiles, and this time he felt it in his groin. 'I'll have my assistant make a booking and send you the details. Pick me up?'

His stomach sank. An image of his rusting, unreliable car flashed into his mind. After only a second of hesitation, Ant cleared his throat. 'I was thinking it probably makes sense to Uber so I can enjoy the wine.'

Smooth, Ant, real smooth.

'Oh, of course. Tetsuya's is better with wine. I just wasn't sure you were a connoisseur.'

He wasn't, and Ant also realised he'd just made the dinner about ten times more expensive. Damn it. But it was better than being caught out in his pathetic excuse for a car.

'I'll have my driver pick you up then,' Alicia informed him.

Her driver. Of course.

Ant knew that, now he was working on one of Sydney's most popular evening news shows, he could well afford the occasional dinner somewhere like Tetsuya's. Jokes aside, his ego hadn't quite caught up to his situation.

'Sounds great,' Ant told her like he was used to all of this. Then he had an ingenious thought. 'How about I wear one of your outfits on the evening?'

Alicia's smile widened, and she clapped her hands together, jumping lightly on the spot. It transformed her from a sophisticated catwalk model to something more reminiscent of a high school cheerleader.

'I knew I liked you for more than one reason,' she said, giving him a wink.

Then she did something Ant was entirely unprepared for.

She leaned in and placed her luscious lips against his with a bright smack.

'See you next week, Antony.'

Ant didn't have the heart to correct her. He hated being called Antony with a passion, and the only people who were allowed to get away with it were his parents.

She stepped back and squeezed his hand quickly before walking away, her supermodel hips moving seductively and with practiced ease.

Ant raised a hand in goodbye. Not that she would see it because her back was to him.

Holy hell. What just happened?

Had Alicia Travers just asked Ant out on a date that wasn't set up? Surely not. It had to be a PR exercise or an opportunity to talk more about her fashion label.

He glanced down at himself. At the silky black shirt he was wearing with the exquisitely matched black trousers. And since when did he refer to trousers as exquisite? What was wrong with him?

Then again, maybe nothing was wrong with him. He'd looked good today, and it wasn't just because of the clothes. He was trim and fit, and in clothes this well designed it showed.

'Huh,' he said to himself.

Sure, he wasn't David Beckham, but Ant was funny and he could also be considered successful. Maybe Alicia saw him in a way he didn't. And maybe, just maybe, it was time he started viewing himself that way, too.

He returned to the dressing room to get his things. Alicia had told him to stay in the clothes if he wanted, and he figured he might as well. He collected his mobile phone and checked for messages. There were a few work emails he needed to review and a message from Jess.

He felt a pang of guilt. It wasn't fair of him to ignore her, especially when she was trying to help. He opened the message.

Check this out!

Below that she'd attached a video of an indoor bike set up in front of a big-arse TV screen.

'Holy shit.'

Ant studied the photo in more detail. It appeared to be taken in his parents' back shed. His parents' previously messy nightmare of a shed.

'Holy shit,' Ant said again. What had Jess done?

Hands shaking a little, Ant typed a message in response.

Are you there now?

Her reply came quickly.

Yep, and will be for a while yet if you want to see this for yourself.

Ant's reply was equally quick.

I'm on my way now.

Chapter Twenty-Six

ANT ARRIVED AT HIS PARENTS' house more quickly than Jess had expected. Stefano was absorbed with riding the bicycle when Ant came in.

'Hey,' Ant said, then stopped to look around in amazement.

Jess also did a double take. Ant was dressed in a perfectly fitted pair of black trousers that showed off his taut backside. They were paired with a matching black shirt made of the sort of luxurious silky fabric you wanted to reach out and stroke. Or maybe it was Ant she wanted to stroke.

She shook her head at herself. Fortunately, Ant was still distracted enough by the tidied shed not to notice. He looked so good. Not that he didn't normally, of course, but today he looked different in a way Jess couldn't put her finger on. Just . . . really good.

'How did . . .' He stopped to survey the space again. 'I didn't answer your messages. I don't understand.'

Jess shrugged, not letting on how proud she was of herself given the state the shed had been in a week ago. 'I figured you were busy, most likely tied up with the show, so I got in touch with your mum directly.'

'But . . . but there must have been forty years' worth of crap in this shed!'

Jess grinned. 'Your mother was dying to clean it out, so I pulled in a favour from a client that works for a charity. I told them they could have whatever your mum didn't want—which was most of it—if they came and helped me.'

'But when?' Ant asked, still sounding dumbfounded.

'A few nights earlier this week,' she answered.

'Why didn't you call me?' Ant demanded.

Jess had expected surprise, but not anger. She decided to tread carefully.

'Well, you work evenings, for one. When I couldn't get a hold of you, I left it up to your mother to get in touch.'

'*She never called me!*'

Jess stiffened in shock. She'd never heard Ant raise his voice before. She stepped forward tentatively, but resisted touching his arm.

'Be quiet!' Ant's father shouted from behind them. 'Can't you see I'm riding through Central Park?'

Jess bit down on a smile. Stefano had been like this ever since Jess and Abi had ushered him in here earlier. Like a kid in a candy store. His eyes had filled with wonder at the equipment Jess had supplied, and as soon as he'd seen the television screen in front of the bike, he'd been hooked.

Jess returned her attention to Ant and lowered her voice so as not to disturb Stefano. 'You'll have to talk to your mum about that. I don't know whether she couldn't get a hold of you or . . .'

'Or she didn't want me to know,' Ant said gruffly. 'I could have helped out, you know.'

Jess felt a surge of indignation swell in her chest. 'I sent you approximately eight messages, Ant.'

His expression turned sheepish. 'Was it that many?'

Jess sighed and chose to push aside the hurt that he had deliberately ignored her, figuring he was stubborn like his father. 'Your father's problems weren't going to go away.'

'Oh, I don't know. He's been determined to hold on to them for years now. What made you so sure that you could solve them?'

Wow, Jess thought, but didn't say it. Ant's father's stubbornness really had driven a rift between them, hadn't it? Instead, she said, 'With my background in rehabilitation I thought that I could help. I figured if he refuses to go to a gym or see a physiotherapist, why not bring the gym to him?'

Ant eyed his father again, then shoved a hand through his hair. 'How long has he been on there for?'

Jess checked her watch. 'About half an hour.'

'Shit. You're going to give him a heart attack.'

Jess smiled reassuringly. 'He's fine. He's riding on a very gentle course that you and I would find extremely easy, and I'm monitoring his heart rate. Come and take a look.'

She led him over to the strange contraption his father was riding on.

'Hang on,' he said. 'This is Dad's bike.'

'One and the same. Your mother told me how much he used to enjoy riding it when he was younger. I had it serviced. Then you take the back wheel off and position it on this trainer, so it still feels like you're riding a real bike. The program provides feedback when you're going up and down hills, and he can change gears and everything.'

Jess couldn't hide the note of pride in her voice from the fact Stefano was loving it so much.

Ant regarded his father with a strange expression. 'We used

. . . that's the bike he'd use when we'd go riding together when I was a kid.'

Jess gestured behind them. 'We kept yours. It's over there.'

Ant turned and his brow creased with emotion. 'Some of my best memories of time spent with Dad were on that bike,' he said softly.

'You could get it serviced,' Jess suggested. 'Set up something similar at your place if you have the room. You can even ride together. Look.' Jess turned and pointed to the screen. 'See those groups of riders? Those are real people riding in real-time together.'

Ant stepped closer. 'That's so cool. And it actually looks like Central Park.'

'It basically is. There are other places you can ride, too. London, Austria, and a made-up world as well.'

Ant glanced back towards Jess. 'I shouldn't have snapped before. I'm sorry. It's just all so surprising.' He gestured to the rowing machine sitting beside the bike trainer. 'Have you convinced him to get on that?'

'I'm quietly confident,' she told him, and Ant laughed a proper Ant laugh. Jess relaxed at the sound. 'I wouldn't have done this if your mother wasn't keen, by the way. I'm helpful, but I'm not pushy.'

Ant shot her a dark look. 'You're a bit pushy.'

'Hi-Jinks wouldn't be where it was today if I wasn't a little pushy.'

Ant nodded. 'Where's my mum?'

'Inside. Cooking. She's informed me in no uncertain terms that I'm staying for lunch. And I think her version of lunch and mine are different. It smells like she's cooking up a storm in there.'

'That's my mum's way of saying thank you. She likes you.'

'And I like her.'

Ant gave her a strange look, then his expression morphed into one of gratitude. 'Thank you. I mean that. I've never seen him want to do anything like this.'

'You've just got to find the right motivation. Everyone's different.'

'Do you think he'll stick with it?'

Jess liked to think Ant's voice held hope rather than doubt. 'Again, I'm quietly confident. I'll drop by a few times a week and—'

'Whoa. We can't expect you to do that for us—'

'I want to, Ant. Really. The benefits of exercise are well-documented in older people who are facing things like Alzheimer's. It won't prevent it, but it can help. I'm keen to get more Baby Boomers partaking in my classes anyway. Think of this as a test case. I might even get a testimonial from your father down the track.'

'Now you're acting deluded, but what do I know? You got him to ride that bike.'

'I'm going to get him to try the rower now, so how about you go inside and say hi to your mum? The less distraction, the better. We won't be too much longer. I don't want to wear him out on his first session.'

Ant nodded and walked towards the door to the yard. 'First me, now him. You're unstoppable, Jessica Jinks.'

JESS AND STEFANO joined Ant and his mother in the kitchen fifteen minutes later. Stefano appeared tired but happy, and went over to what Jess now recognised as his chair at the dining table. He turned the radio on, ignoring them.

'That's him on a good day,' Abi said. 'Well done, Jess.'

'Yes, well done,' Ant echoed. 'Hey, I was thinking maybe I

could join you for his next session? Then you can show me what it is he should be doing, and I can take over from you down the track?'

'Sure,' Jess said. 'I can show you too, Abi, so you can keep an eye on his progress.'

'Watch out, Mum,' Ant said. 'Jess will have you exercising before too long.'

'I've already agreed to try out one of Jess's Hi-Jinks classes,' Abi replied, and Ant's jaw dropped open. Abi put a hand on her hip. 'What? Do you think your mother is too old for Hi-Jinks?'

'No, of course not. I'm just surprised, that's all. I thought you already had your walking ladies to hang out with?'

'They're coming too,' Abi informed him, and Jess hid a smile when Ant narrowed his eyes at Jess.

'What?' she said. 'It's just a few free trial classes.'

'Yeah, and next you'll have them swimming laps like me.'

Jess blinked and stared at him. 'What did you say?'

Ant blinked back and waved a hand at her. 'Nothing. Forget I said anything.'

Jess's eyes widened in delight. 'You've been swimming? When?'

Ant shrugged. 'Just a few times at my local pool. Nothing major. I wanted to try it again because it was the only exercise I actually liked as a kid.'

'That's great!' Jess beamed at him. 'Really great. And you're enjoying it?'

'As much as someone can enjoy exercise, I suppose.'

Jess did a few light jumps on the spot. 'Oh my gosh, you know what this means? I have to eat kale for a week!'

Abi gave Jess a perplexed look.

'Oh, it was just a little bet we had going,' Jess told her. 'If

Ant found himself genuinely wanting to exercise, I said I'd eat kale for a week because he hates it.'

'Shouldn't it be the other way around?' Abi queried.

'Be quiet, Mama,' Ant said quickly, making Jess laugh.

'It's alright, a bet's a bet. I'm going to document it on Instagram. I think I'll have kale pancakes tomorrow for brunch.'

Ant mimed gagging, and she nudged him. 'I've told you, it's not as bad as you think.'

'He was always terrible with his greens,' Abi said, stirring the pot she had on the cooktop. 'Now, Antony. Tell me how the photo shoot went today.'

Ant shot Jess a self-conscious look, and Jess finally realised what was different about him today that she hadn't been able to put her finger on.

'The clothes?' she asked. 'Are those Alicia's?'

Ant nodded and twirled for the women, making his mother roll her eyes.

'Very nice,' Jess said, meaning it.

She was relieved to know that was the reason Ant had caught her attention when he'd first arrived. Clothes designed by Alicia Travers were bound to make an impact. And it was OK to appreciate Ant's good looks, especially now he was growing more confident, Jess reasoned. Just because she'd told him they weren't going to have a relationship didn't mean she couldn't notice him.

'And it went well?' Abi asked her son.

'I'm a natural,' Ant told her with a grin, and both women laughed.

Abi patted his arm. 'I'm sure you are, darling. So when do you see this Alicia next?'

Ant cleared his throat and averted his eyes, focusing on the glass of water in front of him on the bench. 'Next week.'

'Another photo shoot already?' Abi beamed at him, genuinely proud.

'Um, no. It's something else, but nothing important,' Ant muttered, still not meeting his mother's eyes.

'Well, out with it then. What have you got planned? Some other business idea?'

'It's just dinner,' Ant said quietly.

Jess stared at Ant. He still wasn't looking at her. Abi stared alongside Jess.

'Dinner? With Alicia Travers?' Abi's eyes grew wide and a big smile lit her face. Then she seemed to catch herself and cast a quick glance at Jess.

'That's so exciting, Ant,' Jess found herself saying, even though she had a funny taste in her mouth.

'Jess is right,' Abi agreed. 'It's very exciting. I can't wait to hear all about it later next week. But now it's time for food. Can you please set the table?'

Jess might have been mistaken, but Abi seemed to be changing the subject. Like she'd been worried about hurting Jess's feelings at the mention of Alicia. Ant's mother turned her back to them to serve the meal.

Abi was so sweet, but there was no need for her to be worried. Jess and Ant were only friends. And she was happy for her friend. Wasn't she?

It was Jess's turn to shoot a surreptitious look in Ant's direction. He was chatting to his father as he set the table.

Jess wasn't sure why, but she just couldn't see him with someone like Alicia Travers. New clothes and his new look aside, Ant was too down to earth and too genuine for someone like a supermodel.

Jess told herself not to be silly. She didn't know Alicia. She could be the nicest person in the world for all Jess knew. It was just that Alicia didn't seem real. Not fake, perhaps. Just not real. And outside of her own family, Ant was one of the most real people Jess knew.

Still, it wasn't any of her business. Ant could see whomever he liked. Yet Jess couldn't shake the feeling that Ant deserved someone nicer than Alicia Travers.

Chapter Twenty-Seven

'WELL, I think you should still ask him for help with your business plan,' Em said the following week.

Jess, Em and Kat had met up for their regular weekend exercise session down at the beach and they were chatting while they warmed up.

'Definitely,' Kat agreed. 'Seeing as you've helped Ant's parents out, he can return the favour.'

'That's not why I helped them out,' Jess said quickly.

Kat stopped stretching and peered at her. Jess hated it when Kat looked at her like that. Like she was about to be interviewed.

'Why did you help Ant out then?' Kat asked.

Yep. There it was. Interview question number one.

'Because it seemed like the nice thing to do,' Jess explained. 'His dad needs to build some strength so he stops having so many falls, and they really want to keep him in the family home. He'd already scared four physiotherapists away, so I figured I'd give it a shot.'

'You and your passion for exercise,' Kat quipped. 'But are you sure that was the *only* reason?'

Jess turned to face the water, breathing in the salty air she always found so energising. 'He's a friend, I guess.'

'Just a friend?' asked Em, and she shared a look with Kat.

'Yes,' Jess said firmly. 'Besides, Alicia is interested in him. I thought you knew, Kat.'

Kat straightened from the forward stretch she'd been doing. 'No. What are you talking about?'

That was strange. Jess was positive Ant would be telling the whole world about him and Alicia, because that's how Ant was. He loved gloating, even if it was just to get a laugh.

'He went out to dinner with Alicia recently,' Jess told them. 'And it wasn't a business meeting.'

Em's mouth dropped open. 'Oh my God, that's amazing!'

Jess didn't share Em's enthusiasm for some reason. 'Why do you say that?' she asked casually.

Em closed the distance between them and put her hands on Jess's shoulders. 'Because Ant has just become your biggest success story to date. From lazy comedian to supermodel's boyfriend. You've totally got to get him to work on your business plan now so you can promote that angle.'

Jess released a tight sigh. 'That's not really how my brand works. I don't do the whole transformation thing.'

Em threw her hands up in the air. 'You do now! When everyone sees Ant on that Logies red carpet with Alicia and learns that he's there because she's *dating* him, they'll know it's because of you.'

'They will?' Jess asked weakly.

Kat had been listening to the conversation in that watchful way of hers and spoke up. 'They will. Em's right. You should definitely capitalise on this for your business, and I know just the right way to go about it. You need to attend the Logies.'

'Not you too!' Jess protested.

Kat's eyes narrowed. 'What do you mean?'

'Ant suggested it to me the other week, but I said no. I'm not a celebrity or a supermodel. I wouldn't fit in.'

'Yes, you damn well would,' Kat said with a certainty that Jess didn't feel. 'Leave it with me. I'll get you an invite.'

'No. Please. It's not necessary. It's too soon, anyway. It's not going to happen.'

'Leave it with me,' Kat repeated. 'And sorting out your business plan is also necessary,' she added. 'If you don't want Ant to help you because it would be too weird, I have a few contacts I could put you in touch with.'

'Why would asking Ant be weird?' Jess tried to keep her voice neutral.

'Because you seem to think it's weird,' Kat retorted.

'No. I never said it was weird, just that—'

'You weren't sure you were comfortable about it,' Em finished with a knowing smile.

Jess huffed. 'Maybe we should start our exercise session now, ladies.'

Kat and Jess shared another look, and Jess couldn't help herself.

'What?' she demanded.

'It just seems strange that you're so awkward about it,' Em said.

'I'm not awkward,' Jess told them. 'Only I'm not sure it's the professional thing to do seeing as he's my client.'

'It's called quid pro quo. And you've just spent the last couple of weeks at his parents' house setting up a home gym for his father,' Kat pointed out.

Oh, for God's sake, this was getting ridiculous.

'I told you why I did that,' Jess said quietly, because otherwise she'd be tempted to raise her voice at her well-meaning-but-annoying friends.

'Because you're *friends*,' Em and Kat both said at the same time, then they laughed.

Jess didn't laugh. In fact, she felt downright miserable, which made absolutely no sense. Her friends were right. Ant's transformation was going to be a huge boon for her business, and she needed to capitalise on it.

'Ask him,' Kat told Jess when she stopped laughing. 'Seeing as you consider him a *friend*.'

Jess ignored the dark gleam in Kat's eyes.

'I'll think about it. Now stop trying to get out of exercising, you two. Time to warm up. Come on!' Jess set off at a light jog up the beach to indicate that the conversation was over.

JESS AND ANT'S last exercise session came and went, and Jess still hadn't asked Ant for help with her business plan. There hadn't really been a right time, and besides, Ant seemed busy. Not that he'd told Jess that. But she'd happened to notice some more activity on his Instagram account. Another fashion shoot with Alicia. Drinks in the city with Alicia. Exercising on the weekend with Alicia.

Alicia, Alicia, Alicia.

Jess supposed she should have been happy that Ant was continuing to exercise now that the PR exercise was done. Then again, Ant probably didn't have a choice if he wanted to keep a supermodel interested.

Now she was being mean. Alicia could be interested in Ant for more than his appearance.

Jess forced herself to focus as the camera's little red light came on.

'Welcome back to *Sydney Tonight*. We're also welcoming back another guest this evening: Jessica Jinks, the woman behind Ant Monticello's dramatic transformation,' Kat announced.

'I wouldn't say dramatic transformation,' Jess said, being sure to keep her focus on Kat and not on Ant or the person sitting beside him.

'Oh, I'd say it was dramatic,' Alicia said from Ant's other side. 'Dramatic enough to catch *my* attention, anyway.'

They all laughed, and Jess wondered if the camera would pick up that Jess's laugh was fake. Probably not, seeing as Alicia appeared one hundred percent natural on-screen.

Jess had met Alicia briefly in the hair and make-up room earlier. She'd just arrived when Alicia was finishing up, as Alicia was due to go on before Jess to talk about her new fashion range. The supermodel had regarded Jess openly and patted her on the arm before she'd gone to leave the room.

'I like your work,' Alicia had told her.

'Oh, I didn't know you've tried Hi-Jinks,' Jess had said with enthusiasm. Too much enthusiasm, she realised now.

Alicia had smirked. 'No. I meant Ant.'

Then she'd left the room, leaving Jess staring open-mouthed after her. It was due to the shock that Jess's next words were spoken aloud.

'Is she always like that?' Jess had asked.

The hairstylist had raised an eyebrow. 'What? Better than us? She likes to think so.'

Now Jess sat behind the broadcast desk trying to pretend like she belonged and that she didn't hate being on live television. Or that she didn't like Alicia.

That wasn't really fair. She didn't know Alicia. But what she knew so far, Jess didn't like.

Jess forced herself to focus again. They were showing some

of the most recent footage of Jess and Ant working out together on the big screen behind the broadcast desk. Once it was finished, Kat shifted to face Jess.

'Well, my verdict is that Hi-Jinks is a success,' Kat announced. 'Not only is Ant no longer lazy, he's still exercising. That's success in my books.'

'Definitely,' Jess agreed. 'That's what I'm all about. No guilt trips. Just exercise that feels good.'

Alicia reached over and squeezed Ant's bicep even though he was wearing a suit. 'And he sure feels good to me.'

Ant beamed and Jess felt slightly nauseous. Why wasn't Ant being funny? Why wasn't he making a joke of some sort? He should be joking right now, not acting like a loyal puppy.

'So that means Ant is going to the Logies with Alicia,' Kat said for the viewers at home.

'Just try to stop me,' Ant said, still grinning.

'How about you, Jess?' Alicia asked, her voice dripping with sweetness. 'Will you be attending the Logies?'

Jess smiled and tried not to look taken aback. Why was Alicia asking her that question? On national television, no less?

Jess kept smiling and looked over to Kat for some support. Like the loyal friend and practiced presenter she was, Kat turned to face the camera.

'As a matter of fact, Jess *will* be attending the Logies this year, Alicia. The only reason she hasn't mentioned it was because she didn't want to steal Ant's thunder.'

Jess released a tight cough and forced herself to keep on smiling. Oh my God, what was Kat doing? Sure, she'd needed some back up, but that wasn't quite what Jess had in mind. And since when did Jess have an invite to the Logies?

'Oh, how wonderful,' Alicia cried, like she'd just discovered that her best friend was attending. 'I can't wait to see you there, Jess. I'm sure you'll look magnificent.'

Seeing as it was now Tuesday and the Logies were being held this weekend, Jess doubted that very much.

Holy shit. What was she going to *wear*?

Kat shot Jess a surreptitious glance that said, "Calm down. Let me deal with this."

But Jess wasn't dealing with it. Not at all. Inside, she was simultaneously seething and panicking. Who did Alicia think she was, carrying on like that? And as for Kat, was she serious? Had she really gotten Jess an invite?

'Seeing as we're talking about exciting news,' Alicia said. 'Ant's got something else exciting to tell you.'

Jess's inner turmoil halted abruptly as she looked over at Ant.

She could have been wrong, but Ant's smile didn't seem as genuine as it had a moment ago.

'Yes, that's right,' Ant said smoothly. 'When Kat said that I'm going to keep exercising, she wasn't wrong. Soon I won't just be known as Ant the comedian, but Ant—wait for it—*The Champion*.'

Jess saw him give her the slightest sideways glance.

'In this week's breaking news, I've signed up for a triathlon,' he announced.

There was a beat of silence and then Alicia raised her hands to clap animatedly in response to Ant's news. Kat and Jess followed a split second later, albeit not quite as enthusiastically.

At that moment, if someone had asked Jess whether she was on live television, she couldn't have said. Because her mind was too busy racing with the same thought over and over again.

Oh my God, Ant. What have you done?

Chapter Twenty-Eight

AFTER THE SHOW, Jess hurried to the make-up room to collect her things. She just wanted to get out of there. The sooner the better.

Otherwise she'd be tempted to ask—no, not to ask, but demand to know—what Ant was thinking.

You didn't just sign up for a triathlon on a whim! Taking part in a triathlon required weeks and months of dedicated training, not to mention careful eating, to ensure that your body was ready for the challenge.

Jess didn't doubt for a second that Ant was capable of it. What she doubted was his motivation in signing up for it in the first place. As far as Jess could tell, Ant had signed up for the publicity and to impress his new girlfriend. Why else announce it on live television? Jess needed to talk to him to make sure he knew exactly what was involved, but not now and not here.

Not when *she* was around.

Jess could hear Alicia's husky voice talking to someone outside in the corridor. Jess honestly had no idea what Ant saw in the woman.

Apart from her millions of dollars, supermodel body, and her fame, you mean?

Jess growled and shoved her jacket into her bag. She was too hot and bothered to put it on right now.

The more logical part of Jess was vaguely aware that she also desperately needed to speak with Kat about the Logies. In reality, that was far more pressing than Ant's one-hundred-and-eighty-degree turnaround on his attitude to exercise. But Jess was also annoyed with herself and couldn't shake the horrible feeling of guilt that sat in her belly like a lead weight.

It was all her fault.

Jess was the one who had suggested Ant could train for a triathlon. It had been intended to motivate him early on in the hopes that it would prove to him that with dedication and hard work he could achieve anything.

She should have been careful what she wished for. Jess didn't actually think he'd sign up for a damn triathlon. At least, not like this.

She picked up her bag, knowing that in her bad state of mind, now was not the time to make any decisions. What she needed was to get home, get changed into her exercise gear, and go for a run along the beach. That would clear her head and then she'd be able to think clearly.

Jess strode into the corridor, her mind already imagining the feel of the damp sand between her toes and the cleansing sound of the waves crashing to the shore. Which was probably why she didn't notice Alicia.

'Whoa! Slow down.' Alicia caught Jess by the shoulders to prevent her from running straight into her.

'Oh, I'm sorry,' Jess said, flustered.

Wow. Alicia was tall. Jess was neither tall nor short, but she had to look a long way up to meet Alicia's dark gaze.

'I thought you might want to congratulate Ant on his news

before you left,' Alicia said, those dark eyes hard to read. 'Seeing as you're the one who made him into the new man he is today.'

'I will later,' Jess said quickly, darting a look around Alicia. 'But I've got somewhere I need to be now, unfortunately.'

Why, when the woman was so super skinny, did Jess feel like she couldn't step past her?

Jess thought Alicia might have frowned in response. But it was hard to tell because she didn't have any wrinkles, let alone fine lines, so any displays of genuine emotion were obviously limited.

'Huh. OK. So you'll be at the Logies then, will you?' Alicia asked.

Why was Alicia still talking to her? All previous interactions suggested Alicia wasn't remotely interested in getting to know Jess.

'Yes, I'll be there,' replied Jess, not wanting to say much more than that, or to prolong the discussion.

'Huh,' she said again. 'I'm sure Ant will love to have you there.'

'Why do you say that?' Jess honestly wasn't sure where the conversation was going or what Alicia was getting at.

Alicia leaned in. 'For his big moment.'

Jess waved a hand in the air. 'Oh, he doesn't need me there. The results of all his hard work will speak for themselves. You'll make a fine couple on the red carpet.'

Jess swallowed painfully after the last part, her tongue suddenly feeling like she'd inhaled a mouthful of dry ash.

Alicia eased back, her dark eyes squinting at Jess, which Jess supposed was Alicia's version of frowning.

'No, I don't mean his appearance. You know he's nominated for a Silver Logie in the category of Most Popular Presenter?'

'Oh, no, I didn't know that, sorry. But that's really exciting.'

Ant hadn't mentioned it, but then again things had been stilted between them ever since their kiss, and he'd been busy with Alicia.

'It is,' Alicia said with a single nod. 'Particularly if he wins.'

'Do you think he will?' Jess said, her voice holding a note of surprise. She rushed on. 'Not that I think he couldn't win it, just that I think it's pretty hard to win, don't you think? I'm sure he's up against some incredible talent.'

'I'd say Ant is incredibly talented, wouldn't you?' Alicia's voice dripped with meaning.

Jess was aware she was making a mess of this conversation and she really, really wanted to go home.

'Of course he's talented. That's not what I meant. I'm sure he'll do great.'

'Sometimes it just takes someone to believe in you, wouldn't you say?' Alicia asked. 'Like you did.'

Honestly, what was Alicia's game? Jess didn't care if she insulted the supermodel anymore and went to step around her. Alicia caught her by the shoulder.

'Didn't you?' Alicia pressed.

Good God, Jess suddenly felt like she was caught in some bad daytime television soap opera.

'Yes, I did. I believe most people are capable of exercise, including Ant.'

Alicia dropped her hand from Jess's shoulder. 'You were *very* encouraging.'

Jess stared at Alicia, the penny finally dropping. Far out. Alicia Travers was implying that Jess liked Ant. For a split second, Jess feared that Ant might have told her about their one-off kiss, but she dismissed the idea straight away. Ant would never do that. He was too much of a gentleman.

Given Jess had been extremely careful about keeping things professional between them, at least in the public eye, she felt a not-so-nice part of her rear up in response to Alicia's implication. A not-so-nice, *perverse* part of her.

Jess shrugged casually. 'What can I say? Ant's the kind of guy that inspires encouragement.'

You did not just say that! Don't be stupid. Don't go head to head with a supermodel, Jess!

Alicia smiled, but she didn't use her teeth. 'I know, right? And it's nice of you to have been so encouraging up until this point. Lucky he's got me now that things are finished with you two.'

Ugh. The hide of the woman. So what if Jess had no interest in dating Ant? That was beside the point. Just because the woman was a household name didn't mean she could tread all over the regular people like Jess.

'He'll need a lot of encouragement now he's training for the triathlon,' Jess said. 'Some *qualified* help.'

It was Alicia's turn to wave a hand in the air. 'All taken care of. I've got a team of people I'm lending Ant to help him train. My personal trainer, among others.'

Jess almost snorted. Alicia's personal trainer? The only thing Alicia's personal trainer struck Jess as being qualified to do was help her pose and pout for photos if her Instagram feed was anything to go by.

'Oh, so the triathlon was your idea, then?' Jess asked, being careful not to sound too curious.

'Goodness, no! That was all you, Jessica, dear. You really inspired Ant with your unique approach to exercise.' Alicia said the word "unique" like it was distasteful.

Jessica, dear?

The woman might have towered over her, but Jess was

almost one hundred percent certain she could take her down with a few swift moves right there in the hallway.

'But do keep up to date with his progress on social media,' Alicia added, like an afterthought. 'I'm sure Ant would like that.'

'Don't worry, I can ask him myself when we catch up to discuss my business plan,' Jess said, then snapped her mouth shut.

Whoops. Where had that come from? It had just popped out.

This time Alicia really did frown, and it wasn't pretty. It pushed her dark eyebrows down and flared her nostrils, making her look like a recalcitrant child.

'Business plan,' Alicia hissed. 'What's Ant got to do with your business plan?'

At that moment Ant appeared in the hallway, and because Alicia's back was to him Jess saw him first. She seized the moment without thinking.

'Oh, hi, Ant! Exciting news about the triathlon. Hey, you know how you offered to help me with my business plan? Is later this week good for you?'

Never mind it had been ages since they'd discussed it. Jess imagined crossing her fingers behind her back.

Ant slowed as Alicia turned to face him.

'Oh, yeah, that's right,' he said, nodding and looking past Alicia to Jess. 'Sure, I can make that work. Just message me and we'll sort out a time.'

Alicia rushed forward to meet him. 'That's so lovely of you, Ant, and so like you, but don't you think between training for the triathlon and preparing for the Logies, now isn't a good time?'

Jess resisted rolling her eyes.

Ant frowned. When he frowned, he looked much nicer than Alicia, Jess thought.

'No, it's fine. I owe Jess one. I'll make time.'

Alicia stepped in closer to him, putting an arm around his waist. She towered over Ant too, and Jess found herself wondering if Alicia would still wear heels to the Logies.

Alicia smiled. 'Motivating you to exercise isn't a favour for Jess. It's her job, and I'm sure she wouldn't want you to feel indebted. Jess will understand that you're too busy right now and that it might need to wait awhile.'

Ant's frown deepened and a flicker of annoyance flashed in his brown eyes. 'No. I said I'm good. And that wasn't what I was talking about. She did my mother and father a big favour, and I know they'd want me to support her any way I can.'

Alicia's eyes widened. Obviously the fact that Jess knew Ant's parents was news to her. She opened her mouth to say something else, but Ant was already talking to Jess.

'I should have time later this week,' he said.

'Perfect!' Jess said, too brightly. 'I'll be in touch. Now I've got to run. See you.'

Jess turned on her heel and set off quickly in the other direction towards the lifts. The relief at escaping Alicia's unwanted attention was swiftly replaced by a sinking feeling.

What on earth had just happened? Somehow in the space of one conversation, she'd managed to make an enemy out of Alicia and get Ant to help her with her business plan, which she wasn't even sure she wanted his help with anyway.

Jess needed that run along the beach more than ever.

Chapter Twenty-Nine

ON THURSDAY MORNING, Ant made his way over to Jess's apartment. It felt weird returning now that the training sessions were over. And now that he and Alicia were . . .

Whatever he and Alicia were.

Ant still hadn't figured it out. Or maybe he wasn't allowing himself to. On the surface, it certainly seemed like Alicia wanted to be in a relationship with Ant. But Ant had learned long ago not to trust women like Alicia. Not that she'd actually noticed. With her, things only ever appeared to be skin deep. It made it easy, if not somewhat lazy of him, to continue seeing her.

Ant stepped out of the lift and tried to shake off his messed-up thoughts. Jess had been right to friend-zone him. Ant couldn't give her what she wanted. She wanted normal—a husband, kids, and the happily ever after.

The thought of Jess and her happily ever after made his chest ache. He wasn't sure why. Probably because Jess would make such a good mum. He imagined a daughter with those blue eyes and golden hair of hers. The ache in his chest intensified, and for the briefest second, he wondered what it would be like to come home to Jess every day. To their kids.

Stop it, he told himself silently. All he was doing was torturing himself. He'd had a wife and look how that had worked out for him. And kids? Who was he kidding? That was why Alicia was a much better fit for him. The last thing on her mind was settling down.

'Hi, Ant.' Jessica beamed at him when she opened the door.

'Hey,' he said, trying to act natural, when in reality her smile hit him like a ton of bricks.

What was that about, Alicia?

She gestured for him to come inside and he followed her down the hall.

'How's your week been?' she asked.

'Oh, you know. Just the usual.'

She stopped halfway along the hall and turned to look at him. 'Are you alright?'

'What do you mean?'

She shrugged, then resumed walking. 'You don't seem your normal self. I would have expected a joke by now.'

'I'm saving them up for the Logies.'

'Ah, I see. Don't worry, I'm sure when you see my pathetic excuse of a business plan you'll find some more.'

'It can't be that bad. Compared to a lot of businesses, you're already considered a success.'

'I'm just lucky.'

Ant stopped at the entrance to her living area and gestured to the million-dollar view. 'So this is just luck, is it?'

Jess took a second to gauge his meaning. 'No, not entirely.' She sighed. 'You've gotta know, I really don't enjoy working on this side of my business. The planning part kills me. I'd rather be out there helping people or coming up with new workouts.'

'Well, maybe that's part of your business plan—to get people you can delegate the stuff you hate to.'

Jess's lips quirked. 'Did I mention I'm also a control freak?'

'You? I had no idea.'

Jess laughed, and the sound punched Ant in the gut. He'd missed that sound. Not laughter in general. *Her* laughter.

He accepted Jess's invitation to sit at her table in front of her laptop, glad for something else to focus his attention on.

They were quiet while he spent the next twenty minutes reading through her draft business plan. It was good. Really good. Sure, it had a few holes here and there, but she wasn't wrong about being a control freak. She'd thought about all the aspects that were integral to her business moving forward. The next step would be to talk to her accountant and suppliers to cost out the next phase, which might freak her out. But Ant was confident he could convince her it was a worthwhile risk.

'So?' Jess asked, when he was finished.

He couldn't help himself and grinned at her hopeful expression. 'I'm not marking you on it, you know.'

'But if you were?'

He laughed, and that was another punch to the gut as he realised something he'd managed to avoid up until now.

Jess made *him* laugh.

There weren't many people that could. His mum had his measure, and he looked forward to their banter when he spent time at his family home. He always had a laugh with his mates, but that was never often enough these days as they were all busy with work and relationships.

There hadn't been much laughter with Enid. And Alicia?

Ant pushed the thought aside. He was getting surprisingly good at pushing his thoughts aside when it came to Alicia.

'Ant?' Jess asked, still waiting for his response.

Ant put on his best schoolteacher expression. 'It's an

admirable effort, young Jessica,' he told her in a stuffy British accent. 'Plenty of detail and some great ideas, but sadly there's one thing it's lacking.'

Jess wasn't looking hopeful anymore, but worried, and Ant felt a bit cruel. Still, it was necessary for an effective punchline.

'Yes?' she said.

'Kale,' he said seriously.

Ant couldn't help it. He enjoyed the changing emotions that flickered across her face like another man might savour a fine red wine. First there was surprise. Then realisation, followed by an exquisite eye roll. Then came the laughter, so much like a song to Ant's ears that he wished he could record it.

'You. Are. Hopeless,' she said in between breaths while recovering from her laughter.

'No, I'm quite serious,' he said, still talking in the British accent. 'Look.' He pointed at the page where she'd outlined possible ideas around merchandising. 'T-shirts with kale on them is an obvious option that you're missing. Or aprons with an image of kale and the words, *Everything tastes worse with kale.*'

Jess fell into the seat beside him, giggling, and leaned across the table to look at the screen. 'Ooh, I know. I could create a range of smoothie cups! *Rise and kale* could be one.'

Ant nodded approvingly. 'Not bad. Or how about a yoga mat people can do your Hi-Jinks stretches on that says, *Inhale and exkale?*'

Jess shoved his shoulder playfully. 'I love it! You know what? I need to give these more thought, and then can I ask you another huge favour?'

Ant sighed like her request was a burden too heavy to endure, while another part of him rejoiced at the excuse that they'd have a reason to stay in contact.

She twisted to face him in her chair, her knees brushing

his leg.

'I want you to write some taglines for the merchandise I decide on. I want them to be funny and life affirming. The sort of thing that, when people see them, they smile. Just because I take exercise seriously, doesn't mean we can't laugh about it. I want my line of clothing and merchandise to be playful.'

I think I love you.

Ant stood up abruptly and Jess flinched, sitting back in her chair to look up at him.

'But if you're too busy I totally understand,' she rushed on. 'I know things have been hectic for you lately, and you have the triathlon to train for.'

Ant couldn't help himself and snorted. He was still in shock at the unprompted *I love you* thought that he neglected to use his filter. 'The triathlon? Yeah, well I might actually want to sign up for it first before I start training for it.'

Jess stood up to face him. 'What?'

'You heard me. Everyone keeps asking me which triathlon I'm training for, but I haven't told them yet because I still haven't signed up.'

'Oh, thank God!' Jess breathed, then threw herself into his arms.

Ant caught her with a soft "oof", then stiffened as an involuntary zing ricocheted through his system. Holding Jess was like trying to hold on to sunshine. It burned, but it was the best sort of warmth, and it felt like he was glowing from head to toe.

She didn't seem to notice his reaction and gave him a tight hug.

'I'm so relieved,' she told him, her voice muffled by his shoulder. Then she eased back and looked at him. 'I wanted to talk to you about it, but wasn't sure how to bring it up.'

It pained him to do so, but Ant slipped out of her embrace

and stepped back, his body still throbbing with heat. 'Let me guess,' he said dryly. 'You want to train me?'

'Alicia already told me she's got her people on the job for you,' Jess blurted. 'But, ah, of course, if you ever need help, I'm always willing to offer a hand.'

Ant held back a grin. She wasn't a very good actress. Something told him that if he did actually go ahead with this crazy triathlon idea, she'd be dying to help him.

'I wouldn't expect anything less. But that's even if I do one.' He sat back down with a sigh, and Jess did the same. The mention of Alicia and the triathlon seemed to have sapped all the earlier warmth from his body.

'Please don't take this the wrong way,' she said, 'but I was really worried about you doing the triathlon for the wrong reasons. Not that I don't think you're capable of it, of course,' she added quickly. 'It's only that it involves so much time and dedication. You really have to be wholeheartedly committed from the beginning. Ask my brother, Nick. Actually, I can give you his number if you like. I'm sure he'd be willing to chat to you about it.'

This time Ant did smile. He couldn't help it. Everything about Jess's reaction was exactly as he'd expected—and the total opposite of Alicia's.

'What would you class as the "wrong reasons"?' he asked, interested to hear her perspective.

'Um.' She bit her lip. 'You could be doing it for the attention, perhaps?'

He put a hand to his mouth, pretending to be shocked, but it was hiding a grin. 'And when have I ever done something for attention? What sort of person do you think I am?'

Her hand shot out and she rested her fingers on his arm. There was that vibrant heat again. It pulsed through him, making his skin tingle.

'I'm not saying it's not a good reason,' she said, still completely unaware of her effect on him. 'But it may not be one that will sustain you for the duration of the training or for the event itself. Those things take grit.'

He harrumphed. 'And I don't have grit?'

'I didn't say that!' she cried, removing her hand so that he instantly regretted the joke. 'See? This was why I was so scared to bring it up with you. I didn't want to offend you. Honestly, I think after all the progress you've made these last few months, you don't have to prove anything to anyone. Not to the public. Or to yourself. I wanted you to know that.'

Her blue eyes were so clear and earnest it took everything Ant had not to reach over and brush a thumb across her cheek. Perfect. She was just so perfect.

'You're quite the coach, you know that?' he said softly. 'I never did thank you for helping me get fit. So thanks. And for once I'm being serious.'

She shrugged, and the movement struck Ant as shy. 'You're welcome. I try to be supportive.'

'Just so you know, I said I'd do the triathlon for Alicia,' he muttered.

'I did wonder. She suggested it was my idea, though. Just so you know,' she added with a wry grin.

'Oh, did she? Figures. It's not like she made me do it. She just implied in no uncertain terms that it was the obvious next step in my career advancement and to the benefit of our relationship.'

'Oh, for God's sake!' Jess snapped her mouth shut. 'Sorry,' she murmured.

'Quite alright. It seems while I've developed backbone when it comes to exercise, when it comes to women, not so much.'

'Um, can I say something? As your friend?'

God, how Ant hated that f-word. If she weren't so attached to it, he probably wouldn't be in this stupid situation. But she'd made her feelings clear and he needed to respect them.

'Sure you can,' Ant said easily, like he wasn't waging an internal war with himself.

'From what you've already told me, it seems like you're letting your girlfriend boss you around again. You know, like Enid did.'

'That has occurred to me, yes. But in my defence, it's like a disease with me. It really needs a name, like Where Did My Balls Go Disorder.'

Jess cleared her throat like she was trying not to laugh.

'It's a real affliction, I'm telling you,' he went on. 'Painful both physically and mentally. And by the time you realise what's happened and decide to do something about it, they don't just grow back overnight. You need to grow a new pair. It can take months.'

Jess shook her head and laughed properly. 'Has it ever occurred to you that you might be going out with the wrong type of women?' Her eyes went wide and she rushed on. 'Not that I'm implying Alicia is wrong necessarily. It's completely up to you who you go out with.'

'I have a weakness for the popular girls, I'm afraid. I'm sure that's another disorder that needs naming. It all started in my senior year of high school.'

'Did you fall for the popular girl?' Jess asked sympathetically.

'The entire male school population fell for her. Her name was Angie and she truly did look like an angel.' He knew his eyes had probably gone a bit dreamy, but it was inevitable when he brought the memory of her to mind. 'I just never believed she'd want to go out with me.'

'Honestly, Ant, I don't know why you're so down on yourself,' Jess began.

He held up a hand. 'You haven't seen photos from back then.' He pointed to his hair. 'See these beautiful raven locks of mine? Yes, well, they were a lot longer and a lot wilder in those days. It wasn't a good look. More afro-meets-bird's-nest.'

'I'd love to have seen it.'

'I've burned the photos. Anyway, she invited me to be her partner for the school formal and I thought I'd finally made it. I'd suffered years of being teased at school for being the oddball, which I then capitalised on, of course. By senior year, I wasn't cool exactly, but I did have a dedicated fandom thanks to my commitment to being the class clown.'

'I can imagine.'

'If I'd had a soundtrack that year it would have been *Stayin' Alive*, which proves I was out of touch even back then. It was the middle of the grunge era and I still thought disco was cool. Anyway, she shattered my dreams that night when the awards were announced.'

'Oh, no. How?'

It touched Ant that Jess seemed so distressed by his years-old story. Ant hadn't so much forgiven and forgotten, but he had buried it, so when he talked about it now it was as if it had happened to somebody else.

'Angie was named "Most Likely To Succeed", of course,' Ant told her. 'When you look like that how could you not, right?'

Jess didn't appear convinced, but he continued anyway.

'And then they announced my award,' he said with a grimace. 'I won "Most Likely To Be Dumped By The End Of The Night". At first I took it in my stride as I was used to being the subject of the joke. Until I realised those who had organised the awards—the popular kids, of course—knew something I didn't.'

'Oh, no!' Jess cried.

'Oh, yes. My darling Angie had been cheating on me for weeks with one of the year's most accomplished athletes. Turns out funny doesn't beat brawn after all.'

'That's just so mean. You must have been devastated. Not to mention embarrassed.'

'Good training for a life as a comedian, in all honesty. Stand-up comedy can be brutal. Anyway, you'd think I would have had more sense by the time Enid came along. But no. Where Did My Balls Go is a recurring illness, I'm afraid.'

'Hang on. I didn't think Enid was a popular girl. She sounded kind of . . . scary,' Jess said. 'Maybe this affliction isn't as bad you think?'

Jess's sense of hopefulness was actually quite endearing, but unfounded. Ant didn't reply and instead reached for his phone that he'd left lying on the dining table. He brought up the photos app and scrolled through until he found what he was looking for, then handed the phone to Jess.

'That's Enid,' he told her.

Jess's jaw dropped. 'Oh, my . . . she's . . . she's stunning. But I thought . . .'

'You thought because I implied that she might be a lesbian that she wasn't feminine? Tsk tsk. Let's just say if she ever decides to go down that path, she'll be the one with all the looks in the relationship.'

Jess handed him back the phone.

'See, my problem is I get so star-struck when these women show me attention in the first place, that I end up doing virtu-ally anything they say.'

Jess's thoughtful pout turned into a wicked grin. 'Anything?'

He pointed at her. 'Do. Not. Go. There. I'm not proud of my weakness. And on that note, let's get back to your business plan. If I overshare anymore, you'll be tempted to contact the media and sell all my secrets for a nice sum of money. So, where were we? That's right. Kale. I never thought I'd say this, but it's a much better subject.'

Jess sighed. 'I'd never share your personal life with anyone. And if you don't want to do the triathlon, just tell Alicia that. I'm sure she'd understand.'

Ant coughed. 'I think she's the sort of woman who's accustomed to getting what she wants all the time.'

'Oh, well. Maybe it will be character building for her,' Jess suggested, and Ant didn't miss the playful glint in her eyes.

'You don't like her, do you?' Ant was genuinely interested in Jess's opinion.

Sure, Alicia could be temperamental at times, but maybe the reason she was used to getting what she wanted was because she was so driven. Drive was a good quality, wasn't it? And she was easy on the eyes. There was that.

Jess held up her hands, palms facing forward. 'I am not going there, alright? Who you choose to get involved with is your business. Friends don't judge other friends. But just promise me you won't sign up for that triathlon because you feel pressured to. Do it because *you* want to.'

Ant nodded and shifted his attention back to Jess's computer screen, pretending to look over it again. That was just the thing. Ant wasn't sure what he wanted.

OK, that wasn't entirely true.

He still wanted Jess. He was pretty sure that urge was never going to go away. And if his stupid heart was to be believed, he more than wanted her. He was damn well falling in love with her.

But as life—and women like Angie—had taught him, you didn't always get what you wanted. And if a supermodel currently wanted him instead of Jess, who was he to argue?

Chapter Thirty

TO SAY Jess felt out of her depth stepping onto the Logies red carpet the following weekend would be an understatement. The surreal fish-out-of-water experience began the moment her sparkling, strappy gold heels set foot on the ground outside the limo.

There were celebrities in every direction. Some extremely well-known and many lesser-known, but all of them soaking up the attention from the media as naturally as peacocks presenting their feathers.

Except for Jess. Jess felt nothing like a peacock. She felt more like an oversized Christmas bauble. Everywhere she turned her fitted, ankle-length golden dress seemed to catch the light and shimmer. The damn dress was practically alive. When the camera flashes went off, she worried that all the images would show was a blinding reflection. Possibly not a bad thing as she wasn't sure about all the attention anyway.

Jess also felt self-consciously alone. So many of the attendees had come with partners. Kat was here with her fiancé, Matt. Ant was with Alicia. It was like she was a boat without a paddle and she disliked the feeling. But she didn't need a man, right? She was a self-made success story and could stand on her own two feet. In fact, the general chatter on social media and other media channels was that Jess had "made it".

Funny. Jess had thought she'd made it when her business started turning a profit eighteen months ago, but celebrity was big currency these days.

So Jess stood tall on the red carpet, smiling until her cheeks hurt and her lips started to quiver. Eventually, it was with a sense of relief that Jess made her way inside the grand ballroom to take her seat at the designated table, her heels pinching her toes painfully. If she could survive the burn of exercise, she could survive the discomfort of high fashion.

Jess's smile wavered as she saw her other table guests approaching.

A night of Alicia? Now this might be harder to come out of alive.

Kat reached Jess first. 'You look amazing. And you're handling this like an old hand, trust me.'

'You know what they say,' Jess said. 'Fake it until you make it.'

Kat caught Jess's wrist. 'You are not faking it. You're the real deal and everyone knows it.'

Jess saw Kat's gaze drawn to Alicia and quickly looked away, focusing instead on Matt.

'Matt! Looking good as always. You and I can be first-time Logies attendees together,' Jess told him.

He smiled warmly, and Jess found herself returning the smile. It was impossible not to like Matt. Jess wasn't sure if it was because he was an obstetrician—the thought of dealing with women giving birth was enough to make Jess shudder—but Matt was always unflappable.

Matt leaned in to give a kiss on the cheek, being careful to avoid smudging Jess's carefully made-up face.

'Do we receive an award or something once we're done?' he suggested.

'Just wine. Lots of wine,' Kat told him.

'I wish I drank alcohol,' said Jess. 'I could use something to take the edge off.'

Matt looked vaguely alarmed. 'I forgot you didn't drink. You definitely deserve an award after this then.'

Jess smiled. 'I'm tough. I'm pretty sure I can do this.'

'You already have,' Kat said firmly. 'The red carpet is out of the way and that's the hardest part.'

'Thank God,' Jess breathed and sank happily into her waiting chair.

The rest of the night would be all about the entertainment and the presenters at the front of the grand ballroom announcing the winners of the various awards. Provided Jess remembered to appear happy at all times for the roving cameras, there wasn't really much else that could go wrong.

'Hello, Jessica.'

Jess looked up. A long way up.

OK, there was that. Alicia. A statuesque freaking goddess. If Jess looked amazing, Alicia looked . . . other-worldly. Really, how was it possible for one woman to exude that much beauty? Like Jess, Alicia's gown shimmered, but that was where the similarities ended. Alicia's dress was gunmetal grey, but calling it that didn't do the colour justice. It moved with her body like a second skin, the grey deepening to shades of blue in the right light. And every light was the right light, of course. The low V neckline showed off her ample cleavage, but in a sophisticated, elegant way. Jess hadn't seen the back of the dress, but she already knew Alicia's back would be on display. And why not? When you looked like that, everyone would be staring at you.

Jess rose from her chair and attempted to smile. It almost appeared genuine after her earlier stint on the red carpet.

'Hi, Alicia. You look fantastic.'

'Alex Perry. How could I not? And you're wearing?'

Jess named the designer she'd never heard of before this week, but whom Kat had assured her was a big deal. Thanks to Kat, Jess was apparently on trend.

One of Alicia's dark eyebrows arched in response. 'Lucky girl. I suppose it does suit you, if you like that sort of look.'

Jess opened her mouth, but nothing came out. After all, when you didn't have anything nice to say it, was better to say nothing at all.

'You look stunning, Jess,' Ant's deep voice announced as he stepped out from behind Alicia.

Jess hadn't noticed him standing there until now. But Alicia was so tall he must have been there the whole time. Jess noted Alicia had indeed worn heels tonight, sky-high ones.

'Thanks,' Jess replied, glad for the interruption.

It was only then she took in his appearance properly.

Oh, my.

'You look amazing,' Jess blurted, then caught herself. 'I mean, I'm used to seeing you in a suit on *Sydney Tonight*, but this is next level. Very dapper.'

Dapper was the polite way of putting it. Ant was like a character from a nineteen twenties movie. He wore a black jacket with tails, a bow tie, and a crisp white shirt with his dark hair slicked back to complete the look. It was the first time Jess had seen his wayward locks tamed. It served to highlight his distinctive facial features and his olive skin with the expression lines Jess had become familiar with. She'd never call them wrinkles or worry lines because they were the result of laughter. And perhaps it was the suit, but Ant's brown eyes appeared darker than usual. Almost dangerous.

The edge of Ant's lip quirked. 'Dapper? I was going more for gangster.'

Kat cleared her throat beside Jess. 'The only thing dangerous about you is your punchlines.'

'Ah, but my punchlines can be very sinister when the occasion calls for it.'

Alicia's nostrils flared.

What was her problem? It was just small talk.

The model shot Ant a meaningful look and they both sat down at the table. Jess resisted frowning. It was like watching a well-trained animal and it made her feel slightly sick to watch it.

Kat caught Jess's eye and they all sat down, too. Fortunately, Jess was seated beside Kat on one side and Ant on the other. Being seated next to Alicia wouldn't just have been painful, it would have been hard work.

Alicia immediately engaged Ant in discussion, so Jess chatted comfortably with Kat and Matt until the awards ceremony began. Even so, she couldn't help but notice the way Alicia dominated Ant's attention. Any time he attempted to comment to Jess, presumably to draw her into the conversation, Alicia would quickly find a way to demand his focus. On Alicia's other side was the producer of *Sydney Tonight*, and she seemed to have no issue involving him in whatever they were talking about.

Kat brushed Jess's arm. 'Forget about it.'

'It's just so . . .'

'Obvious?' whispered Kat. 'Yes, I know. It's just jealousy. Don't worry about it.'

'Of me?' Jess squeaked.

Her high-pitched reply caught Ant and Alicia's attention, and Kat smiled.

'Just an exercise joke,' she said casually, and brushed Jess's arm again. 'Jess is such a good sport about my continued resistance to exercising.'

Alicia smiled, except it wasn't really a smile. More like a curled top lip.

'Yes, well, Jessica is right to persist. You're skinny, but you could tone up. Many of my model friends are the same.'

Kat's fingers dug into Jess's arm. 'And Hi-Jinks is the best way to go about it.'

'Oh, I wouldn't say that,' Alicia replied. 'There's plenty of other, more *proven* methods, just ask my personal trainer.'

'Well, Jess is *my* personal trainer,' Kat said, giving Jess a meaningful look. 'There's a reason her exercise regimen is taking the country by storm.'

'Fads never really appealed to me,' Alicia said, plucking at her dinner roll with her painted nails. So far, Jess hadn't actually seen her eat it, only play with it.

'Each to their own,' Jess said brightly. Knowing that Kat wouldn't back down, she quickly changed the subject. 'I mean, look at Ant. He's into triathlons now.'

Alicia's demeanour instantly shifted to one of pride. 'Oh, I know. He's so inspiring to watch.'

'You watch him train?' Kat asked dryly.

'Hey,' Ant cut in, '*I* watch myself train now, I look so good.'

And with that everyone laughed, and the mood at the table lifted. Ant winked at Jess and she gave him a grateful look. It reminded her of his perfect timing when he'd come to dinner at her parents' house.

The lights dimmed and music filled the big space, the low bass notes of a musical introduction penetrating Jess's chest.

'Oh, they're starting,' Jess exclaimed. 'How exciting!'

Alicia gave Jess a derisive look and turned away to view what was happening at the front of the room.

Kat grinned. *Jealous*, she mouthed.

Jess shook her head. She still couldn't believe it herself, so she put the strange thought aside and concentrated on the presentation.

Chapter Thirty-One

EVER SINCE HE'D sat down at the dinner table, Ant had felt awkward.

Ant hated feeling awkward.

It was a feeling he remembered only too well from his school days, and one that he went to extremes to avoid now that he was an adult. Usually the feeling was alleviated with a good joke. Or several of them.

Not tonight. Tonight Ant knew that no amount of joking on his part would prevent him from appreciating the painful truth of his predicament.

To his left sat the country's most beautiful woman, his date for the evening.

And to his right sat Ant's perfect woman.

Yep, he was royally screwed, and not in the way he wanted.

Why oh why couldn't he be happy with Australia's top model? A fierce beauty who wanted him to succeed as much as he did.

Because the woman on his right thought he had absolutely nothing to prove. Because the woman on his right laughed with him and made him laugh. Jess had a different beauty. It shone from the inside out, like the sun breaking through the clouds. Her beauty was natural and innate, not carefully curated like Alicia's.

Only Jess had made it clear that she wanted more than he could give her, so now here he was pretending to be captivated by a supermodel who in reality bored him to tears.

Ant hadn't expected Alicia to be so boring. Initially he had been attracted to her because the old cliché of the dumb model wasn't one that applied to her. Alicia was smart as a whip, had serious ambition, and was impressive in front of an audience. Only she didn't seem to have a sense of humour. Or not one that Ant had discovered yet.

And to Ant's mind that made her the dullest person in the room.

Ant reached for his wine glass. It had already been a long night and the awards ceremony wasn't even half over. He couldn't wait for it to finish. He should have been excited about the Most Popular Presenter award that was yet to be announced, but he couldn't sincerely believe that a comedic sidekick on an evening news show would take the prize.

A few weeks ago Ant also would have been thrilled at the prospect of ending the night in Alicia's arms. But like the rest of her, Alicia was astoundingly uninteresting in the bedroom. It was as if she expected to be admired in the bedroom as well as outside of it. That made things very one-sided. Namely, she lay there, and Ant did all the work. Three months ago Ant would have worried that he was the problem. But now he was in the best shape of his life, so it didn't make sense. Was it asking too much for him to expect a bit of ardour from her?

He was so deep in thought it probably explained what happened next.

The first time Ant heard his name, he barely heard it. He

was still trying to figure out why Alicia was so unenthusiastic. It was almost as if she didn't enjoy sex. Was that even possible? Ant had heard about women that had no sex drive, but surely Alicia wasn't one of them. She was Alicia Travers, for God's sake. One of the sexiest women alive.

The second time Ant heard his name, he became aware of it only because of the thundering applause.

'Oh, my God, Ant! You won! You *won!*' Jess jumped up beside him, clapping wildly.

Ant blinked and looked up at her. 'Huh?'

Her smile was so bright it hurt his heart. 'You won, silly! You won the Silver Logie!'

From his other side, Alicia's arm snaked around his and she hissed, 'Stand up. Now.'

Ant shot up from his seat in shock, slipping out of her grip.

Holy fucking crap. He'd just won the award for Most Popular Presenter! No way.

He stared at the others standing around the table, clapping loudly for him, their smiles as wide as Jess's.

It started to sink in. 'Oh, wow. Oh . . . *fuck.*' He ran a hand through his hair, forgetting it was slicked back with whatever awful substance Alicia's hair stylist had insisted on using, and ended up with an oily hand.

Alicia caught his arm and lowered it. She was smiling like the others, although if you looked closely it didn't reach her eyes.

'You need to go and accept your award now,' she said in a low voice.

Ant breathed out. So this was real. It was really happening. An oddball comedian who had taken a job on a nightly news program to add what the producers had called "a human element" had just been voted by Australians as their favourite presenter.

Ant threw his head back and laughed. He laughed long and deep, until it reached his belly, and boy did it feel amazing.

Alicia tugged on his sleeve like an annoying child and said through clenched teeth, 'Antony, what are you doing? Go and accept your award.'

He felt his temper flare, dampening some of his unbridled joy.

'That's Adonis to you,' he told her, his voice laced with sarcasm.

He heard Jess laugh on his other side, not at him but with him. He glanced over at her.

Her eyes were lit with joy and she was still clapping.

Jess leaned closer, still beaming. 'Congratulations, Adonis!'

Ant still wasn't thinking straight and made the mistake of thinking she was leaning in to give him a congratulatory kiss, so he leaned in, too.

Jess's eyes went wide in surprise and she tried to step back.

It was too late. Ant overbalanced and grabbed for her so that he wouldn't stumble. And now it wasn't Jess's cheek in front of him anymore.

Her lips were.

They kissed. On the lips. For the whole world to see.

Ant had just kissed Jess instead of Alicia.

Jess sprang back, her eyes so wide it was like looking at the sky on a cloudless day.

Kat stepped in behind Jess's shoulder. 'I suggest you kiss Alicia now.'

Ant swung around desperately and caught Alicia by the waist, ignoring the way her dark eyes flared with anger. He dipped her backwards, like they were performing a tango move, and kissed her long and hard and with a substantial amount of tongue.

Alicia finally managed to extract herself. 'The presenters are waiting.'

Ant nodded, avoiding her gaze because her tone of voice made his balls shrink in fear. He plastered a wide smile on his face and made a show of walking to the front of the ballroom to accept his award, waving at the audience as though they were loyal subjects.

When he arrived on stage, he gratefully accepted the award.

'Well, that's possibly the best reaction to winning a Logie I've seen to date,' Sonia, the well-known lifestyle presenter announced. 'I can't wait to hear your thank you speech.'

A ripple of laughter filtered through the audience.

Right. Speech time.

While Ant never in a million years expected to win the award, he had prepared a speech because, well, jokes.

He recalled the speech from memory. Gushing in all the right parts and making everyone laugh at every available opportunity. He thanked the show's producers for giving a comedian a shot. He thanked Kat for putting up with him. His parents for raising him. He joked about how he'd known he'd officially made it when Alicia started dating him. How he was still in denial that someone as amazing as her was with him.

When Alicia met Ant's eyes across the ballroom, most of the fury was gone and she nodded approvingly. It was almost like her body language was saying, "Good boy."

The realisation stung, and instead of saying one final thank you and getting his backside offstage like he should have, he ad-libbed.

'And, ah, you're all probably wondering why I kissed Jessica Jinks.'

The buzz of the audience faded immediately and you could hear a pin drop.

'I just got a bit overexcited for second and turned right when I should have turned left. I hope you'll forgive me. And Alicia, you're still talking to me, right?'

The audience laughed, and Alicia waved her hand as if to say it was all water under the bridge. After all, she was a super-model. She didn't have to compete.

'But before I go, I also want to thank Jess. She trained me and toned me for three months straight, laughing at my jokes. All because she believes in the idea that anyone can get fit. Even me. Hell, look at me.' He waved a hand in front of himself with his free hand. 'I'm in the best shape of my life and I intend to stay this way.'

A few audience members whistled and called out.

'I know, right? I still can't believe it when I look in the mirror either. I'm a new man.' He leaned into the microphone and in a Darth Vader voice added, 'Soon you will know me as *Triathlon Man*.'

Waiting a beat for the expected laughter, he went on. 'I'm also Alicia's man, obviously. Just so we're clear.'

More laughter. Ant bowed once, twice, to the resounding applause, and then gratefully let the presenters sweep him offstage before he could say anything else incriminating.

Chapter Thirty-Two

JESS WONDERED if it was possible to die of embarrassment. While Ant had taken responsibility for the kiss, she felt as if a big part of it was her fault, too. She'd just been so excited about him winning the award. So ecstatic. It had seemed entirely natural for her to lean in and give him a congratulatory peck on the cheek.

Except Ant hadn't even had a chance to kiss his girlfriend yet, and she was muscling her way in and trying to kiss him.

And when she'd realised what she'd been about to do, she'd tried to shift back.

Big mistake.

One lip-smacking, massive mistake.

'Are you sure you wouldn't like a drink?' Matt said softly from beside her.

Jess sighed. All she'd wanted to do after the awards ceremony finished was to go straight to her hotel room, but Kat had insisted she come along to the after-party. Jess knew that it made sense. Act like nothing unusual had happened and everything would be all right.

But it wasn't all right. Because Jess had *wanted* to kiss Ant. She'd wanted to be the one to congratulate him first. To be the one that he turned to when something went right or wrong. But she wasn't. Jess had missed her chance, and now it was Alicia's job. Ant had made that fact perfectly clear up on stage when he'd accepted his award, and it stung more than a little bit. Not that Jess could really blame him for his words. Jess had been quite clear all along that she only wanted to be friends with Ant, and he'd only been attempting to smooth over a very awkward situation.

'Stop trying to make her drink alcohol, you're a doctor,' Kat said.

'I don't have any other pain relief with me,' Matt replied.

'Pain relief?' Jess asked. 'What are you talking about?'

'Um, perhaps you haven't seen your face?' Kat asked. 'I feel like having another drink on your behalf.'

'Oh, I'm sorry. I should probably just go—'

'No,' Kat said firmly. 'Not yet. Wait until a few others start to leave, and then it won't look like you're trying to escape.'

'Well, I want to,' Jess said morosely.

'I think you're overreacting,' Kat said. 'Ant's the one who is going to have to live down the gaffe, not you.'

Matt nudged her. 'I don't think that's why Jess is so upset.'

Kat frowned. 'Then why . . . *oh*. Shit. Why didn't you tell me you still had feelings for him?'

'Still?' squeaked Jess. Jess had never, ever, told Kat about anything that had happened between her and Ant, especially given she was Ant's co-host.

Kat levelled her with a serious look. 'Oh, come on. Like it wasn't half obvious. Only I thought you'd put that all to bed when Ant started seeing Alicia.'

Jess didn't have the heart to protest and instead lifted her shoulder in a half-hearted shrug.

'You know, I convinced myself that my next-door neighbour *wasn't* the hottest man to walk the earth for a full month before I kissed him,' Kat told her. 'It's called denial, Jess.'

Matt smiled. 'Trust Kat. She's exceptionally good at denial.'

It was Kat's turn to nudge Matt. 'Yes, I am. Which is why I know this isn't you worrying about your reputation.'

'We kissed,' Jess blurted, then looked around desperately for a waiter. Even if it was only water, she needed a drink to help swallow these stupid thoughts instead of saying them.

'Well, yeah,' Kat said dryly. 'I think the whole world got that, thanks to the television coverage.'

'No,' Jess whispered. 'Before tonight.'

Kat's eyes rounded, but only for a second. Then they narrowed, and she simultaneously shuffled Jess into a dark corner of the room while shooing Matt away with her other hand.

'I'll, ah, be back in a minute,' Matt said, and took his leave.

Kat looked around them, and satisfied that there was no one nearby to hear them, said in a low voice, 'Why didn't you tell me?'

'Um, because you're Ant's co-host?'

Kat's dark eyes flickered with hurt. 'But I'm your friend first and foremost.'

Jess sighed, feeling horrible. 'I know, and I'm sorry. I'm just so sorry about this entire mess. I've ruined Ant's big moment. And I'm pretty sure Alicia already hated me, but now she's bound to detest me even more.'

Kat sighed too, her gaze softening. 'Jess. Trust me. No one could hate you. She's just jealous.'

'How? Why?' Jess cried then, at Kat's alarmed expression, lowered her voice. 'She's *Alicia Travers*.'

Kat smiled, and it was kind. 'And you're Jessica Jinks. Haven't you figured that out by now?'

'I don't look like her,' Jess protested.

'No, you don't. You don't need to. Because you're *Jessica Jinks*. Anyway, we need to back up a sec. When did you kiss Ant? Does Alicia know?'

'Well, not unless Ant has told her.' Jess's blinked. 'Oh my God, you don't think I kissed Ant while he was going out with Alicia, do you? I'd never do that!'

Kat's smile was still kind, and she squeezed Jess's arm lightly. 'I didn't think so. Was it just a kiss? Nothing else?'

'Just a kiss.' Then she paused. 'It was a very nice kiss.'

Kat grinned and raised an eyebrow.

Jess huffed. 'Alright. It was the *best* sort of kiss. Happy?'

'If that's the case, then why was it only a kiss?'

Jess rested her back against the wall in defeat. 'Because I friend-zoned him.'

'What? Why?'

'Because Ant and I aren't well-suited. Everybody can see that.'

'OK,' Kat said slowly. 'Break that down for me, will you?'

Jess huffed again and straightened. 'Because Ant's divorced and has no plans to marry again, and I do. One day. With the right guy.'

'OK,' Kat said again.

'What?' Jess demanded.

'Now is probably a good time to point out that I had no plans to marry either,' Kat told Jess, her eyes twinkling. She raised her left hand and the large diamond solitaire twinkled at Jess, too.

Jess crossed her arms. 'Your point being?'

Kat laughed. 'When it's the right person, you write your own rules.'

Jess collapsed against the wall again, suddenly feeling teary. 'I thought I was doing the right thing. I thought it wasn't fair to lead him on and to have a relationship with him if we wanted different things. I also thought it wasn't very professional of us to get involved with each other. I thought . . . oh, *fuck*. I don't know what I thought.'

Kat rubbed Jess's shoulder. 'That's the problem with love. Thought doesn't really get a look in. It's all about the feelings.'

Jess sprang off the wall like she'd experienced an electric shock. 'I don't *love* him!'

Kat tilted her head thoughtfully in response.

'No, I don't,' Jess repeated. 'I mean, he's gorgeous and funny, and we laugh so much when we're together. And his parents are the best, and my folks even like him too, which I'm really surprised at. I thought they'd write him off as a shallow celebrity, but they keep mentioning him all the time, even now that I've finished training him. Sure, I might miss him a bit now that we don't get to see each other regularly.' Jess paused. Reconsidered. 'So I might miss him a lot. But he's a good friend. That's natural, right?

'And he was really helpful with my business plan,' she went on. 'He's even happy to help me with some taglines, which is really nice of him.'

'Like you helped out with his dad?'

Jess waved a hand at her. 'Oh, that was nothing, really. I was happy to help.'

'So you think he's gorgeous, do you?'

Jess stopped at the change of subject and stared at her friend. 'Yes. So? I think Chris Hemsworth is gorgeous, too. It doesn't mean I'm going to marry him.'

'When did you realise you found him gorgeous?'

Jess narrowed her eyes at her friend. She knew that tone of voice. That questioning tone of voice.

'Who? Chris or Ant?' Jess replied lightly.

Kat rolled her eyes. 'Ant.'

Jess shrugged. 'Oh, I don't know. It's not like I ever thought to myself one day, "Hey, you know, Ant's really gorgeous, isn't he?" He just is. Like Chris Hemsworth.'

'So from the beginning, would you say?'

'Sure,' Jess said. 'I guess.'

'*Before* his transformation?'

Jess threw her hands up in the air. 'Honestly! I don't know why everyone keeps calling it that. He was just as lovely before all the training as he is now. It's not like he suddenly became hot by losing a few kilos and developing some muscle tone.'

'But Alicia didn't notice him until he did.'

'Well, Alicia's a . . . *you know*. I don't have anything nice to say, so I'm not going to say it. If Alicia hasn't figure out what a great person Ant is inside and out, then she's . . . not a nice person. It's not all about his exterior.'

'Not a nice person?' Kat appeared to be holding back a smile. 'In what way? You don't think she's looked past his appearance?'

'Well, obviously she must know that he's funny. She'd be a . . . not a nice person not to know that. But Ant's super intelligent. He hides it well, but he is. You don't have a quick wit like his without being smart. He's driven, too. Again, not that he makes a big deal out of that either. He's also sensitive. He pretends he isn't, but he is. Really, I don't think Alicia knows Ant at all if we're being honest.'

'And you do?'

'Well, yeah, we're friends.'

Both of Kat's eyebrows lifted slowly. 'I'm curious. How did you say that kiss felt again?'

Jess scowled. 'It's pointless to keep bringing it up.'

'Except it was the *best* sort of kiss. Funny. If you were just friends, I would have thought kissing Ant would feel like kissing your brother.'

Jess shuddered involuntarily. 'Oh, God no. It was nothing like that. It was really hot. Very sexy, actually. But completely comfortable, too. Like we'd known each other forever, you know? I think that's why it took me by surprise. I was so surprised I got carried away for a moment before I managed to stop myself.'

'Yes. I do know. Because that's how it feels when I'm with Matt.'

Jess released a whimper.

'And I love Matt,' Kat finished.

Kat really was very good at presenting a compelling argument.

'I don't . . . oh shit,' Jess breathed. 'You think I love Ant, don't you?'

'Does it kill you to see him with Alicia?'

'Yes,' she replied miserably. Jess covered her face with her hands and mumbled the words she'd been too scared to admit.

Kat tapped Jess on the shoulder. 'I'm sorry. I missed that.'

Jess removed her hands and looked desperately at her friend.

'I said I'm such an idiot. I've loved him all along and now it's too late. There. Are you happy?'

'No, because you're not.'

'Well, I don't see what the hell I can do about it. I missed my chance. I'm not going to ruin his chance with someone like Alicia if that's what makes him happy.'

'Because you love him?'

'Yes! Stop making me say it! It hurts too much.'

'See. Here's the thing. I don't think Ant looks too happy at the moment either.'

'What do you mean?' Jess asked.

Kat turned and gestured to the opposite corner of the room.

When Jess saw Ant it felt like her heart stopped beating in her chest. He was surrounded by several other celebrities all chatting happily, probably congratulating him on his win.

Gosh, she missed him. So much. She missed their exercise sessions. She missed the ways he'd find to goof around and make her laugh. Jess had always found exercising fun, but with Ant it was even more so.

She missed their text messages. The banter. The flutter in her chest she'd get when she'd see there was a message from him. But they'd dropped off in recent weeks since he'd become involved with Alicia.

She missed being able to bounce ideas off him about Hi-Jinks. She missed the way he tried out his jokes on her.

Jess sighed.

'Look closer, Jess,' Kat instructed. 'Does Ant look happy to you?'

Jess glanced over at him again. Actually, Ant appeared to be letting the others talk, which was unlike him. Surely after winning an award like that he'd be grinning from ear to ear and holding the floor?

'Now look over there,' Kat told her, nodding to a different part of the room.

'That *bitch*,' Jess breathed.

'She's not so nice now, is she?'

Jess didn't bother to reply. She was too busy staring in shock at Alicia, who currently had her arm around a popular actor's shoulders. Jess blinked when she saw the actor's hand snake around her waist and caress her hip.

With a sense of panic, Jess's gaze shot back to Ant.

Ant watched Alicia with a forlorn expression.

'Oh my God, I have to distract him,' Jess whispered. 'I'll catch you later, OK?'

'No problem. I need to go find Matt.'

Jess barely heard her. She was too busy hurrying over to the other side of the room.

Chapter Thirty-Three

'ANT. HI!'

Ant looked away from Alicia and blinked.

'Jess. Hi.'

His heart sank at the sight of Jess, and he was glad he wasn't the type to blush with embarrassment. Not only had he managed to dangerously upset his girlfriend, he'd thrown Jess into the spotlight for unwanted reasons. He knew how difficult Jess found it to be on camera unless it was planned. Now there were going to be many, many unplanned images of him and Jess all over the internet and tabloids tomorrow.

The group of men he'd been chatting to made room for Jess, and all of them smiled. It was hard not to when she was wearing that slinky dress. The after-party was being held in a low-lit function room of the hotel, but Jess still shone like the sunshine.

One of the men, a producer for a lifestyle show, congratulated Jess on Ant's recent transformation. Ant knew how much Jess hated that term, but she accepted the compliment as graciously as he knew she would.

He also didn't miss the way the guy next to him eyed Jess up and down. Patrick Waite. He was a smarmy television presenter on a long-running home renovation show.

Ant wasn't even sure why he was talking to them. When Alicia had stormed off earlier, he'd been forced to work the room, pretending that he was enjoying the accolade of being awarded Most Popular Presenter when what he really wanted was to be alone.

'So, ah, Ant, I've got a few people I want to introduce you to,' Jess said, when she'd finished chatting to the producer. 'Do you mind if I whisk you away?'

Ant nodded, disguising his curiosity. Jess had been terrified of attending tonight on account of her not being a celebrity—even though everyone else thought she was. Ant couldn't think who it was Jess wanted to introduce him to seeing as she didn't actually know that many people here personally.

He let himself be led towards the outdoor courtyard connecting to the function space.

Jess turned to face him and Ant swallowed. When would it get easier to be around her and not want her so much?

'Ant,' she whispered. 'Do you want to get out of here?'

Ant wasn't sure he'd heard her correctly. 'What?'

'Do you want to leave?'

'With you?' he gaped.

She shoved him playfully on the shoulder, but her eyes darted left and right nervously.

'Nice try,' she said. 'No, I just meant that you don't look like you're having that much fun anymore, and I don't know many people here, so I thought maybe we could escape together.'

'Without Alicia?'

Jess's gaze shifted over his shoulder and her mouth flattened.

He answered his own question. 'Yeah. Good point. I think she's busy.'

He hated the sympathetic smile she gave him, but the idea of leaving this place with her cancelled most of that out.

'It's probably not a good idea to leave together,' he told her.

She grinned. 'You know, that hadn't even occurred to me.'

He found himself grinning back. 'So, what's your plan?'

'I'm in room five fourteen. Meet me there in five or ten minutes.'

His grin faded. 'You want me to come up to your room?'

There was that nervous expression again. 'Yes. I thought we could sit on my balcony and chat. You can have a drink and I can . . .'

'Order dessert?' Ant joked.

He knew Jess didn't drink, and he'd never seen her eat junk food. The thought of her indulging in a decadent dessert made his mouth water—and it wasn't because he was hungry.

'Maybe,' she said noncommittally.

'If you promise me that you'll order something off the dessert menu, then I'm in.'

'They don't serve kale, you know.'

'I know.'

He knew his eyes held a challenge. Hers held amusement.

'You want to see me eat dessert?' she asked.

'Something rich and gooey and full of calories.'

'And here I was thinking you were nice. I do eat dessert occasionally, you know.'

'I've never seen it.'

'Just because you've never seen it doesn't mean it doesn't happen.'

He raised an eyebrow. The thought of Jess eating something like sticky date pudding with ice cream had just lightened his mood considerably.

'Alright. It's a deal,' she said. 'See you soon.'

With that, she flashed him a smile and left him standing there wondering what the hell he'd just agreed to.

They were friends. Just friends. She'd made that clear right from the beginning. Going up to her room wasn't risky. It wasn't forbidden. It was just two friends hanging out together.

He pushed aside the thought that Alicia would kill him if she found out. As if to prove a point, he forced himself to seek her out in the crowd. There she was, still flirting outrageously with that actor, Drew Callagher. His gaze hardened.

Yeah, something told him that she wouldn't notice. Still, he retrieved his phone from his trouser pocket and punched out a quick message.

Heading out for some fresh air, but you stay here and mingle. I won't wait up.

He dropped his phone back into his pocket and walked towards the foyer.

JESS PACED her hotel room nervously. Inviting Ant up had seemed like a good idea. Anything to get him out of that room so he wouldn't have to watch Alicia's punishment.

Jess knew that's exactly what it was. She wasn't like Alicia in any way, but she understood women. And Alicia was currently making Ant feel guilty for his accidental behaviour earlier. The least Jess felt she could do was help distract him.

'But in your hotel room?' Jess said out loud.

In retrospect, it wasn't one of her better ideas. But there weren't really many alternatives. Ant was a celebrity. He'd just won an award, so sharing a drink elsewhere in the hotel would only add to the rumours that would already be swirling after their unintended kiss. Going out somewhere in public wouldn't be any better.

So the hotel room it had to be.

Jess glanced down at her dress. God, the damn thing was bright. She'd contemplated taking it off, but changing out of it would have seemed strange.

Jess stopped pacing and looked around for something to do while she waited. She saw the room service menu propped on the desk and snatched it up.

She was deciding between the mud cake and a custard tart when there was a soft knock on the door. She padded over to the door barefoot—her dress might be staying on, but her heels had been the first to go. She opened the door a crack.

'Room service,' Ant said in a low voice.

She smiled and let him in quickly, both of them darting glances out into the hallway to make sure no one else was around.

They both laughed awkwardly as she closed the door.

Ant's gaze dropped to her dress momentarily, then back to her face. 'You're kind of overdressed for dessert.'

Jess blinked, not sure that she had heard right.

He slapped his forehead with a loud smack. 'Oh my God, I can't believe I just said that! I did *not* mean it in the way you think.' His dark eyes locked on to hers desperately. 'Is your mini bar full?'

She gestured to the small fridge. 'Be my guest.'

He went over and crouched down in front of it, the black trousers he wore showing off his backside nicely.

Jess looked away self-consciously and strode over to the balcony with the room service menu still in her hand. She settled herself on one of the chairs positioned to take in the view of the skyscrapers that made up the skyline of the Gold

Coast. Beyond their twinkling lights, the expanse of famous beach lay in the distance, dark and dormant in the evening light. The nearness of the ocean relaxed Jess somewhat.

Ant joined her on the balcony and dropped into the chair next to hers. He'd taken his suit jacket off, as well as the tie, and the shirt was now open at the neck. In the dim light, she could just make out a scattering of dark hair against his olive skin.

Jess returned her gaze to the coastline again, not entirely sure where to look.

Ant reached over and picked up the menu sitting in her lap.

'Hmm,' he said, taking a long swig of beer that made his Adam's apple move up and down.

Jess imagined kissing it, so she focused on the view again, her palms suddenly sweaty. God, what was wrong with her? She needed to get a grip.

Her own words came back to haunt her. *I've loved him all along and now it's too late.*

'How about I pick?' he suggested, breaking through her tormented thoughts.

She turned to stare at him, glad for the distraction. 'I thought I'd get to choose.'

'I don't think so,' he mused, putting his beer on the floor of the balcony. 'Let's see.'

'That doesn't seem fair,' Jess interrupted. 'Seeing as I hardly eat dessert.'

His eyebrow quirked in response. 'Don't you trust me?'

'No!' She laughed.

He shot her a wicked grin and Jess's stomach clenched. Maybe dessert wasn't a bad thing. It would take her mind off being here alone with Ant.

'Let's see,' he said again. 'Mud cake. It definitely has to be mud cake.'

Jess hid a relieved smile, because that had been her choice, too. Instead, she said, 'You're cruel.'

'Kale smoothies are cruel.' He stood up and went over to the hotel room phone to place the order.

'Congratulations again, by the way,' Jess said when he returned.

'For what?' he replied innocently.

She smiled at him. 'Most Popular Presenter, of course.'

He looked like he was about to make a joke, so his next words surprised her.

'I can't believe it,' he said.

'Believe it,' she replied firmly. 'You deserve it.'

'Thank you,' he said, falling silent.

They sat quietly, studying the view.

'You know,' Jess said after a while. 'I think we just had a serious conversation.'

'Weird, wasn't it?'

'No,' she said simply, which shut him up again.

He cleared his throat after another minute or so. 'Just so you know, I'm really sorry about—'

'I wanted to kiss you, then I thought better of it. You over-balanced. It just happened. Don't worry about it.' Jess immediately cringed and mentally slapped herself for the slip.

Ant's eyes appeared to darken. 'You *wanted* to kiss me?'

'Sure.' Jess was careful to keep her voice light. 'To congratulate you. You know my stupid touchy-feely tendencies. Only I realised too late that Alicia should kiss you first, so I panicked.'

He looked away. 'It's OK. No harm done.'

'Except for pissing off your girlfriend big time and the national news coverage tomorrow.'

Ant shrugged. 'She'll get over it.'

Jess gave him a sideways look. 'Um, will she? I don't think she's used to being ignored.'

'Drew Callagher isn't ignoring her,' Ant pointed out.

This time Jess fell silent. Ant didn't sound as distressed as she'd expected about Alicia's attentions being elsewhere. It was almost as if he didn't care. Did he care?

She gave him another sideways glance. He didn't look distressed either. More like resigned. Or accepting.

Oh, far out. Had their accidental kiss ended his relationship with Alicia? If Alicia was all over Drew for the entire world to see, then that seemed pretty conclusive, didn't it? You didn't drape yourself all over a famous actor at an industry after-party when there were cameras everywhere if you didn't want to be seen.

Jess's first emotion was guilt. It was a thick, heavy feeling that threatened to suffocate her if not for another lighter feeling creeping in at the edges. Relief.

There was a knock on the door. Jess jumped up, eager to have something to do and something else to think about.

When she walked back in with the plate in her hand, Ant's eyes lit up.

'This is brilliant,' he said, like a boy who had just been given free reign of the candy store.

'No,' Jess corrected. 'It's ginormous. There's no way I can eat all of it.'

'Then I'll help you. But you start.'

Jess sat down and put the plate on her lap. Oh, boy. The mud cake was so dense it felt heavy on the plate. Fine chocolate coated the top and a thicker layer of chocolate icing stuck the bottom half and top half together.

'Are you going to look at it all night?' Ant asked.

'I don't know where to start.'

'Here.' Ant reached over and picked up the cake fork, then

carefully extracted a thin wedge of the cake from top to bottom.

'You've done this before,' Jess said.

'A time or two. You want to get all the layers in one mouthful. It tastes better that way.'

Jess expected him to hand her the fork. But he didn't do that. He reached over and held it in front of her mouth.

Something in Jess's chest fluttered. She thought it was her heart, but it could have been the breath in her lungs. She wasn't sure.

'Here,' he said, his voice soft.

Their eyes met. Yes, it was definitely her heart. And it wasn't fluttering anymore. It was thundering in her chest like a runaway train.

'Ant—'

He silenced her by shoving the mouthful of cake in her mouth. It was such a shock that Jess breathed in when she should have chewed.

She coughed violently, her body making sure she didn't inhale the cake. Unfortunately, that meant spraying crumbs of cake all over the balcony as well as Ant.

'Shit,' Ant swore, jumping up.

He threw the plate onto the side table and it landed with a clatter. Jess slapped a hand to her mouth to prevent any more projectile bits of cake landing on him. Ant bent down and hit her on the back roughly.

Once she could breathe again, Jess began to giggle.

Ant's eyes were the first to smile. Jess knew the exact moment they did because the little happy lines in the corner of his eyes started to do a dance. Then his mouth twitched.

Jess kept giggling.

'Smooth, real smooth, Ant,' he muttered, still looking at her.

Then he smiled properly.

And something in Jess broke.

She stood up, not breaking his gaze. With her shoes off, they were almost the same height. Just the right level to reach over and . . .

'Jess?' he asked, his eyes holding a question. He rubbed his hands down the side of her bare arms and Jess shivered.

'Jess?' he said again, less certain this time.

Jess reached up and ran her fingertips over his slicked-back hair. Ant's eyes flickered closed and his chest rose as he inhaled a tight breath.

Then she ruffled his hair and his eyes fluttered open again, like a shocked butterfly. She grinned at him and arranged his hair so that the waves dropped forward over his forehead.

'There,' she said, satisfied. 'That's better.'

Ant's eyes went soft, and they dropped to her mouth. 'You've got some cake . . . here.' His finger wiped the side of her lip. Jess caught his wrist.

'Ant?' she said softly.

'Yeah?' He was still focused on her lips.

She released a shaky breath.

'I really did mean what I said before. I wanted to be the one to kiss you first tonight,' she whispered.

His eyes locked on to hers. They weren't soft anymore. They flared with heat. With need. Jess felt her body respond, a longing pulsing deep in her core.

'Like this,' she said.

Then she placed her hands on his cheeks and planted her lips on his.

Chapter Thirty-Four

ANT TASTED of beer and warm spice and chocolate cake. Wait, the chocolate cake was probably her. Anyway, he tasted good. Better than good. Better than last time. Better than the best.

He kissed her deeply, like she was everything. Like she was the only thing that existed. It banished any thought of Alicia or the fact that they might still have a relationship, because they obviously didn't if Ant was kissing her like this.

Jess didn't waste any time exploring him. Her hands travelled to his toned shoulders, then over to the ridges of muscle rippling across his back as he moved. She found herself annoyed at the white piece of cotton for coming in between them.

Instead of stepping away as Jess feared he might, Ant's hands dropped to her waist and squeezed her hips tightly. Jess melted against him, and he groaned into her mouth. The material of her dress was thin, and she could feel everything. The buttons on his shirt. The strong planes of his chest, which was the evidence of how hard he'd been working to get fit. And against her stomach, the hardness of his need for her.

Jess tilted her hips in response. He didn't groan this time, he growled, and the throbbing need pulsed up and down her thighs like an electric current.

He gathered up her dress so it was the height of a mini skirt, then one of his hands slipped underneath. His thumb stroked her through her panties and they clung to her because she was so goddamn wet, and still there was too much fabric everywhere getting in the way.

She grabbed his shoulders. 'Inside. Now.'

Ant broke away, his eyebrow arched in a question. 'Is that an order?'

'If you want me naked, we go inside now.'

Without another word, Ant went inside, waiting for Jess to join him. Once she did, he closed the door and swept the curtains shut. She turned so her back was to him.

'Can you undo me?' she asked.

She thought she heard him exhale, and the next thing she felt was his hand on her shoulder and then the gentle sound of her zip being lowered. She stepped out of her dress and lay it carefully over the back of the chair. It was a designer label after all.

She turned to face him.

Ant's chest rose and fell as if he'd just run a marathon instead of undoing a zip. Jess glanced down at herself self-consciously. All she wore was a lacy black bra that was mostly see-through and a matching pair of panties.

Jess knew she didn't look like a supermodel. She wasn't particularly tall. She didn't have big breasts. She was toned and fit, and that was the way she liked it, but whether Ant preferred her to a supermodel, Jess had no idea.

'Um, you're staring,' Jess said. 'Have I still got cake on me?'

Ant blinked, like he'd been woken from a trance.

'I'm staring because it's you,' he said, like that explained everything.

'Well, I guess I am naked,' she quipped.

Ant's eyes darkened to smouldering coal. 'No, you're not naked. Yet.'

Jess sucked in a sharp breath as he stepped in and dragged his lips across her bare shoulder. It left a trail of fire on her skin.

'See?' he murmured. 'Naked.'

Then he lowered his mouth to her breast and suckled her through the lacy fabric until her nipple was a hard peak.

'Not naked,' he said.

'Ant,' she breathed, her body trembling as if a million electric currents shimmered all over her skin. 'Please.'

His eyes met hers. 'Please what?'

She couldn't find the words. Now she was the one who felt like she'd run a marathon.

His lips curled. 'Please what?'

She shot him a desperate look. 'Please take it off.'

'Your wish is my command.'

He reached around and undid the clasp. Jess shrugged the bra off with a keen sense of relief.

'Fuck, Jess. *Fuck.*'

Then his mouth was on her again, his tongue circling her nipple in lazy strokes, and Jess felt so full and heavy she thought she was going to burst. Her fingernails dug into his shoulders, but he didn't seem to notice.

She writhed beneath his touch, and his hands slipped down to hold on to her waist, one of his thumbs playing with the elastic on her panties.

'Oh, Jesus, Ant. Would you just take them off?' she begged.

Ant broke away with a big grin. 'Damn. You're bossy. But that suits me, because I want to know exactly what you want.'

A part of Jess swooned, then blissed out at his words. Jack had always been so demanding during their relationship. It wasn't like things hadn't been good between them. They'd just been . . . predictable.

'Take your shirt off while you're at it,' she told him.

His grin broadened. 'Sure thing.'

Jess watched him unbutton his shirt, her heart hammering in her chest like she'd just sprinted along the beach.

Ant dropped his shirt to the floor and looked over at Jess uncertainly. A part of Jess's heart broke off and shattered. That this man, this beautiful man, could be so unsure of himself killed her. He was muscled without being buff, and his dark chest hair led a tantalising trail beneath his trousers.

'Come here,' she said.

He stepped in, his eyes still uncertain, and she feasted on his mouth, brushing her breasts against his chest deliberately to tease him.

'Damn, Jess,' he breathed.

It was wrong of her, but she enjoyed the note of pain in his voice. He wiped the smile right off her face when he slipped a hand beneath her panties and between her legs.

She doubled over as his finger found her and circled her restlessly. She shuddered and bowed forward like a tree in a wild breeze, gripping his shoulders to stay upright.

'You like that?' he whispered in her ear.

'Yes,' she hissed as his finger dipped into her wet folds but didn't venture inside. 'Ant, please.'

'So polite, sweetheart. Tell me want you want.'

Instead of telling him, she grabbed his wrist and pushed

his finger slowly inside her. It was exquisite, but still not enough.

He released a shuddering breath and moved his finger inside her while his thumb continued to circle outside. She bucked her hips to angle him deeper.

Ant's eyes were as wild as his hair. 'Like this?'

Jess nodded, the need building inside her with every stroke of his finger, and every time he entered her deeper. He reached around and clenched her backside to hold her in place, and she used his grip to move herself up and down.

'Fuck, Jess.'

'I want that, too,' she told him boldly.

He pressed his forehead to hers, moaning softly.

'Are you still hard?' she whispered, wondering at the confident words that were leaving her mouth, but also not caring.

Ant made a strangled noise deep in his throat. 'Honey, I could cut glass with the erection I've got going on in my pants.'

'Good. Then imagine it's moving inside me right now. Fast and deep, Ant. That's how I want you to touch me.'

He inhaled another shuddering breath and did as she instructed, moving his hand relentlessly against her until the selfish part of Jess just wanted to take, take, take everything he had to give. And he wasn't even properly inside her yet.

The thought sparked the heat that had been building inside her, and she clenched around him as the feeling threatened to become too much. She squirmed and tried to shift away, but he had a firm grip on her and he pulled her down. Again and again. Over and over. Then his thumb. Oh, holy hell, his thumb was the best sort of intense.

Suddenly the heat had nowhere to go. It flashed and exploded into a burst of light so bright it rocked her body from head to toe, sending shock waves through her. And still his thumb kept tormenting her while his free arm moved to hold her up.

With a gasp of breath, Jess moved towards the bed and Ant followed, only drawing out of her when she collapsed on top of it. She lay there shuddering, aftershocks trembling through her.

'Oh, wow,' she breathed.

Ant stood above her, grinning happily. 'I'll say.' He looked down at his hand. 'I'm no loser in the bedroom, but even I didn't know my hand was this talented. It just needed some instruction.'

Jess giggled. 'Very talented.'

'Maybe it needs a name—'

'No!' Jess cried, and they both laughed.

Her laughter stopped when her gaze drifted to his trousers.

'Take your pants off.'

'We don't have to—'

'Now, Monticello.'

'OK, then.'

He swallowed and lowered his pants, then stood in front of her naked. Shrugged.

'Don't shrug,' she told him, and flashed him a smile. 'Adonis.'

He swallowed again. 'Don't tease me.'

'This. From a comedian. Come here, my Italian God.'

Jess knew that when it came to guys, sometimes nothing you said mattered. You had to make your point through actions.

Ant moved forward and Jess sat up. He swallowed a third time.

'Oh, you happened to notice my position, did you?' she said coyly.

Then she reached out and took him in her hand. Ant definitely had nothing to worry about. No, not a thing.

Her hand swept up and down the length of him, enjoying the weight of him in her palm. The hard, unyielding power of him.

When she stroked the underside of the tip, his head lolled back and he released a ragged breath.

Smiling to herself, she closed her lips around him while he wasn't looking.

His head snapped up, and he stiffened. 'Fuck me.'

If her mouth hadn't been busy, she would have said, "Oh, I will."

Instead, she stroked him with her tongue. Sucked and lapped at him like he was sweeter than the sweetest dessert. His thighs flexed and hardened like the rest of him. She ran a palm across the taut muscles.

'My, you've been working out, Adonis,' she said between strokes.

He released a bark of laughter. 'So I have.'

'I hadn't noticed until now.'

Another bark of laughter.

Then Jess swore.

'What? What is it?' he demanded, stepping back.

'I don't have a condom.'

Ant frowned. 'Shit. Wait. I think I do.'

He turned and grabbed his trousers, giving Jess an eyeful of his bare arse. Working out, indeed.

He swung back with a look of victory. 'I had one in my wallet.'

They stared at each other. So. They were really doing this.

Hell, yes. They were doing this. She couldn't remember wanting anyone as much as she wanted Ant right now.

She gestured to his lower half. 'I can keep going—'

'Uh-uh. I'm good. If you're OK with that. I think I'd rather . . .'

'You think you'd rather what? Say it, Adonis. You wanted me to tell you what I want. Return the favour.'

'Geez, you're not as sweet as I thought you were,' he said with a lopsided grin, looking a little like he'd won the lottery.

'Is that a problem?' she asked sweetly.

'Hell, no!'

'Then say it.'

Yes, she wanted him so much. But she wanted him to be himself with her. Sensitive. Sweet. Hard. Soft. Demanding. Giving. Whatever he wanted to be. Jess had no intention of making the same mistake other women had in his past by dictating who he should be.

He came closer and stroked her cheek with the palm of his hand. And as always, that thumb drove her wild.

'I want you,' he whispered.

Jess bit her lip. 'How?'

'I want to be inside you.'

'No, I mean, *how* do you want me?'

His mouth rounded in a small "o". 'I get to choose?'

'Depends. If it's too kinky, then no.'

He considered her words with a crooked smile. 'Then how about on your knees facing the wall?'

She flashed him a wicked grin. 'See? You do know what you want. And that sounds good to me.'

She scrambled up onto all fours and got into position at the bedhead. She heard the condom wrapper crinkle.

'Good to me?' he muttered. 'It's sounds fucking awesome to me.'

She laughed. She should have known being in the bedroom with Ant would be just as much fun as out of it.

The bed shifted as he climbed on and came over to her.

She felt his breath tickle the back of her neck and she sighed as his lips brushed her shoulder. A finger traced the path of her spine, and she gripped the bedhead tightly.

His teeth grazed her shoulder and his hand came around to cup her breast.

'Oh, Ant,' she sighed.

'Oh, Ant, what?' he said darkly.

She grinned at the wall. 'Oh, Ant, I want you inside me, pretty, pretty please.'

His palm swept across her stomach, and lower still until his fingers dipped between her legs. It should have been sore from his earlier attentions, but it already ached for more of him.

She arched her hips back. An invitation.

He rested his forehead on her back and the tip of him pressed against her.

'Jessica,' he breathed, then he entered her, slowly, reverently.

She arched back more, taking as much of him in as he was willing to give. She felt the part of his anatomy he claimed not to have move against her, and it drove her wild. She used her hands to brace herself and pushed into him.

He buried himself inside her, his teeth biting into her shoulder. Then he was moving inside her, lighting up all the sensitive nerve endings that had been waiting in expectation. But still it wasn't enough.

His hands grabbed her hips. 'I don't want to hurt—'

'More, Ant. Please give me more.'

His fingernails dug into her and he drove into her harder, faster, deeper until he reached that spot that ached for him. That needed him.

She matched his rhythm, meeting each stroke and pushing him to go even harder.

'Far out, Jess, this isn't a workout. You're going to break me.'

'No, I'm not. You've got this. I'll take as much as you can give.'

He groaned, long and loud, like it was the last thing he wanted to hear. But his body rose to the challenge and now it was a race. A race to fulfil each other.

His hand gripped her wrists against the wall. His other hand held her hip. He was in control and she loved it.

She pushed her backside into him so her hips were almost parallel with the bed.

'Jesus, Jess, I'm not sure—'

'You. Got. This,' she said between gritted teeth, because that spot inside her was swelling with something so sweet it was verging on painful.

'Fine.'

He dropped her wrists and grabbed on to her hips again, all pretence of being polite gone.

Oh boy.

There it was. The everything.

It swelled again, and this time it overflowed, rushing outwards from the centre of her. As the ecstasy ripped through her, she cried out like a woman possessed, her body convulsing wildly.

Ant nuzzled into her shoulder and held on for dear life, the wave invisibly flowing from her to him, and he trembled and pulsed with his release.

When it passed, Ant eased out of her and they fell onto the bed beside each other.

'Holy. Shit. Now I know what my sex life was missing,' he muttered. 'Fitness.'

'And a woman.'

Ant slapped her leg lightly.

'Can you move?' Jess asked.

She saw him smile at the ceiling. 'Don't want to. I'm good.'

She laughed and the heady feeling reverberated around her body like the orgasm had.

'We'll have to move sometime,' she said.

'No time soon, though.'

He threaded his fingers through hers and lifted her hand to his mouth, placing a kiss on the back of it so she quivered.

'Sounds good to me,' she whispered.

Chapter Thirty-Five

THEY'D BEEN DOZING for around half an hour when they were woken by a phone pinging.

Jess reached out for hers, which was sitting on the bedside.

'Must be yours,' she muttered, putting it back down. She sounded sleepy and slightly drugged from the post-sex high.

Ant groaned and rolled off the bed to find his trousers. He found his phone in one of the pockets and sat on the edge of the bed to read it.

It was from Alicia.

'Shit,' he said, before he could stop himself.

Jess sat up. 'What is it?'

He didn't reply and read the message.

Where are you? I'm back at the hotel room and you're not here.

'Shit,' Ant said again. He checked the time. It was only midnight. Ant had expected Alicia to be out a lot later than that.

Jess joined him at the edge of the bed. 'Ant? Is everything alright?'

He turned the screen off quickly.

'It's fine,' he said, standing up. 'It's just Alicia. I'm really sorry, but I'm going to have to go.'

'Go?' Jess stared at him blankly.

Oh shit, he thought again. He'd thought he'd be able to slip out later and spare them both the awkwardness. 'Yeah, I can't just desert her.'

'And why not? She seemed to forget you quite easily.'

'I know, but she's back at the hotel room and I should go to her.'

'To tell her it's over,' Jess said.

It was his turn to look at her blankly. 'What?'

Jess reeled back. 'Oh my God.'

Ant didn't know what he'd just done to upset her, but whatever it was he wanted to take it back. He crouched down in front of her.

'Jess?'

'You weren't going to end things?' she whispered.

He stared at her, too scared to talk.

'Oh, my God!' she cried, and scrambled to the other side of the bed like he was a poisonous spider. 'I thought . . .' She put a hand to her head. 'I thought things between you were over?'

'No,' Ant said slowly.

'But you just slept with me!'

'Yes,' Ant said equally slowly. Then he realised something much too late, and he immediately hated himself. No, he more than hated himself. He loathed himself with every fibre of his being.

He climbed onto the bed to go to her.

Jess recoiled and scrambled off the bed so that she was standing on the opposite side.

'This was a one-night stand?' she demanded.

Once again Ant chose not to say anything, because he was scared to. He pushed a hand through his hair. Fucking hell.

He had no idea what this was.

Now it occurred to him that Jess had thought things with Alicia were over before they'd made love. He'd never told her that. He'd never even told her he had any intention of that.

But this was Jess, he realised, and it was like his heart suddenly flip-flopped and stopped beating.

Jess would never have a one-night stand. That was something Ant did. Not her.

Shit. Shit. *Shit.*

He hadn't thought. He'd just reacted. She'd kissed him, dammit. She'd pressed that perfect body against his. And he hadn't thought about a goddamn thing after that.

'Ant, say something!'

'I don't know what to say.'

'Say you're not going back to your hotel room,' she said.

'I can't just leave her waiting for me. She'll think something's wrong.'

'Something *is* wrong, because you just slept with me.' Jess let out what sounded like a sob, but she wasn't crying, she was pacing the room. 'I was a one-night stand. I'm so stupid. I should have known. You told me all along you didn't want the same things as me, and I didn't listen.'

'Jess. Wait.' Ant rounded the end of the bed and she stopped pacing, looking a bit like a cornered animal. She appeared as desperate as he felt, and somehow he had to make things right.

'Jess,' he said again. 'Let me fix this. Let me go talk to her.'

'To end things?' Her voice was so full of hope that his heart fractured a little.

'Is that what you want?'

'Of course it's what I want! I wouldn't have slept with you otherwise!'

Ant stared at her. She was breathing heavily, her chest rising up and down like it took her an extreme amount of effort to look at him right now.

'You want me?' he asked softly.

It sounded like Jess suppressed a moan. 'You're asking me that? After . . .' Her gaze travelled to the bed where he'd had her pinned against the wall earlier. 'After that?' she finished.

'Yes,' he said, then huffed. 'No. You know, I don't know! This still feels like a dream to me, Jess.'

'Yeah, and currently it's turning into a bad one.'

His phone pinged again, and Jess glared at it. Flashing her a look of regret, he picked it up again.

I'm sorry about tonight. I overreacted. Where are you?

Ant's heart sank. He couldn't just ignore her. Earlier doubts about their relationship aside, he had no intention of being nasty just because Alicia had acted like a spoiled princess tonight.

Yeah, and cheating on Alicia with Jess isn't nasty?

God, what a mess. How had things suddenly become so screwed up? Jess hadn't wanted him. She'd friend-zoned him. She'd made it clear they weren't suited.

Ant lowered the phone. 'I need to go. I'm so sorry.'

Jess gestured to the bed with a stricken look on her face. 'And this?'

'I don't know, Jess. It was wonderful. Beyond . . . anything. But I don't see how it can change things.'

'How can it not change things?' she whispered.

Ant stepped in and put his hands on her shoulders, knowing that he probably looked as stricken as she did.

'Because you said yourself that I'm not right for you.'

'What if I've changed my mind?'

He closed his eyes. Not long ago, Ant would have given anything to hear those words from her. A future with Jess was as unbelievable to him as world peace or an end to famine. But now she was saying it was a possibility.

Except he knew deep down in his heart that it wasn't. He'd been a coward about her the entire time, and now it was important he showed some courage.

So instead of saying he'd changed his mind, because a part of him would always want her no matter what, he told her the truth.

'You deserve better than me, Jessica Jinks.'

She shook her head.

He squeezed her arms. 'No, you do. Don't deny it. You deserve someone who will rock your world in every way. Who will give you the big, fancy wedding. The brood of kids. The family man. Not the comedian who works odd hours and then goes on tour for weeks on end, leaving you alone to try to manage your business and the family. I'd give that to you if I could, but I can't. Being a comedian is who I am, Jess. I can't change that.'

She was still shaking her head. 'I don't care. None of that matters. We'll make it work. I have a big family to support me. Your mum would support me, too. I know she would.'

'No, Jess, no.' He pressed his forehead against hers, breathing in her sweet scent like she was a drug. Knowing that it would probably be the last time. 'Jess, there's something you need to know. You remember my mum told you she was the younger woman?'

Jess frowned, obviously confused about what Ant's family had to do with any of this. Ant still wasn't sure he'd made sense of it either, but he knew that it was important.

'My mum wasn't just the younger woman. She was also the *other* woman.'

Ant let that sink in. He watched as Jess's eyelashes fluttered as she blinked, like they wanted to fly away from here.

'Your father cheated?' she asked.

Ant nodded. 'On his first wife, yes. They had four children together.'

Jess blinked again.

'I have two half-brothers and two half-sisters.'

'I didn't know.'

'That's because we never see them. Dad cut off all contact with them when he divorced. He provided for them financially, but that was all.'

Jess gaped at him. 'You're serious? How could he do that?'

'I don't know,' Ant said genuinely. 'I didn't find out about them until I was fifteen, until Mum slipped and told me about it one day. Dad never planned on telling me.'

'But why? And why would they have you if he didn't want anything to do with his other children?'

'I was unplanned,' he said. Saying it all these years later still made him feel numb. 'Mum says it was a happy surprise because she'd always wanted a child, but I know that Dad didn't. I'm pretty sure he loved her too much to ask her to give me up, but I definitely wasn't what he wanted. If not for me being an "accident", Mum would have given up what she truly wanted for my dad. So don't you see, Jess? I can't let you give up the things you want for me.'

'But they *love* you,' Jess said fiercely. 'I know they do.'

'Mum does,' Ant agreed. 'Dad barely tolerated me. I think because there was only one of me it was easy for him to ignore me. It was always about Mum for him. She's all he ever wanted.'

'Oh, Ant, I'm so sorry. I had no idea.'

Ant grimaced. 'Yeah, it's not something I generally tell people about. It's so far from your happy family it's ridiculous.'

'Have you met your half-brothers and sisters?'

'Yes, I have, but only a couple of years ago.' After many years of wondering, he'd finally worked up the courage to make contact after his divorce. He wasn't sure why it had felt important to do so at that point in his life, but it had. 'I begged Mum to give me their details, and she did on the proviso we didn't tell Dad what we were doing. I get along quite well with one of my brothers and one of my sisters. We keep in contact, and I've been to a couple of their kids' birthday parties. It was nice. Kind of like your family, you know?'

'Oh, Ant,' she said again.

He dropped his hands from her shoulders. 'I'm sorry, too, but not for that. I'm sorry about tonight. I shouldn't have slept with you like this. I know you'd never have a one-night stand, but I've wanted you so badly for so long and when you kissed me . . . you're all I want.'

Jess's eyes filled with tears, but it was like they were scared to fall. 'I want you too, Ant.'

He closed his eyes because it was easier than looking at her. 'I want you so much, Jess, it hurts. But if I let myself have you, I'll suffocate you. I'll stop you from having the things in life that you want, all because I want you so much. Like my father. I can't do that to you.'

She shook her head again, and a tear finally dislodged and trailed down her cheek. 'No, Ant. That's not right at all. I *know* you. You're not like that. You're nothing like your father.'

'I married Enid because she didn't want children,' he said firmly. 'I can't make you give that up.'

Jess had stopped moving. She didn't say anything. She just stared at him.

'And now I've cheated on my girlfriend with you, because .

. .' The reality of the situation slammed into him like an out-of-control car. He'd just made Jess the other woman. 'Holy shit.' He stared at her in her shock. 'I'm. Just. Like. Him.'

Jess started to speak, but he shook his head at her.

'I'm sorry, Jess. I know I don't deserve your forgiveness, but I hope one day you'll be able to. I've got to go.'

Or I'll hurt you more than I already have, he thought, but didn't say.

His urge to flee was unstoppable. Not from her. From himself.

He left her standing there. Wide-eyed. Wounded. And it was the hardest thing he'd ever done. But it was the right thing.

He closed the door gently on his way out and the sound of her stifled sob felt like someone had plunged a knife into his heart.

But he didn't turn back.

Chapter Thirty-Six

JESS THREW herself into her work. When she wasn't taking classes or running a one-on-one session or posting on social media or developing new recipes for her followers, she was working on her business plan. She spoke to suppliers about her range of clothing and merchandise. Held meetings. By the end of the month, she'd partnered with one that offered the right combination of customer service and cost-effective pricing.

She'd like to say she never thought of Ant. But she did. He crept into her thoughts at the most unexpected times. His broad smile flashed into her mind when she was sprinting up and down the beach. The memory of his lips on hers rattled her when she was making her morning smoothie. He was there constantly in a million little ways that added up to one massive heartache.

She wanted to hate him. She tried to hate him. But she couldn't. What he'd done wasn't right, but she understood his reasons. They were stupid reasons, she regularly thought to herself, mainly because it didn't seem fair. It was like Ant had shut an entire part of himself off because of the family he'd been raised in. Like he'd never allowed himself to even entertain the idea of kids or a happy family because of his father.

Then Jess would grow angry at Stefano, but that didn't last long either because Jess had grown to like Stefano, too. She wasn't sure why he'd been so cold to Ant growing up. Stefano was occasionally abrupt around Jess, but never mean.

And who was Jess to say what Ant wanted? Maybe she was projecting her own ideas of happiness onto Ant. He could be a fulfilled person without kids. Except now she'd had time to reflect on them, his words didn't make sense. None of them did.

I married Enid because she didn't want kids.

Enid didn't want kids. He'd said nothing about himself. It was like he'd chosen Enid because then he wouldn't have to think about it.

She also recalled the night of their first kiss. He hadn't told her, "No, I don't want kids". He'd said, "I've never seen myself having kids."

Or maybe Jess was reading too much into everything.

Nothing about the entire situation made any sense. But she supposed that it didn't have to. It wasn't hers to figure out. Things with Ant were over now, including their friendship. That was the part that hurt the most.

Jess didn't tell Kat about the one-night stand. She didn't tell anyone. Instead, she told Kat that after a brief chat on the night of the Logies, they'd both retired to their rooms separately. So the fact that Ant was still with Alicia was expected. Jess made the excuse to Kat that she'd chickened out about telling Ant her real feelings. That it wouldn't seem right to do so when Ant was in a relationship with another woman.

The other woman.

That was what Jess was. Even though it had only lasted one night, Jess hated herself for it. Ant was right. She *did* deserve better. She deserved better than being someone's dirty secret. If she was ever going to find The One, it wasn't going to be as a result of an unplanned night of passion where neither of them had stopped to consider the consequences.

Despite her determination to put it all behind her, Jess found herself viewing Ant's posts on Instagram. He wasn't as active as she was, but usually every week there would be a new update. Interestingly, most of them were related to work or his triathlon training. Jess supposed it made her selfish, but the fact that there wasn't any mention of Alicia eased some of her pain.

He'd probably decided his private life was best kept private from now on, and Jess could totally understand that. She'd never aired her personal life for the entire world to see, and her posts were always related to Hi-Jinks.

Aside from the occasional sneaking glance at Ant's posts, she thought she'd started to put him behind her. That all changed with the message she received one Monday evening.

Jessica. I hope you don't mind me getting in contact. Stefano has been asking for you. If he wasn't such a grumpy old man I'd suggest he misses you. I know you're busy, but if you can spare the time to drop by for a cup of tea, we'd love to see you. Abi.

Jess didn't reply straight away. She left it an hour—a long, agonising hour of wondering what to do. Then, with a huff, she'd replied.

Abi. So lovely to hear from you. I hope you are both well. I'm really busy, but I will see what I can do and will be in touch.

She should have just said no, that she didn't have the time. But she did genuinely like Ant's parents and she was interested to know how Stefano was getting on with his exercises. She could have asked, of course, or called them. Instead, she left it open because that seemed like the right thing to do. Then, at the end of a busy day of classes later that week, Jess finally relented and asked if they were free for her to drop over. She knew for a fact Ant wouldn't be there because he was filming the show. Another night alone in her apartment going over a business plan she'd already pored over a million times didn't seem like a reasonable excuse to avoid his parents.

Abi replied straight away and said they'd love to see her.

'COME IN. COME IN.'

Jess let herself be ushered into the small terrace house. Something about the homely space dissipated the nerves that had been swirling in her stomach on the drive over there.

'You've come at a good time, actually,' Abi told her as Jess followed her up the hall. 'Come to the back shed and see Stefano. He's just finishing up on the bicycle. I tell you, he loves that Central Park circuit in New York. Probably because he went there himself as a young man. I don't know if it's the exercise or the memories, but afterwards it just lights him up.'

'Has he had any more falls lately?' Jess asked Abi when they reached the back garden.

Abi stopped walking and turned to face Jess, her brown eyes full of pride. 'Not one. He's a lot more stable on his feet. Plus, he seems to be having more good days than bad days. I can't thank you enough for what you've done, Jess. I know we can't stop him getting older, but . . .' She pressed her lips together, suddenly emotional. She reached over and grasped Jess's arm. 'But I thought with every day that passed that more and more of my Stefano was slipping away. And now he's not. He's here more than he's not, and it's wonderful.'

Jess smiled, feeling close to tears herself. The picture Ant painted of his father was so different to this man that Abi was so obviously in love with. Jess wished she could understand it. Was that why she'd agreed to come here today?

Abi let go of her arm and Jess shook off the thought, following Ant's mother towards the shed. It wasn't any of her business who Ant's dad was then or now. It was his family. Not hers. And she and Ant weren't in a relationship. They were barely friends now, so it was better for Jess to stay out of it.

When she stepped inside, Jess found herself stopping and staring.

'Whose bike is that?' she asked.

Next to Stefano's a second bike was set up that hadn't been there before.

'That's Ant's old bike. He got it fixed, bought himself a trainer, and comes over to use it a couple of times a week. He says it's to help train for the triathlon, but I don't know, it doesn't seem like very effective training to me.'

'How do you mean?'

'Well, he's figured out a way that both him and Stefano can ride at the same time, so he goes around the courses with his dad. At the slow speed Stefano rides, it won't be doing Ant any benefit.'

Jess felt all the breath leave her lungs. Ant was riding with his father? She didn't have time to formulate a suitable response, because Stefano called out to them.

'What are you nattering on about, woman?' He was too focused on the screen to turn to look at them.

'I said,' Abi told him a loud voice, 'that you have a visitor. Jessica is here to see you.'

Stefano immediately stopped pedalling and twisted slowly in his seat. When he saw Jess, his dark eyes lit up.

'Jessica! Bella ragazza! Where have you been? We've missed you.'

Abi nudged Jess. 'See? I told you he has a soft spot for you.'

They watched him get down from the bike carefully—and steadily, Jess noted—and walk over to them. He stopped in front of Jess, a big smile transforming his usually sullen expression into something else entirely. He put his hands on her shoulders and kissed each of her cheeks, Italian style.

Jess blushed brightly.

Stefano frowned. 'You've lost weight. You look too skinny. Have you been eating?'

Jess wanted to frown too, because she was having a hard time reconciling the old man's concern for her with the picture Ant had painted of his childhood. 'I've been eating, Stefano. Just working very hard lately, that's all.'

'Too hard,' he said. His voice was raspy and well-worn like the rest of him, but there was no mistaking his disapproving tone.

'Then you must stay for dinner, Jess,' Abi told her.

'Oh, no—'

'You must,' Stefano said. 'Then I know you've had a good meal today.'

Jess shot Abi a helpless look, and Ant's mother simply shrugged.

'I always make too much,' she said. 'You know we'd love to have you.'

Jess relented, and they returned to the house once Stefano had turned off the screen linked to the bike. Inside, Jess let them direct the conversation. She didn't want to bring up the subject of Ant, and they didn't seem inclined to either, which was a relief. Instead, they spoke at length about her business and about how much Stefano was enjoying riding. By the time dinner was over, Jess was feeling so full that she was keen to move, so she stood up and started collecting the dishes.

Abi stood up, too. 'No, no. You mustn't. You're our guest.'

'Please, it's no trouble. I'm from a big family. I'm used to doing my fair share.' Jess took their bowls over to the sink located opposite the dining table.

'Eh. Big family, you say?' said Stefano. 'How many?'

'Five children altogether,' Jess replied easily, knowing already what was coming next.

Stefano's eyebrows rose like surprised caterpillars. 'Five, eh? And where are you in that?'

'I have four older brothers.'

'Four big brothers!' Abi said. 'My dear, that must have been challenging.'

'Oh, no. It was pretty good, actually. They all looked out for me, and I learned a lot tagging along after them.'

Abi nodded. 'Probably why you're so competent now.'

'Shh. Don't tell my brothers that. They already have big enough egos.'

Stefano let out a bark of laughter, but his smile faded as suddenly as it came. 'Four brothers. I had four brothers.'

Abi reached over and stroked his hand. 'Stefano came from a big family, didn't you?'

'Was this in Italy?' Jess asked. After everything Ant had told her, Jess was more than a little curious, but was careful to keep her voice neutral.

'Yes,' replied Abi. 'I never met them, unfortunately. I was born and raised here in Australia, but Stefano emigrated and left his family behind.'

'Did you ever go back to visit?'

Abi looked at her husband. His eyes appeared distant, like he was remembering something that wasn't in this room. She shook her head. 'Sadly, no. It was such a big trip and a lot of money. Not to mention time away from his business. We always said when we retired . . .' She sighed. 'By then, they were all gone.'

Jess glanced at Stefano, who still appeared to be some-where else. 'Oh, I'm so sorry to hear that.'

Suddenly, Stefano slammed a fist onto the table and Jess jumped, dropping a bowl into the sink. It clattered loudly.

'I'm so sorry,' Jess said, shaken. 'It didn't break.'

'Here.' Abi rushed over and took the bowl from the sink and placed it into the dishwasher. 'Let me finish.' She glanced back at her husband, who was now frowning. His fist was still resting on the table. 'Stefano, dear? Why don't you go and turn the television on now? That police drama you like so much is about to come on.'

'Eh?' He blinked, and it was like he was back in the room again. 'Oh, yes. I don't want to miss it. Excuse me, Jessica. You can join us if you like.'

Stefano stood, moving like an ancient tree might creak in a gentle breeze, but Jess was glad to see he still seemed sure of himself. When he'd left to go to the other room, Jess went to collect the other plates from the table.

'I'm sorry if he scared you, dear,' Abi said, still rinsing dishes. 'He has mixed memories of his childhood in Italy. You never know if it's the good or bad ones that he will remember.'

'I'm sorry. I didn't mean to bring it up, but when he asked me about my family—'

'Please, no harm done.'

They were quiet for a minute while they cleaned.

Abi glanced over at Jess. 'Have you seen Antony lately?'

Jess looked away and bent over to place a plate in the dish-washer. 'Not lately, no.'

'Because of Alicia?'

Jess straightened slowly, feeling old like Stefano all of a sudden. 'Um, well, she is his girlfriend.'

'Pfft.' Abi scrubbed a pan angrily. 'Some girlfriend. We haven't even met her.'

'You haven't?'

'No.'

It was horrible of her, but it made Jess feel better somehow. She wasn't sure why.

'I was hoping you two were becoming more than friends, to be honest.' The scrubbing seemed to relax.

'Oh, no,' Jess said quickly, glad Abi's back was to her because her cheeks were flaring. 'We've always been friends.'

Abi nodded and scrubbed harder again. 'My Ant. He never makes good decisions when it comes to women, I'm afraid.'

'Alicia's very accomplished,' Jess said weakly, the compliment leaving a bad taste in her mouth. However, most parents would be extremely proud if their son was dating one of the country's most successful models, so it seemed strange that Abi wasn't.

'Pfft,' she said again. 'She's all wrong for him.'

'You haven't met her,' Jess said softly.

'I don't need to. A mother knows. Ant needs someone that he can put down roots with. Not some flighty, self-obsessed model. Someone he can start a family with.'

'He does?' Jess said doubtfully.

Abi frowned at Jess's tone of voice and stopped what she was doing to turn to face her. 'What has he told you?'

See, this was why coming here was a bad idea. Jess should have just kept her curiosity to herself and her constant niceness in check.

Jess bit her lip. 'That he doesn't want children.'

Abi growled and returned to the pan, which Jess was sure had been scrubbed clean a while ago. Jess touched her arm tentatively.

'I'm sorry. That's probably not what you wanted to hear if you were hoping for grandchildren.'

Abi threw her hands up in the air sending soap suds in all directions. 'I don't care about that! I care about Antony, and he'd be happier with a family, I know it.'

Jess decided to dispense with politeness for a change. 'He seems determined to believe otherwise.'

Abi looked to the ceiling like the heavens held answers they didn't, then wiped her hands on a towel. 'It's his father's doing, unfortunately.'

'He might have mentioned that, too,' Jess said very softly, even though Stefano was in the next room and his hearing wasn't very good.

Abi straightened. 'He did?'

Jess nodded. Abi exhaled a long breath and gestured for Jess to sit down at the table.

After they were seated, she said, 'Did he tell you anything else?'

'He said that things with Stefano weren't great when he was growing up.'

'They've never been great,' Abi said in a low voice. 'I tried for years to get Stefano to talk to Ant. To explain why Stefano found things so hard, but male pride is a strange beast.'

'Do you think it would have made a difference?'

Abi didn't answer. She was studying her hands intently. 'Life never turns out the way you expect it to. Sometimes it's better than you could ever have hoped. Other times you're faced with difficulties you never could have imagined.'

Jess nodded. She knew she'd led a relatively sheltered life so far. She was from a good home and a good family. There were no dark family secrets that she was aware of.

Abi reached over to pick up a napkin sitting on the table like her hands needed something to do. 'Did Ant mention I was the other woman?'

Jess didn't know what to say, so she just nodded.

'Anything else?'

The only other thing Jess could think that she was referring to was Stefano's other family, but how did you bring that up in conversation?

'Your expression tells me that he did,' Abi said knowingly. 'He doesn't talk about it with anyone, you know.'

'He doesn't?'

Abi shook her head. 'No. So either he trusts you very much, or he's using it as an excuse to keep his distance.'

'I'm not sure,' Jess replied awkwardly, although she suspected it was both.

Abi sighed again. 'Do you care for my Antony, Jessica?'

'Yes, of course—'

'Uh-uh. You know what I mean. I'm not expecting you to tell me what's in your heart, that's for you to know. But I'd like to know if you could care for him the same way he cares for you.'

'We're just friends—'

'And I'm not an old woman. Denial is a horrible affliction, I assure you. I've seen the way he looks at you.'

'Then, yes,' Jess whispered. 'Not at first, I didn't. I thought we were just friends, but then my feelings started to change.'

Abi nodded like it was the answer she'd been expecting. 'Sometimes the heart knows before we do. Our minds take a while to catch up.'

'But Ant is with Alicia now.'

She fell silent at Abi's stern look, which told Jess all she needed to know about Abi's thoughts on that matter.

Abi reached over and patted Jess's hand. 'I'm sorry my Ant is currently running in the wrong direction. I think it's time I did something I should have done long ago.'

Jess's eyes widened in alarm, regretting being so honest

with Ant's mother. 'Oh, no. It's best if we just leave things. I don't want to interfere in Ant's love life.'

Abi patted her hand again. 'No, I agree. But it is time for me to deal with some family business that should have been aired long ago. Then maybe Ant won't feel the need to run so much.'

Jess stared at Abi, unsure what to say or do. She knew one thing. She shouldn't have come here tonight. She didn't want to be responsible for dredging up family difficulties or making things harder for Ant than what they already were.

'My dear, don't look so worried. The things I speak of were at play long before you came along. Stupidly, I thought Stefano knew best.' She grimaced. 'Men never know best.'

Jess managed a weak smile. 'Try telling that to my brothers.'

Abi grinned and stood up. 'Life would be so much easier without them, wouldn't it? But then that would be boring. Come on, I need to fatten you up with dessert before you leave.'

Chapter Thirty-Seven

ANT KNEW something was off even before he arrived at his parents' place for dinner. They'd been at him for weeks to bring Alicia over so they could meet her. But when his mother had gotten in contact earlier in the week, Alicia's name hadn't even come up. Instead, she said that his presence was required on Sunday night and her tone brooked no argument.

Alicia hadn't been happy. They'd already organised to attend a dinner with her friends the week before. When he explained that he wouldn't be coming, she was furious. As he was learning, her fury was usually short-lived, and she started asking questions about why she wasn't invited. He made excuses, saying it was a dull family affair involving relatives he hardly knew himself, even though it was a blatant lie. Aside from his uncle, they didn't have distant relatives, but Alicia didn't know that. After a while she stopped questioning him. Then she began making comments about what a great night she was going to have with her friends, as though she was trying to make him jealous of missing out. Actually, that was exactly what she was doing, Ant knew now. For one of the most beautiful women he'd ever known, she seemed to require constant assurances of her beauty and importance. Or maybe she was a narcissist.

Every time Ant wondered why he was still with her, the image of Jess's stricken face came to mind and the urge to leave Alicia disappeared. By staying with Alicia, he wouldn't be tempted to run back to Jess. To tell her that he loved her. How deeply sorry he was that he'd hurt her. But it always came back to that one thing—he couldn't give her what she needed in a relationship, so he was better off with someone else.

He wasn't proud of his motives. He knew they were far from noble. He had no illusions about Alicia either. She liked the notoriety of being with someone who had won a popular TV vote. He was the man of the moment. Ant suspected when his time in the limelight faded and the country moved on, Alicia would, too. Hopefully by then Jess would have as well.

'There you are!' Ant's mum opened the door for him when he arrived.

He frowned when he heard voices coming from the back of the house.

'I thought it was just going to be us?' he asked.

'I never said that, and you never asked. Come on, my pot will boil over.'

Ant felt a tingle of wariness at her reply. His mother was being deliberately obscure, and Ant couldn't think who the voices belonged to.

His question was answered a second later when he stepped into the back living area. He froze in the doorway.

'Antony, look at you!' A large old woman with dark, grey-flecked hair held back in a neat bun bustled over to him and engulfed him in a hug.

'Maria?' he said warily.

It was a name that was never spoken in this house. The name of his father's ex-wife. The shock of seeing her in his family home rendered him unable to say anything more than that.

She eased back and patted his cheeks. 'And Tobias and Mia are here, too. You've met their children before, I believe?'

Still stunned, Ant looked over at his half-brother and sister standing near his father, who was seated at the table. Seated around him were four children—Carly, Matthew, Anna and Tina. If Ant's memory served him correctly, the children ranged in age from four to about ten. They were all focused on a snakes and ladders board on the table and his dad was rolling the dice.

'Hi Ant,' the kids chorused when they saw him, but they didn't get up as they were obviously too absorbed in their game.

What the hell?

He looked desperately across to his mother for some reassurance that this was all a dream. This sort of happy family scene didn't occur in their household. With emotion in her eyes, she turned the gas down on the pot cooking on the stove and came over to him.

'I invited them here tonight because it's finally time some family myths were put to rest,' Abi said in a low voice. She caught Mia's eye, and Mia nodded.

Mia clapped her hands. 'Come on, kids. Aunty Abi says Stretch, the cat, is outside somewhere, and he needs his dinner before we have ours. Can you help me look for him, please?'

The littlest girl, Tina, jumped up. 'I love Stretch! Where is he?'

Mia smiled at her youngest daughter. 'Aunty Abi says he likes to hide beside the garbage bins. Let's see if he's there.'

'Ew, naughty kitty.'

'Come on,' said Tobias, giving his son Matthew a nod and then catching Ant's eye.

Matthew stood up and pointed at Stefano. 'I'm winning right now. Don't go all sneaky on me and try to move me down a snake while I'm gone.'

Stefano held up his palms and gave Matthew an innocent look. 'What? Me?'

'I'll keep an eye on him,' Abi promised.

Ant watched all of this wordlessly, still frozen to the spot until everyone but his mother, father and Maria had filed outside.

'Come and sit,' Maria told him warmly, leading him to a nearby chair.

Ant remained standing next to the chair, feeling like he was having an out-of-body experience. Aunty Abi? His dad playing a board game with his grandchildren? What the fuck was going on?

A grandparent playing a game with grandchildren might be normal in another household, but not in this family. Especially when, as far as Ant knew, his dad had nothing to do with his grandchildren until today.

'Sit, sit.' Maria flapped around him like a mother bird.

Ant finally sat.

His mother and Maria shared a look.

Maria spoke again. 'Abi tells me you don't want children.'

Ant gaped at the two women and then across to his father, who appeared to be avoiding his eyes and was studying the dice in his hand.

'Antony?' Abi said softly.

'Mum, what the hell is going on?' Ant said much too loudly.

Stefano flinched and gave them a look of uncertainty, then returned his attention to the dice.

'There's no need to yell,' Abi said. 'Maria and I felt it was time to discuss our family history.'

Maria and her? Since when did Maria and his mother talk regularly? His mother was the other woman, for God's sake.

Maria studied Ant as if she saw something he couldn't.

'When your father and I emigrated to Australia, we were both running.'

'Yes, I know,' Ant said shortly. 'Life in Italy was tough, I get it. Dad reminded me about how poor his childhood was a million times when I was growing up.'

Maria's eyes filled with sadness. 'It wasn't just poverty we were running from, Antony. I was pregnant with another man's child and risked being disowned by my family.'

'What?' Ant breathed.

'Tobias's father is not Stefano. He was another young man I loved desperately, but my parents forbade me to see. When I fell pregnant, the boy I thought I loved refused to have anything to do with me.'

'I'm . . . I'm sorry.' Ant glanced outside.

Tobias wasn't his half-brother after all? The revelation cut deep because he was the one from his father's first family that he probably felt closest to.

'If not for your father, I don't know what I would have done,' Maria said.

Ant's eyes returned to her. 'What do you mean?'

'He offered to marry me and take me to Australia so that we could start a new life here. We didn't love each other, but in time we thought we could.'

This was all news to Ant. 'Forgive me,' he said. 'But why would my father offer to do that? Were you friends?'

'Just a neighbour,' Maria said softly.

Abi cleared her throat. Stefano looked up at Abi and Maria, careful to avoid Ant's eyes. His expression told Ant that

Stefano was having a good day, and that he was mentally present in the room with them. He'd been having more good days since Jess had gotten him exercising.

'My father was a cruel man,' he said gruffly. 'He used to beat us.'

His face contorted with something Ant guessed was grief, but he wasn't sure because he'd never seen his father show such emotion before.

Abi nodded, like that was all she needed. 'Your grandfather didn't just beat his children, Antony. He was emotionally abusive, too. He would starve them as punishment. Stefano always got beaten the worst because he'd try to protect his younger siblings. Your father had a difficult upbringing.'

Difficult? Ant's had been difficult. Stefano's sounded far worse than that.

'I'm sorry,' Ant said, his voice rough.

Stefano nodded his head, but didn't meet Ant's eyes.

'When we came to Australia, things were hard,' Maria explained. 'Your father worked several jobs to help us get ahead. As you know, we had more children.' She smiled. 'We didn't ever love each other, but we became good friends. Things were going well until Stefano lost one of his jobs. That's when he started the business. Things were very hard financially. He started drinking. He became verbally abusive. Then one night he lashed out physically.' She glanced over at him, as though she felt bad for even bringing it up, but Ant felt outraged on her behalf.

He glared at his father. Stefano's bottom lip appeared to waver, and he kept playing with the dice in his hand.

Maria sighed. 'After that, he would still drink. But never at home. He became very distant, and we rarely saw him.'

'That's because he met me,' Abi told them.

'It was like he was a whole different person all of a

sudden,' Maria said. 'I knew something had happened. I had my suspicions right from the start, but I let it happen because Stefano seemed more like the boy I'd left Italy with. But still there was the distance from us.'

Abi sighed. 'I'm ashamed to say that for a long time I didn't know about Maria and the kids. Stefano made me feel like the only woman in the world. But when I found out, I was furious.'

Stefano looked up at his wife, his dark eyes full of regret.

'So I marched right over to Maria's and told her what had been going on. There was no way I was going to be the other woman and break up someone's family.'

The corner of Ant's mouth lifted slightly. He could just imagine his small but determined mother doing exactly that.

Maria reached over and grasped Abi's hand. 'We confronted him together.'

'How did that go for you, Dad?' Ant said dryly, unable to keep the words to himself.

Stefano grimaced. 'Not so good.'

Maria barked with laughter. 'It wasn't good for any of us, but your father broke down. He told us how much he loved Abi and how he wanted to be with her. He then said something that made us reassess everything.'

Abi squeezed Maria's hand. 'He said he didn't want to be a father anymore. That he wasn't fit to be. That he thought it was better for the children's sake if he wasn't around in case he . . .' She looked guiltily at her husband. 'In case he hurt them.'

'So I agreed to a divorce,' Maria said. 'So long as your father continued to support us, which he always did.'

Abi reached over for a shoebox sitting on the table Ant hadn't noticed before.

'These are a few of the letters your father sent to your half-brothers and sisters when they were growing up. Take a look.'

With uncertain hands, Ant opened the box. It was stuffed full of letters. He opened one. It was to Mia from his father. He opened several more. His hands shaking, he carefully returned them to the box.

'You know when your father had to work on weekends?' Abi said. 'He usually wasn't working.'

'He was visiting us,' Maria finished. 'And he never hurt us again. Ever. Those early days were hard, and if not for the alcohol I don't think it would ever have happened.'

'So that's why Dad never drinks alcohol?' Ant asked his mother.

She nodded. 'I helped him break the habit early on.'

'Then why . . .' Ant struggled to find the words. 'Why keep his other family from me?' *Why make me think I wasn't wanted?* he wanted to add, but didn't.

Stefano cleared his throat and they all fell quiet.

'I couldn't do this.' He waved his hand in the air. 'The big family. It was too hard. Brought back too many memories of my own family. If I was the visiting father, I felt more like a loved uncle and could separate myself from it.'

'You never laid a hand on me,' Ant said. 'Ever.' His father had never been warm or loving, but Ant knew without a doubt his dad would never hurt him like that.

Stefano stared at him. His dark eyes had always seemed unfathomable to Ant when he was growing up, but now they welled with tears.

'That's because I never . . .' He coughed and a tear spilled over. He swiped it away. 'I never let myself get close enough to.'

Ant's own eyes filled with tears. That his father was admitting to keeping him at arm's length seemed to fill a hole he'd never let himself admit to. After all, he had a father growing up unlike some of the other mates his age. What did he have to complain about, really? That his dad was a distant, grumpy old bastard? Ant had never wanted for anything.

Except for his father's companionship.

Ant was standing up, his chair scraping on the tiles, before he realised it. He went over and crouched down beside his father.

'You would never have hurt me,' he told him.

Stefano shook his head, his bottom lip quivering. 'But I could have.'

'No,' Ant said firmly. 'No, you wouldn't. Not from what Mum and Maria tell me. You adored Mum. You still adore her. You worship her. I always felt like a third wheel because you loved her so much.'

'I'm sorry,' Stefano grunted.

'I thought you hated me,' Ant said in a small voice he barely recognised.

Another tear spilled from Stefano's eyes, and he reached out a hand towards Ant. It shook, but not from old age. He cupped Ant's chin.

'You are so full of light and laughter, my boy,' he said in a pained voice. 'So much like your mother. I never wanted to extinguish that because of my demons.'

Ant eased back on his heels, out of Stefano's grasp, and rubbed a palm across his mouth. He dared another look at his father.

'And all these years I thought you didn't think I was funny,' Ant joked.

Stefano's eyes lit with surprise, and then he threw his head back and laughed, the warm sound reverberating around the small kitchen. The sound unfurled some of the aching pain in Ant's chest, and he smiled and stood up.

Stefano inhaled a ragged breath after his laughter subsided. 'Things are different now. If it had been now, I would have gone and spoken to someone. Gotten help. Your mother helped me though.'

Abi shook her head sadly. 'But it was never enough.'

'Back then we weren't allowed to talk about our demons,' Maria added. 'Carrying them takes a heavy toll.'

Stefano studied the dice. 'Of course I said no when your mother wanted everyone here today. But then she told me how you don't want children.' He looked up at Ant. 'That should be your choice. Not a choice made because of who your family were or are.'

He paused and everyone remained silent, waiting for him to go on. Stefano rarely said much, so no one wanted to prevent him from saying what he wanted to.

'The only reason I kept my other children from you was because I didn't want you thinking you were an afterthought or an accident. You may have been a surprise for your mother and I, but my children are my proudest achievement even though I had so little to do with them. Including you.'

Ant sat back down, feeling unsteady on his feet.

'I missed out on so much because I was scared,' Stefano said darkly, glaring at the snakes and ladders board.

'Scared of what?' Ant asked, finding it hard to imagine this gruff man being scared of anything.

Stefano met his son's eyes. 'I think you know, because you fear it, too. I was terrified of becoming like my father.'

'THANKS FOR COMING WITH ME TODAY,' Jess told Kat and Em, who were waiting with her at the edge of the beach.

'What? And miss Triathlon Man himself?' Kat quipped. 'Not likely.'

'Mmm,' Em agreed, taking in all the people on the small beach.

It was more of a cove than a beach, located not far from Manly Harbour where the famous Sydney ferries came and went.

'It's hardly a chore to stand here and watch the competitors warming up,' Em added.

Kat quirked an eyebrow at Em. 'I didn't know you were into athletes.'

'Men, Kat. I'm into men.'

They all laughed, and Kat shook her head.

'Well, I'm definitely impressed,' Kat said. 'Participating in a triathlon is hardcore and Ant scores points just for all the training. It's relentless. He's been up super early for weeks. Then he goes home to grab a quick nap so his eyes aren't hanging out of his head by the time the show airs in the evening. That's dedication.'

'You should be proud, Jess,' said Em. 'He wouldn't be here today if it wasn't for you.'

Jess's gaze settled on Ant. He was standing around with some of the other competitors, stretching. They all wore full-length wetsuits ready for the swim component of the triathlon. The event started with seven hundred and fifty metres in the water, which on its own required good fitness. After that, they would return to the beach and run just under three kilometres. Then it was on to a bike for a twenty-one-kilometre ride, and then five more kilometres of running to finish.

Jess looked away, taking in the picturesque view of the ocean in the early morning light. Ant's wetsuit clung to him like a second skin and somehow Jess calling him Adonis didn't seem like a joke to her anymore.

'But, wow, it's early,' Kat said, yawning, breaking through Jess's thoughts. 'I definitely get friendship points for this.'

Em nodded to the other side of the beach. 'It's not too early for her, sadly.'

Jess had been trying to keep her attention away from where Alicia was standing with several others. She had one of them holding a phone up and taking a photo of her posing against the backdrop of the water. In shiny black leather boots, tight-fitting black jeans, and an off-the-shoulder T-shirt, she looked overdressed for the beach.

'Ugh,' Kat said. 'That woman is hard work. I can't believe he's still with her.'

Em gave Jess a sideways look. 'Have you asked him how things are going?' she said to Kat.

Kat screwed her nose up. 'No. There's nothing worse than people asking you about your personal life when you're in the public eye.' Kat also gave Jess a sideways glance. 'He doesn't really talk about her, though. I'm not sure if it's deliberate.'

'It's OK, you two,' Jess told them. 'I'm not jealous.'

'No,' Kat corrected, 'you're single-handedly working yourself into the ground so you don't have to think about him.'

Em nudged Jess. 'That's what happens when you're about to become a well-known television personality.'

'Stop it, both of you,' Jess protested.

'What?' Em asked. 'Can't I be excited for you? Having your own segment on one of Australia's highest rating lifestyle shows is a big deal.'

'Thanks,' Jess said self-consciously.

Kat rolled her eyes. 'Stop downplaying it. This is a big step for you.'

'I know, and I'm trying not to think about it.'

'It will be easier than live television,' Kat told her. 'You can do multiple takes and you'll get to know the crew like you did when you filmed the segment for our show.'

'Except Kat has me going on live television again,' Jess complained.

Kat waved a hand in Jess's direction. 'That? That's nothing. You'll be on-air for maybe ten minutes while you plug your new segment on our network and Ant carries on about how great he is for completing a triathlon. Anything to distract him from his greatness.'

'You know I still don't like live television,' Jess told her.

'I'll swap with you,' Em said.

'With what?' Jess asked.

Em sighed, and it was a big sigh for Em, who was usually upbeat. 'I'm a bridesmaid at a family wedding. Again.'

Jess's face lit up. 'That sounds lovely! Why would you want to swap that?'

'Because it's like the three-hundredth time I've been a

bridesmaid, and every single time my father tries to set me up with somebody inappropriate.'

'Maybe he'll suggest someone nice this time,' said Jess hopefully.

'And maybe the man of my dreams won't be an arrogant developer hell-bent on making money and destroying the environment.'

Jess's face fell. 'Oh.'

'I'm sensing a theme?' asked Kat.

'Oh, yeah. There's a theme alright,' Em complained. 'They're all usually entitled know-it-alls who think they are God's gift and can't appreciate an intelligent woman that has a mind of her own.'

'Oh,' Jess said again. 'Sorry. You can come on *Sydney Tonight* if you like.'

Kat tapped Jess's arm with the back of her hand. 'Oh no you don't.'

'It's alright,' Em said, sighing again. 'I'll just take along a decoy.'

'A decoy?' Jess asked.

'Yeah, I'll bring a date I know my father will hate so much he'll forget about trying to set me up with arsehole number one hundred and twenty.'

'Sounds fun,' Kat said lightly, and they all smiled. 'Hey, I know, let's get a selfie of ourselves and post it on Jess's account and title it, "It's so early even Jess isn't up for exercise."'

Jess laughed. 'I'm not sure about that, but yes, let's get a selfie.'

They crowded around Jess's phone, Em muttering that if she was going to be made famous on Jess's Instagram account, she would wear sunglasses even though it was barely light.

They snapped off a few shots and were so busy critiquing them that Jess didn't notice Ant approaching.

ANT PAUSED a few feet from the women. So Jess had come. When he'd texted her to ask, he wasn't sure what sort of response he'd get. For once he didn't attempt to make a joke of it.

Hi Jess. I hope you don't mind me getting in touch. I've invited Kat to attend the triathlon this weekend and was wondering if you'd like to join her? It would be nice to see you there.

Her reply had come a few hours later and it was simple and non-committal.

I'll think about it.

He supposed it was all he deserved, and it was probably the best he could hope for.

He never stopped thinking about her. He thought about her at work. He thought about her during training. He thought about her when he was with Alicia.

Ant swallowed the familiar distaste that surfaced when he attempted to reflect on his relationship with Alicia. He knew he was a coward for staying with her, but like leopards found it hard to change their spots, apparently so did cowards.

He pushed the thoughts out of his mind and stopped in front of them.

'Hey, ladies. Thanks for coming. I'm starting to feel like a celebrity or something.'

Kat snorted. 'Like you need a bigger head, Mr. Most Popular Presenter.'

'Hi,' Jess said quietly.

Ant tried to sneak a better look at her and failed, because once his eyes were on her, he couldn't look anywhere else.

'Hey,' he said, transfixed.

She looked amazing, as usual. She was wearing her

uniform of black leggings and one of those fitted exercise brand tops that she lived in. She obviously hadn't gone to any special effort with her clothes this morning, but Ant knew without a doubt that she was the most beautiful woman on the beach.

Em cleared her throat and stuck her hand out. 'Hi. I'm Em. One of Jess and Kat's neighbours.'

Ant shook himself and took her hand. 'Oh, the penthouse lady? Nice to meet you.'

Em's eyebrows rose and Jess giggled, the adorable sound making Ant's stomach twist.

'Penthouse lady?' Em said. 'I like the sound of that.'

'Em.' Jess tugged her friend's jacket. 'You know that's also a dirty magazine, right?'

Em didn't even blink. 'Yeah, I got that.'

They all cracked up, and Jess blushed. Ant's stomach twisted tighter.

'Uh, anyway,' he said, 'I can't linger because I'm so big and important now, but it's really cool that you're all here. Hopefully I won't embarrass myself.'

'Oh, I'm depending on it,' Kat said.

'Hello, ladies.'

The sensation in Ant's stomach went from a sweet, painful tug to one of nausea.

He turned to face Alicia. 'Hi. I was just coming to see you.'

'Well, I found you first.'

He ignored her unimpressed look because it was something he was growing used to lately. He put his arm on her elbow and went to lead her away.

'I've got to get back to the start line,' he said.

'Off you go then.'

Ant hesitated. There was no way he was going to leave

Alicia with Jess, even with Kat around. Kat wouldn't let things get too awkward, but still.

Alicia directed her gaze to Jess. 'Congratulations on your television debut.'

'Oh, thanks. It's nothing,' Jess said humbly.

'No, it's quite something. First your Instagram following, then Ant, now this. It's worked out so well, I'd almost suggest you planned it.'

Jess frowned. 'What do you mean? How would I have planned it?'

'Well, that little kiss at the Logies certainly got you some attention, didn't it? Plenty of producers in the room that night.'

Jess gaped at Alicia, and Ant grabbed her elbow more firmly this time.

'Come on, Alicia. Let's go.'

Alicia shook him off. 'I'm not ready to leave.'

'I'm sorry, Alicia,' Jess said quietly. 'I think you've mistaken me for somebody else. I'm not that strategic. I kissed Ant that night by accident.'

'By accident?' Alicia sneered. 'Give me a break. I know when a woman is throwing herself at my boyfriend.'

Kat went to step forward, but Jess shook her head.

'I wasn't throwing myself at him,' Jess said more loudly. 'But you're right. I wanted to kiss him.'

Everyone fell silent. Ant stared at Jess. Alicia was glaring. Jess didn't flinch.

'It was wrong of me to do it like that in public, but I wasn't thinking,' Jess continued.

Alicia stepped in closer to Jess, towering over her. 'You *wanted* to kiss my boyfriend?'

'Yes,' Jess said simply.

Obviously this wasn't news to Ant—their night in the hotel

room had put any doubts about that to rest—but it was certainly news to Alicia.

'You bitch,' Alicia snarled.

Jess shrugged. 'Yes, I guess I am. But then I don't suppose you're much better.'

'Excuse me?' Alicia was doing that weird flaring nostrils thing that Ant noticed her do when she didn't get her way.

'Well, going out with Ant has been kind of strategic for you too, hasn't it?'

'I don't know what you mean.'

'It's funny. You mentioned producers earlier, and I've gotten to know the one on my show quite well these last few weeks. It turns out he knows the folks involved in organising the Logies quite well.'

'What's your point?'

If it was any other time, Ant would think from Jess's tone of voice that she was having a casual conversation, but there was an icy cold glare in her eyes.

'Mmm,' said Jess. 'And he said you also know them. In fact, you had a pretty good idea of how the public vote was swaying prior to the Logies.'

Alicia raised a slim shoulder in an offhand shrug. 'If you're in the public eye, you keep your finger to the pulse with what the public is thinking. It's part of our job. I don't see what the big deal is.'

Jess stepped in so her sneakers were almost touching Alicia's boots. Ant had the distinct impression he was witnessing a deer take on a tiger, but something told him the tiger was underestimating the deer.

'My point is, that you knew Ant was going to win that Logie.'

Alicia huffed. 'Of course he was, he's so talented.'

'*Before* you started going out with him,' Jess added.

Alicia huffed again, but it came out more like a cough. 'How could I possibly know that? The voting doesn't finish until just before.'

'OK, well, you wouldn't have known for sure. But I was told Ant was a shoo-in to win this year, apparently. The network was pushing for it, and you knew that.'

'I was?' Ant said dumbly.

Kat rolled her eyes at him, then spoke up. 'Jess makes a good point, Alicia. Was that why you decided to get him to model your clothes?'

'And so what if I did?' Alicia threw back. 'It was always going to be someone high profile.'

'And you only go out with people who are high profile, is that right, Alicia?' Kat finished.

Obviously deciding Kat wasn't someone she wanted to take on, Alicia directed her dark glare towards Jess again. 'You're just jealous. You missed grabbing Ant while his star was rising and now you're regretting it, but I got there first.'

'Ant's star power has nothing to do with the fact I wanted to kiss him,' Jess said quietly.

'Oh, come on!' Alicia cried, her haughty demeanour slipping momentarily. 'Why else would you want to kiss him?'

Kat and Em stiffened, and Jess flinched. She swallowed and shot Ant a pained look.

'Yes, Alicia,' he cut in, his voice low. 'Why else would you want to kiss me?'

Alicia looked between them. Her eyebrows barely moved thanks to her cosmetic surgeon, but her wide eyes gave her away.

'Alicia?' Ant said again.

Her face transformed into a broad smile, the sort she regularly put on for the cameras. 'Ant, that was terribly blunt of me. It wasn't how it sounded at all.'

'Let me guess,' Kat interrupted. 'It was an *accident*?'

Kat's words hung in the air between them. Kat crossed her arms and stepped closer to Jess. Em did the same. Ant reassessed his initial impression of the women. They weren't deer at all. They were a pack of lionesses and Alicia was a gazelle.

Alicia puffed out her chest in annoyance. 'Come on, Ant, these women are deluded. You have to get ready for your race.' She put an arm around his waist.

He shook her off, his anger getting the better of him for the first time in . . . well, ever.

'Fuck off, Alicia.'

She blinked and froze. 'What did you just say?'

'You heard me,' he said.

'We'll talk about this afterwards,' she snapped. 'You need to focus on your race.'

'There's nothing to talk about,' he shot back. He quickly glanced at Jess, wondering if he was about to say too much, but said it anyway. 'And for the record, I wanted to kiss Jess, too.'

Alicia's top lip curled so high it was actually quite impressive.

'I knew it! You've wanted to fuck that little fitness bimbo the entire time, haven't you?'

Ant crossed his arms like the others. 'Don't talk about Jess like that.'

'It's OK, Ant,' Jess interjected, her jaw jutting out defiantly. 'You don't need to protect me. And for the record, Alicia, we've already slept together. Apparently Ant prefers fitness bimbos to models.'

Alicia's top lip may as well have leapt off her face in hatred, but the lip filler weighed it down. 'You son of a bitch. You deserve her. Fuck you and this stupid race. Some of us don't need to exercise like addicts to look good. You can have her.'

Alicia stormed off along the beach and they all watched her go. Her ability to flounce while her boots sunk into the sand was equally impressive.

Ant made a show of feeling his balls through the wetsuit and the woman stared at him awkwardly. He winked at Jess.

'Huh. There they are. It turns out my balls have been there the entire time, I just didn't know it.'

Jess grinned back at him and it was better than the sunrise.

Kat nudged Jess. 'You slept with Ant.' It wasn't a question, more like a demand.

Jess flushed bright pink. 'I probably shouldn't have said that, but I was so angry it just slipped out.'

'At the Logies,' Ant admitted.

'*No!*' Kat sounded generally surprised for a change.

'Yes,' Jess whispered.

Kat looked between them. 'Then why on earth are you still with Alicia? And why have you been working like a woman possessed? Was it that bad?'

Jess blushed so brightly she could power the sun.

'Ah, no, it definitely wasn't bad,' Ant said, sparing Jess the embarrassment of answering. 'I've just got some, ah, issues, that make it hard to be in a relationship. I felt Jess deserved better.'

Kat stepped in and prodded Ant's chest with her forefinger. 'Do not talk to me about issues, Monticello. I've got a list of issues as long as my arm when it comes to relationships and now I'm engaged. It's no excuse.'

Ant darted a look at Jess. 'No, it's not. I'm starting to see that now.'

Her finger pressed into his chest harder. 'And it's up to Jess to decide who and what she deserves, you hear me? Even if it's a clueless, lazy comedian like you.'

Jess laughed softly and put her hand on Kat's shoulder. 'He's not lazy, and it's OK, Kat. I've got this. Thanks.'

Kat threw Ant one last threatening look and stepped away to stand with Em.

'You need to go and do your race,' she said to him.

'Race? What race?' he joked. 'Is that what I'm here for?'

She smiled, then looked like she was about to touch him, but didn't. He felt the absence of her touch keenly.

'Yes,' she said.

'Can we talk after? If I can still move?'

She was still smiling. 'Yes.'

'Forgive me.' He grabbed her by the shoulders and planted a kiss on her mouth, then ran off before she could chastise him.

'I'll be waiting for you!' she called out.

His heart swelled in his chest, and he suddenly understood what all the early mornings and the sore calves and disciplined eating was for. He'd told himself it was to keep himself busy and his mind off Jess. He'd told himself it was because he wanted to prove to himself that he could it. That it was a challenge.

But now he understood. While Alicia had been the one to suggest it for the publicity—no surprises there—it was obvious now that Jess was the real reason he'd agreed to do it. He wanted to show her that he had what it took to be good enough for her. That he deserved her.

And now he was going to prove it.

Chapter Thirty-Nine

FOR THE ENTIRE RACE, Jess wondered if she'd said too much. Not to Alicia. She was past worrying about her. Ever since Allan, her new producer, had told her that Ant had been a shoo-in for this year's Logie award, Jess had been concerned about Alicia's true interest in Ant. It pained her to think it, because Jess thought Ant was wonderful inside and out. But someone like Alicia? Everything seemed so stage-managed with her. And then when Alicia had the audacity to accuse Jess of being manipulative in front of Ant, she'd seen red.

'Remind me not to get on your bad side,' Kat said later when they were waiting in the carpark near the finish line at the top of North Head.

The rocky outcrop was a protected heritage area that was open to the public for coastal walks, which took in the view of Sydney Harbour and the city. Today one side of the road was cordoned off for the triathlon participants.

'Why?' Jess asked.

'You are fierce,' Kat told her. 'You took on Alicia without blinking. Why didn't you tell me about the Logies thing?'

305

'I wasn't certain,' Jess explained. 'But I wondered. And then she gave me the opportunity to ask.'

'Opportunity?' Em scoffed. 'That's an interesting definition of opportunity, if you ask me.'

Kat tilted her head to look at Jess. 'This wasn't your first run-in with a mean girl, was it?'

Jess smiled. 'You could say that. There's something about me they don't like.'

'Yeah, you're too nice and gorgeous and they can't compete,' Em told her.

'Maybe. It wasn't Ant's first run-in with a mean girl, either, but I hope it will be his last.'

Kat reached over and squeezed Jess's hand. 'I hope so, too. Are you going to give him a chance?'

'I'd like to, but we need to talk about some things first.'

Jess still remembered Kat's advice about writing your own rules when it came to relationships, but Jess needed to be realistic. She still wanted kids and she needed Ant to know that. The last thing she wanted was for him to change his mind because of her. But she also didn't want to lose him again. She honestly had no idea what the solution was, and it was terrifying.

So Jess watched the race with a tight knot in her stomach, growing more and more nervous as they waited for the runners to make their way towards them.

What if their feelings for one another weren't enough? What if they still couldn't make it work?

'Hey, there he is,' Em told them, pointing to Ant behind a few runners in the distance.

Jess squinted and found herself counting. 'Oh my God! He's in the top ten!'

'Eighth to be exact,' Kat said.

'Holy shit!'

Kat and Em stared at her.

'What?' she said. 'I believe in him, but I never expected him to be this good. And if you ever tell him that, I'll kill you.'

Kat and Em grinned, and Kat nodded appreciatively. 'You know, I like this new side of you, Jess.'

Jess didn't reply. She was too busy watching Ant. Wow, he looked amazing. He appeared tired, and she could just make out the frown lines from a distance because he was concentrating so hard, but his footfalls were sure and steady.

'Come on, Ant,' she whispered to herself.

'Unbelievable,' Kat said. 'His ego isn't going to fit inside the studio after this.'

They fell silent, waiting for the runners. Several of them sprinted past, the finish line in view. They were the clear winners. Ant was with a few other runners further back. As they drew closer, Ant looked up and spotted Jess.

His expression went from one of concentration, and Jess suspected a bit of pain, to being lit up with delight.

She jumped up and down on the spot, clapping loudly. 'Come on, Ant!'

Em put her fingers in her mouth and wolf-whistled.

Ant grinned, and all the doubts swirling in Jess's mind and belly stilled for a moment. She loved him so much. Surely they could make it work somehow? They had to.

As if he read something in her expression, Ant blinked.

It was only a second, but it was long enough to distract him.

He missed seeing a small pothole in front of him, and his foot landed squarely in the centre of it. His ankle twisted gruesomely, pulling his foot from beneath him, and he went down. Hard.

'Oh my God!' Without hesitating, Jess sprinted over to him, her heart pounding.

He lay on the ground curled up in a tight ball, moaning.

'Fuck,' Kat said, arriving not long after.

Ant groaned and attempted to move.

'Don't,' Jess barked at him, and he stilled.

Em came over to them and Jess shot her a panicked look. 'Go get the first aiders. Quick.'

'On it.' Em jogged off.

'Have to . . . finish,' Ant muttered.

'Oh, no you don't. You need to lie right there until help comes,' Jess ordered.

Ant tried to push himself up off the ground.

'What are you doing, you moron?' Jess cried. 'Please stay still.'

Ant looked like he was trying to grin, which was when Jess noticed the gash on his face. He must have hit it when he'd gone down. Jess winced.

'I like how I'm a moron, but you still say please,' he said. Ignoring her earlier instructions, he managed to sit up.

'Oh, Ant, you're bleeding.'

He looked down at himself like he was only registering the damage for the first time. The side of one arm had some nasty gravel burn and was bleeding as well. So was his knee, which had taken the brunt of the fall when he went down.

'Awesome. War wounds,' he said, sounding proud of himself.

Jess huffed and stood up. 'Stop kidding around. You're hurt.'

'I'll live. Now help me stand up.'

'Are you serious? You've definitely got a twisted ankle. It might even be broken. You're staying where you are.'

'Nope. I'm finishing this race.'

'You are not finishing this race,' Jess shot back.

'I'm finishing this race,' he repeated.

'You don't need to finish this race,' Jess protested.

Kat watched on in amusement.

'Look,' he said gruffly, shifting to stretch his legs out in front of him slowly. 'I discovered I had balls this morning. I'm going to finish this race.'

'For God's sake, Ant! I know you have balls. I've felt them!'

Kat slapped a hand over her mouth and walked off, her shoulders moving up and down in silent laughter.

Ant grinned again. 'Yeah, I remember that. It was kind of nice from memory. Now help me up.'

Jess sighed. 'Really, Ant? Really?'

He levelled a serious look at her, and Jess's next protest died before it could leave her lips.

Oh my gosh. He wants this. He really wants to cross the finish line. It means that much to him. Despite her worry about his injuries, Jess felt a stab of pride.

Ant had called himself lazy when they first met, but he wasn't anything close to it. He was passionate and driven and funny and maddening, and Jess was rather fond of his balls, too.

'Alright,' she said. 'But on one condition. The first aider checks you out, and then we help you walk across the finish line.'

'My balls are shrinking a bit,' Ant admitted.

'I'll make it up to them later,' she shot back without thinking, and he grinned harder.

'OK, here we are.' A middle-aged woman arrived with another man holding a first aid kit. 'Oh, Ant. What have you done to yourself?'

Ant nodded at Jess. 'It's her fault. She distracted me with her beauty.'

Jess shot him an unimpressed look, then turned to the others. 'He wants help to get across the finish line, but I think he's hurt his ankle really badly. Can you check it first? I don't want him to do any more damage.'

The man and woman crouched down in front of him and surveyed his wounds.

'Nice job, Ant,' the guy said.

'I thought so. I'll look good on-air tomorrow night.'

They shook their heads at him, and the woman touched his ankle gently. 'OK. Tell me when it hurts.'

Ant hissed and drew his leg back. 'Hurts.'

The woman looked up at Jess. 'Definitely sprained. Possibly broken. I'd recommend an X-ray. But we can help him to the finish line provided he doesn't put any weight on it.'

They helped him to stand up.

'I can help him if you like,' Jess offered.

'No, you walk in front,' Ant said, hopping awkwardly on his good leg while the others walked with him slowly.

'Why?'

His grin was wicked. 'Because I like looking at your arse.'

Jess flushed red and averted her eyes. She wondered if there would ever be a time when he couldn't tease a blush from her. 'It can't hurt that much then,' she called back.

It was only about fifty metres to the finish line, but it took them a few minutes to get there. Em and Kat clapped along with Jess when they arrived, as well as the other club members and competitors waiting in the carpark.

They took Ant over to a fold-out chair and carefully lowered him into it.

'Thanks,' he breathed, the lines in his face betraying the pain he was in.

Some of the other competitors came over to them.

'Well done, Ant,' said a blonde woman. 'You came eighteenth after all that.'

'Awesome effort,' another guy said, shaking Ant's hand.

Ant smiled, breathing heavily but looking happy. He looked at Jess and patted his lap. 'Sit down.'

'You're hurt—'

'Now, woman. I want to hold you. You're my prize.' His warm, brown eyes were filled with expectation.

Well, then. Jess looked around self-consciously, and Kat gestured for Jess to move. When Jess hesitated, Kat rolled her eyes and clapped her hands.

'Alright, give them some space everyone. Monticello wants to state his undying love, and it's going to get creepy.'

The others laughed and did as they were told, moving away to chat quietly.

Ant pointed to his lap.

'You're bossy now you've found your balls again,' Jess told him.

'It's great, isn't it?'

It was actually, so Jess went and sat carefully on his lap. Ant put his arms around her and nuzzled her shoulder.

'I've missed you,' he murmured. 'Miss me?'

'Some.' When he eased back and gave her a sharp look, she grinned. 'OK, a lot. But you were busy with bitchface, so I kept my distance.'

Ant mimicked a hissing cat. 'I like it when you're jealous. That was my whole evil plan, you know. Make you jealous until you scared her off.' His expression turned serious. 'Actually, I was a coward. I have no idea why I was with her. I think it was so I would stay away from you. And now here we are again.'

She nudged him with her shoulder, but her smile trembled a bit. 'We still need to talk about things . . .'

'I want a future with you, Jess. I want children, too. With you. I always have. I was just too scared to admit it to myself. Because when it comes to you, I want everything.'

'I . . .' Jess opened her mouth. Closed it. Opened it again. 'You do?'

'Yep.' He tucked a strand of hair behind her ear. 'I need to update you on some family stuff, but basically I'm loveable and awesome and my dad thinks I'm funny, so it's all good. Turns out he had some dark family shit he's been hiding all these years.'

'Oh my goodness,' Jess breathed. 'I'm so sorry.'

'I'm not. Wait. That came out wrong. What I meant is I'm sorry for what happened to my dad, but I'm glad he finally opened up about it. It made me realise I'm not going to turn into him.'

'You're not your dad, Ant.'

'I'm getting that now, but I've been slow on the uptake, OK? I'm going to need guidance. Lots of guidance.'

She ignored the innuendo. 'You really want kids?' she asked softly.

'With you,' he replied firmly. 'Little Jesses running around everywhere sounds phenomenal. Not to mention mini Ants. How cool would that be?'

'Terrifying.'

He kissed her on the cheek. 'But we'd need to get married first.'

'I thought you said—'

'Forget what I said. I've been an absolute fool. How could I accurately measure my view on marriage when I married the wrong person? I need to marry the right person before I decide whether marriage is worth all the fuss everyone thinks it is.'

'And you think I'm the right person?'

Ant smiled and cupped her cheek, his thumb stroking it gently. That damn thumb was going to be the death of her, Jess was sure of it, but it would be a happy death.

'What do you think?' Ant whispered.

'Yes.'

'Oh, and just so we're on the same page,' Ant added. 'I'm your right person, right?'

Jess rested her forehead against his and giggled. 'Yes.'

'Good. Now what's a guy got to do around here to get a proper kiss?'

Jess eased back and surveyed him. He was sweaty and dirty and bloody, and his hair was all messed up, but he was hers.

'Oh, I don't know. Participating in a triathlon and nearly killing yourself ought to do it,' she told him.

'Damn. You're hard to please. I'll have to work harder in the future.'

She placed a kiss on his forehead. 'No, Ant. You're perfect, just as you are.'

His brown eyes softened. 'I love you, Jess.'

'I love you, too.'

And then they kissed for such a long time that they didn't see any of the other competitors reach the finish line.

Acknowledgments

I wrote this book during the global pandemic. If not for Jess and Ant, I think I would have gone way crazier during lockdown. This book became a wonderful escape for me, made more so by Ant's humour. I don't know why, but I've always wanted to write a comedian hero. Perfect timing, Ant.

Despite being written in the safety of my office, there is a list of people that I need to thank for helping me to get Self Made out into the world. My A-Team: my beta-readers Sarah, Donna, Milia and Nicki; my long-time editor, Laura; plus my proofreader, Rebekah.

As always, thanks to my boys for their loving support. You make this possible xx

To my readers: I hope that you enjoyed Self Made as much as I enjoyed writing it. Now, more than ever, having access to entertainment and the opportunity to escape reality for a little while is super important. So, thank you for purchasing this book. Supporting authors is a big deal, because it means we can keep writing more books to keep you entertained! Thank you.

They've got no time for love. But what if love finds them first?

Em Georgiou looks like the sort of girl you take home to your family. But she's got a PhD to finish and a career to kick-start first. And besides, Em likes men too much to settle down— much to her father's exasperation.

Joel Scott doesn't do relationships. He's too focused on his architecture business. So when his hard-to-please, cut-throat developer client suggests that he 'gets to know' his daughter Em, Joel is prepared to add the spoiled daddy's girl to his to-do list for the sake of his career.

Except Em is way more capable than her father gives her credit for. And she's certainly not the type of woman you strike off your to-do list.

Can Joel convince Em that he's not just trying to impress her father? Or that you can fall in love when you don't want to... even if it involves facing up to a dark past you'd rather forget?

Join Belinda's newsletter

AND RECEIVE A FREE EBOOK!

Sign up to Belinda's newsletter to be kept up to date about her latest book releases, news and specials.

To say thank you, you'll receive a **FREE copy of HEARTSTRINGS a Hollywood Hearts novella** valued at $1.99, which was rated 'A' by Smart B*tches, Trashy Books!

Sign up here: https://dl.bookfunnel.com/98v02gbzho

About the Author

Belinda Williams is a marketing copywriter who allowed an addiction to romance to get the better of her. She writes contemporary romance including romantic comedy and romantic suspense featuring good guys. She's occasionally tempted by bad boys, but prefers to write strong women characters and men with big hearts.

Her other addictions include music and cars. She's a music lover who sings lead vocals in a covers band and her eclectic taste forms the foundation for many of her writing ideas. She also has a healthy appreciation for fast cars and would not so secretly love a Lamborghini. For now she settles for her son's Hot Wheels collection.

When she's not obsessing over word count, she can be found counting laps at her local swimming pool or taking on yet another renovation project in her Sydney home, where she lives with her husband and son.

Belinda loves to hear from her readers! Connect with her below: